A Stirring from the Depths

Kait Waterhouse

This is a work of fiction. Any resemblance to actual persons, living or dead or actual events is purely coincidental. Although real-life locations or public figures may appear throughout the story, these situations, incidents, and dialogue concerning them are fictional and are not intended to depict actual events nor change the fictional nature of the work.

Published in the United States of America October 2025 by Kait Waterhouse.

Cataloging-in-Publication Data is on file with the Library of Congress.

ISBN Paperback 979-8-9930112-2-6

Ebook 979-8-9930112-1-9

Author website: http://www.kaitwaterhousewrites.com/

Editor: Tara Sexton

Cover Design: Fay Lane

Formatting: Juliet Bridges

To the women in my life—
you carried me here.

Contents

A note from the author   ix

Glossary and Pronunciation Guide to Irish
Terms   xi

Prologue   1

Chapter 1   3
Iona

Chapter 2   11
Cian

Chapter 3   17
Iona

Chapter 4   25
Iona

Chapter 5   31
Cian

Chapter 6   38
Iona

Chapter 7   46
Cian

Chapter 8   52
Iona

Chapter 9   64
Cian

Chapter 10   77
Iona

Chapter 11   87
Cian

Chapter 12   98
Iona

Chapter 13   112
Iona

Chapter 14   126
Cian

Chapter 15   141
Cian

Chapter 16   150
Iona

Chapter 17   162
Cian

Chapter 18   172
Iona

Chapter 19   179
Cian

Chapter 20   182
Iona

Chapter 21   192
Iona

Chapter 22   204
Iona

Chapter 23   212
Cian

Chapter 24   215
Iona

Chapter 25   224
Iona

Chapter 26   233
Iona

Chapter 27   242
Iona

Chapter 28   250
Cian

Chapter 29   261
Cian

Chapter 30   269
Cian

Chapter 31   277
Iona

Chapter 32   285
Iona
Epilogue   296

Acknowledgments   301
About the Author   303

Dear Reader,

Please be aware, *A Stirring From The Depths* is dark and at times includes content that may be too upsetting for some to continue any further. Please know it is my wish that you take care of yourself, first and above all. At the risk of spoiling some future surprises in order to protect you, I am going to list the content/trigger warnings here: animal cruelty, violence, nudity, blood, profanity, death, alcohol use, depictions of mob brutality, murder, depictions of sexism, use of firearms.

I believe this list is complete, but if in your reading you feel I've missed one, please reach out to me as I wish to protect all of my wonderful readers.

Sincerely,

Kait

Glossary and Pronunciation Guide to Irish Terms

Abhainn—River, pronounced *AH-win*

A chuid—My portion, pronounced *uh khwid*

Anamchara—Soul friend, pronounced *AU-nim-khar-ah*

Bean chéile— Wife, pronounced *ben kay-la*

Bean sigh—Faerie who warns of death, pronounced *ben shee*

Cailleach—Crone, pronounced *CALL-ee-och*

Creathnach—Dulse seaweed, pronounced *kraw-hen-acgh*

Each-Uisce—Water horse, Kelpie, pronounced *acgh-ISH-ka*

Mo mhuirnín—My darling, pronounced *muh MOOR-neen*

Seanmháthair—Grandmother, pronounced *SHAWNA-wa-hair*

"YEA AND IF SOME GOD SHALL WRECK ME IN THE
WINE—DARK DEEP,
EVEN SO I WILL ENDURE...FOR ALREADY I HAVE
SUFFERED FULL MUCH,
AND MUCH HAVE I TOILED
IN PERILS OF WAVE AND WAR..."
—HOMER

Prologue

P lumes of crimson bubbled and churned among the black waves. Shouts from men above the water were garbled, a language those beneath did not speak. Regardless, the bellowing message was clear. Everywhere there was panic. Fish scales swirled in a metallic frenzy, gleaming from the dull moonlight. Seals and porpoises propelled themselves through the currents, lapping at the fish, and trying to escape the heavy nets as they sailed down over them. The sea was tinted a deep and terrifying shade of red. Then, all at once, the blood that rained from above thinned to pale rust. The alien voices drifted further and further away from the cove, and all who remained below, drifted dazedly into darkness.

Long after the sea had calmed, its waters still and inky, the seals returned. To any who witnessed, it would appear as any other feeding ritual. Sleek, muscled bodies spun through the water. The only sound aside from the hush of the waves was a cacophony of clicks which purled out behind the seals' sharp teeth, signaling where to go. Down they went. One after another, each following the one before, lungs full of air, ready to dive below.

The first to dive nudged its snout against the black layer

covering the cove floor. Clouds of muck billowed out around the ghostly figures. The others knew to stay back; to watch and wait. The clicking grew even more riotous as anticipation rose. Fins flexed and whiskers twitched.

A spring of sulfurous water erupted from where the seal had dug down. A surging column of bubbles exploded out from the sea floor. The pod jerked away, flippers jetting their bodies out to make room for what was about to happen. A thin tendril of olive-green seagrass began to unfurl from the bubbling well. Soon, more and more writhing tendrils of kelp and weed bloomed out of the spring. The seals clicked to one another as they dodged and rolled around the quickly growing forest. They weaved their way back to the center, where the spring still gushed madly. All around them, swaying banners of seaweed stretched up to the cresting waves, reaching for a sun that had yet to rise.

Finally, within the jet of frothing water, a massive kelp frond the shade of blood emerged, slowly curling around itself, as the ocean whirled around it. The seals stilled as the spring waned and the blood kelp grew more and more broad. Each moved in closer, hesitant but eternally curious. The crimson frond eddied and curled into almost nothing before it withered and fell to the bottom.

Left in its place was a seal whose coat was black as the blackest velvet. Unblinking eyes like obsidian peered out at the pod.

She'd come.

"LIMITLESS AND IMMORTAL, THE WATERS ARE THE
BEGINNING AND END OF ALL THINGS ON EARTH."
—HEINRICH ZIMMER

Chapter One

IONA

The weight of the stone blade was hardly noticeable in my palm. Silently, I hauled my body out of the water. Seawater beaded down my bare arms. The wooden hull of the boat let out a groan under my weight, but by then, I'd already made my move. One hard slash with my fisted dagger sent its mass of tangled nets sailing down into the depths, no longer connected to the ship's rigging. I looked up, scanning the deck. The men on the boat remained completely unaware; smoking their pipes and humming drunkenly in the dark. The combination of drink and sea lulled them into complacency while I did my work. Tonight, I wouldn't need to spill any blood.

I released my grip on the railing and allowed myself to begin sinking into the ocean, when my wrist was seized, then tugged harshly, yanking me up and onto the deck. A large, ruddy faced man with wide cheeks and a barreled chest let out a sharp hiss as he took in my appearance. He dropped my wrist to move his hands in a strange gesture to the top of his head and then across his chest. He was clearly unprepared to see a half-woman, half-seal sprawled in front of him.

My coat was wrapped around my waist, allowing arms and a human torso to work for me as I did the sea's bidding. Below my navel was a tail, blubbered and tapered with two clawed flippers on its end. I used his moment of shock to my advantage, swinging out wildly, channeling all my strength into driving my knife through his eye. His jaw hung slack, and his body began to topple down over me.

But I was quick— and strong.

Time had taught me, and lessons learned over lifetimes made me what I was. I wrapped both forearms around his neck and pulled him over the side with me. We plunged into the sea in an exhilarating rush. Once back in the ocean, I released his corpse, and stared into the man's remaining eye, blank with death as he sank downward into the dark.

The bones in my arm still seemed to reverberate with the impact of hitting his skull with my knife. I flexed my human fingers even tighter around its hilt, squeezing hard enough to sting the palm of my hand. The killing calm lay heavy on my frame, an old feeling as familiar as the heft of my coat. One less human was one more life saved, that I was sure of. My destiny was an unending journey, my path awash with the blood of greedy men.

I slipped the bit of netting tied to my blade around my neck, then reached down to my waist and threw the sealskin hood over my head. In a moment, soft pink flesh became a hardy hide, deep as a winter solstice night and plenty thick enough for these waters. My human facade melded into one with wide black eyes, sharp canines, and a snout perfect for holding air while swimming into the depths, out to find my kin.

I pulled myself through the icy water and delighted in the cold as it curled around my seal body. The rushing sensation of soaring through the ocean at the highest speeds felt like what I imagined flying was for the gulls.

Freedom.

Bubbles raced out through my nose, collecting on the edges of my whiskers. Herring lurched away from me, frantically flitting through the waves to avoid my teeth. The sea opened herself to me as I happily jettisoned through her inky waters, until I reached a familiar outcropping of steepled black rocks, tipped with pale lichen at the highest point and slick with sea spray below.

Dark shapes moved about anxiously on its surface, a deep murmuring in chorus carried on the waves to my ears. If I didn't know better, I might think the land itself had become a writhing mass. As I ascended above the current, my seals clicked and snorted, slapping flippers against the rock in greeting. Their breath clouded around them in the cold. I waded out of the sea, pulling my hood away from my face. In a moment I was on two human feet, walking briskly towards the sheltered overhang.

Removing my coat was a simple enough matter. As swift as a thought, it obeyed my desires. There was an innate connection between my coat and my body. Though it was not physically attached to me, it was a part of my being in every fathomable way.

I was a creature of the *in-between*, belonging to neither world fully, but I supposed I liked it that way. When I wanted my coat hung open, my features became that of a woman with dark hair and eyes. I could walk on land with human legs and use human hands to my advantage. Or I could keep my coat tight around me and remain like my beloved seal kin. My appearance meant little to me. There were merely times in which my duty required one or the other. Fingers and fists made protecting my flock a bit easier than relying solely on large canines and the sheer force of my seal body. Being a powerful beast of the ocean held its own advantages.

Years of pounding waves and storms had carved a half-moon indentation in the black stone where my family resided. The monolithic rock was a silent sentinel, guarding over my flock when I was afar. This smoothed alcove was a perfect place to keep watch and sleep undisturbed by sea spray or wind. It was my preferred shelter. After navigating the seals that littered the surface of our island, I nestled down, leaning back against the rippled stone. I ran a hand around the heft of my hair, bringing it over my shoulder while I pulled in a deep breath. The cool weight of my blade between my breasts rose and fell with each exhale and inhale. Sleep would arrive soon enough.

Three pups flopped their way towards me, wishing to share the shelter for the evening. They enjoyed these human fingers as well. Perfect for scratching beneath chins and the soft flesh of their bellies. They knew I could not deny them their pleasure. I clicked gently, welcoming them in. Soon, I was firmly cushioned between them, each snoring and dazed after soft, freckled hands gently stroked their sides. The ocean lapped rhythmically against the rock, and besides the occasional snort or tremor from the massive seals readjusting their bodies, the night was still. The full moon hung above us all, silently staring down at me—silvery and cold.

How many full moons had it been since my first? How many more until my last?

I knew only one thing: I was a vessel for the ancient force within me. It was heavy and wrathful. It lapped against my insides and whispered into my being. It was all I was or would ever be. The sea birthed me out of pain and rage over the destruction of her children. I was to do what she could only manage through storm and wave: stop those who tainted her waters with blood and unnatural death. There was no choice to be had; it seemed to be innate—this burning need to protect, to kill any and all who threatened these gentle beasts. My body acted with a will outside of any conscious thought. It had always been so, since the day I was thrust from the abyss. I leaned back against the rock, allowing the soft bodies curled around mine to lull me to rest.

Sometime in the night, I must have pulled my coat tightly around myself, unconsciously changing from woman to seal. I could be swift like smoke once I slid into the waves, but the transition from land to sea was always somewhat cumbersome —dangerous—while in this body. After scanning the perimeter for any signs of peril, I hauled myself into the water. Green-black ripples shimmered out from the impact of my body sliding into the sea. The sky was a grey pearl and a dense fog hung low around the rock, obscuring much of the horizon from view. It was as if all that existed above the ocean was our home, and the seals who had yet to stir from sleep. The world we felt safest in, the one that fed and raised us, existed below.

I dove down deep. Bubbles danced before me as I exhaled. It was never warm here, but this body was made for the frigid temperatures. A mere human could survive no longer than an hour before succumbing to grave illness or death. That was a blessing in itself. We were protected by the water, but nowhere was truly out of reach for those beasts.

Humans.

They snatched up our food in their nets, desecrated our sacred spaces with their stone fortresses. They murdered, stripping skin from bone, life from body, in minutes. My kin were safest in the ocean, and safer still with me.

I circled the small pod of seals now, my fins churning the water in eddies. We swam as a unit, whistles and clicks signaling where the fish and crab were hiding among the kelp. A seal's life is one of peace— sleep, hunt, bear pups, and swim. To swim was to live. It was *everything*; the purest act of existence. We were sleek, graceful, weightless. Free of all that could fetter us. Moments of natural violence occurred around food and mating, or perhaps if a shark or whale were in the mood for seal flesh— and only then. It was a life of necessity, and of sheer will. That any one being should think they hold dominion over such unassuming creatures was unforgivable.

In my years attached to this life, I'd grown intelligent, and cunning. The seals looked to me for guidance and safety, knowing in their own way that I came to this world for them. They followed me, looked to me to protect them, keep them from all the harm I could. My purpose was to guard them with all that I had, and so my existence was one of solitude. Living in the in-between meant I lived inside my own head. The voice my human form could employ had hardly ever been given the chance to speak, though I was skilled in all the languages I'd heard man speak. It was quite beneficial at times. The sea had sought to give me even footing against humans by gifting me a coat and a mind full of words to wield like a weapon.

I once wondered what would happen if I should stray from my flock, or from the sea entirely. If I left my coat behind and walked among those on shore. Yes, humanity was full of black-guards who cared little for others, but there had been a time when a pair of pale eyes and a striking figure had beckoned me to land, to see if there was a different sort of life waiting for me. He was so beautiful, so enticing and lovely that I truly contemplated letting my coat—the most precious, singular thing I would ever possess—be lost to the sea. I was foolhardy enough to think I could be anything other than what I truly was. I learned my lesson, and from then on, knew to stay well away from man.

I learned what cruelty humans were capable of. I had witnessed helplessly when they had taken from me.

There was no amount of time or atonement that would ever clear them of their crimes.

And so, I clung to my claws and my dagger, and learned to welcome the killing calm.

"THE SEA THAT BARES HER BOSOM TO THE MOON;
THE WINDS THAT WILL BE HOWLING AT ALL HOURS,
AND ARE UP GATHERED NOW LIKE SLEEPING FLOWERS;
FOR THIS, FOR EVERYTHING, WE ARE OUT OF TUNE."
—WILLIAM WORDSWORTH

Chapter Two

CIAN

I could hardly contain my excitement as I made my way to our meeting place. I pulled my midnight cloak close, though I wasn't cold in the least. It was merely a gesture to keep my hands from wildly fidgeting about in anticipation. For *she* would be there—the young lass who'd snared my attention the very moment I laid my eyes upon her bonny figure. Since then, every night we'd come together at the castle ruins.

She'd steal out from her home, unbeknownst to her Da, then by starlight alone, we would find each other. It had been weeks of meeting in secrecy like this. Each night I'd felt surer than the last that she was destined to be mine. My bride. It was in the way her delicate fingers curled around the nape of my neck, sending chills ricocheting down my core. Her lips, full like Cupid's bow, whispering sweet nothings in my ear. My heart beat a heady rhythm in my chest.

It was clear she had become just as thoroughly ensorcelled by me. With every evening together, she grew more bold in her affections. It was all I could do to maintain her innocence, if only just barely. My fingers wrapped themselves more deeply within the folds of my cloak as I came round a crumbling stone arch, the very breath stolen from my lungs at the sight of her.

My bride, *bean chéile*.

Her bright, eager eyes paired wonderfully with a luminous grin that spread across her round face as our gazes met. She broke into a sprint across the path. In a moment she was wrapping her slender arms around my waist, peering up into my eyes.

Her voice was a breathless song. "*Mo mhuirnín*, the day lasted so long. Felt like I would never get these arms of mine around you."

I couldn't help but smile down at the beauty before me. My lips trembled with feverish anticipation. There was no time for me to utter any words, only time enough for embracing, for kissing. I placed my hands on either side of her face, soft skin caressed by my thumbs before I leaned forward and took her mouth to mine.

Ah.

She was eager; almost too eager. Our lips tangled together in a clash of growing urgency. I pulled away slightly, watched as she panted, lips still parted and begging for my return.

"My darling. S'not right for us to dwell in the shadows as we have. Let's take our love out of the darkness. Let's make right of this. Will you be my wife?" I let my eyes bore deep into hers, willing the words out of her. Her eyes fluttered in shock for a moment, before that beautiful smile unfurled once more.

Arms squeezed my middle even tighter as she cried out in joy. "Yes! Let us be married at first light. Let us be husband and wife. I was afraid you would never ask." Her voice was shaken, muffled beneath my cloak. My heart jumped up into my throat.

At last.

"We don't need to wait until morning, my dear. I know where we can be wed this very night." I curled my fingers around her chin, pulling her glance back to me. She bit her bottom lip, and I knew full well she was afire with the idea that we could be husband and wife, sharing a marriage bed within the hour. Her eyes smoldered blue fire, and it took all I had in me not to take her then and there. Instead, our lips melded together again, her mouth opening to me. My tongue swept in, deepening our passion. Her body pushed hard against mine, and I knew she was ready.

"Come, I'll take you there, my bride." Her fingers found mine, joining us flesh to flesh. My skin felt electric, alive with longing and passion. Weeks of this feeling built inside of me, the sheer desire. I tried to keep my growing sense of urgency under control, but it wasn't long before I found myself tugging her arm behind me as I all but raced to the shore of the riverbank.

"Will we be handfasted? Who is going to perform the rite?" My bride's voice was a giddy gurgle behind me. I sensed a sliver of apprehension in her words. I needed to get her to the river before her anticipation soured.

"Yes, my beloved, we will be handfasted and bound to one another, for all the days and nights of this world. Just a little farther along this way, my darling. Not long now until we may know each other." I turned back to smile at her, reminding her of all *that* would entail. She blushed and my stomach clenched with ecstasy. I helped her climb down the steep hillock just before the rocky bank. The night was still, save for the distant rumble of waves crashing against the black cliffs, and the hush of the river, my *abhainn*, as it flowed to the sea. My bride was self-consciously straightening her skirts and rearranging her pale curls around her shoulders. I stood speechless before her beauty, pale and full like the moon.

"Here we are my love, not long now until we are wed." I reached out my hands to her, and she took them obligingly. That gorgeous smile spread again like fire. She looked up into my eyes, searching for something. Before she could ask, I pulled her to me once more.

"Are you ready?"

Wordlessly she nodded her head, granting me all the permission I needed. "Come. Be my bride."

I walked slowly backwards, leading her with my gaze, guiding her ever so gently. Into the riverbed, the water lapped at my legs, welcoming me home. She did not look away as her hem sank to the stones beneath the water. She did not look away when we were waist deep, the chill turning my lovely bride's lips a pale grey. She did not look away when I pulled her to my side as I changed into my true form. Sleek, massive, and dark with slick *creathnach* tangled all about my mane. She did not look away when I pulled her under the water altogether. I did not see her, but felt her slender fingers cling to my neck, as I swam down into the depths, the black waters overcoming us entirely.

When we reached our home, she was still looking out with her crystalline eyes, but the woman was no more. Another bride, fleeting as fire and storm. The rush, the joy— torn away in a moment. The ache inside me was sharp as a blade and yet it was a dance I could never see the end of. No matter how brief, or how the pain of broken promises of forever tore at my heart. I beheld my lover's gaze one last time before the current pulled her from me forever, taking her so that she might dwell lifelessly in the waters forevermore.

I glanced up to see the Moon's wavering glow far above the river. She looked down on me in her sad sweet way, beckoning me up from the depths, away from my cottage. Lovely and solemn, the moon was one I never could tame. The one who knew my secrets well, and yet still seemed to shine with all her might so that I could continue in my ways, old as the hills— though not as old as she.

The columns of swaying *creathnach* around my door waved a slow farewell. I was still thrumming with the instinctive thrill of completing the only task I had ever been given.

Take a bride to the water, give her to the depths, and begin again.

How many wives had I wed to the river? It was a question to which I didn't care to know the answer. There were things in the world that existed for dark purposes, to uphold the balance between the Seen and Unseen. It was an endless gift to live between. It ached something terrible though, at times like these, when the thrill of warm kisses and bodies pressed together must end so quickly. I found myself feeling a familiar sort of hollowness as I ascended from the bottom of the river.

Up the sloping bank, out to more shallow waters. My hooves silently navigated the stones that dotted the river's edge. I filled my chest with air once again, letting the glacial water coursing through me trickle away to nothing. Standing on the shore of my *abhainn*, I shook once as a beast, and then, I was no longer hooved and maned. Instead, I stood perfect— and human.

"HE WHO LETS THE SEA LULL HIM INTO A SENSE OF
SECURITY IS IN VERY GRAVE DANGER"
— HAMMOND INES

Chapter Three

IONA

The pups chirped all around me as I jumped into the ocean. I pulled my human legs up to my chest, creating a wild splash to soak the little ones. When I re-emerged, they were still humming with joy over the trick. A grin spread slowly across my face as I took in their innocent glee. Pups as young as these wouldn't be ready to swim for a few weeks yet, but they were safe here on this rock. I hadn't seen any humans try for this stretch of terrain. Too many jagged edges hidden beneath the swells to sink their ships.

The sun was milky yellow, slowly burning its way through the morning fog. The day was growing warmer. Waves lapped against me, gentle and familiar, like a mother's embrace, I supposed. Tiny diamonds of light sparkled off the ocean's surface. As I looked out at the horizon, my breath caught in my throat when my gaze was captured by something I did not recognize.

On shore, barely more than a brisk swim away, was something glistening beneath the sun. I had to shield my face from its blinding glare. I peered back around to my flock, watched as a seal or two sauntered towards the water's edge, some already diving and surfacing to catch their breath before continuing the hunt for food. The pups seemed to be the only ones watching me at the moment. One cocked his head, those round, obsidian eyes waiting to see what I would do about the mystery on land. After scanning the horizon a dozen times for any sign of man and checking to be sure my kin were all accounted for, I decided to go and see for myself what this strange glowing object might be.

I pulled my seal skin over my human body. My beautiful black coat cascaded over my arms and head. It fused with my body in a swift wave of change. Fingers and toes became flippers. Whiskers lengthened before my eyes, and suddenly I was swift beneath the waves once more. I rarely left my flock for any period of time, but the sea was calm today, a sort of peace hanging in the air that signaled I was free to stray. So little in my life was truly mine, it only seemed fair to be able to slip away now and again to see what I could for myself.

The swim proved to be greater of a distance than I initially thought. The fog must have impeded my judgment. I watched the sea floor beneath me as I flew through the ocean. Crab and seaweed dotted the rocky bottom, along with constellations of dark sea stars, piled neatly together as they feasted on barnacles. Pale anemone waved up to me with their long finger-like tendrils. Seals cannot smile, but my heart beat hard within my body and a feeling like sunshine flowed through me. The small wonders hidden to many showed themselves to me. It was a gift, and in that moment, I felt lucky to receive it.

I neared the rocky coastline, the strange object still shining in the sunlight. I remained submerged save for my face. To any watching from the shore, they would only see a sable seal with black inquisitive eyes, nothing more than a creature of the sea. Before I removed my cloak, I turned back in the water to see our rock. The dark stones sparkled in the morning, but I was so far away. My family appeared only as small specks surfacing then disappearing again into the waves. I wouldn't stay long.

I swam as close to the shore as I could get without beaching myself and took one last look around to be sure I was alone. When I was certain, I let my sealskin slip from my body. With only a thought, it slid down my now human arms, opening from the center of my torso like a man's jacket without buttons. I pulled my hood back, and slowly made my way to land.

The rocks covering the shore were jagged and slick with rock weed and toothy barnacles, but I was used to this terrain. I crouched, using my hands to keep from falling, eyes ever searching for danger. Once I cleared the largest of the rocks, the remaining ground was made up of dark pebbles and drying seaweed. I felt comfortable enough in my solitude to stand fully on my feet. I still wore my coat around my shoulders, though it hung open in the front.

The object that captured my curiosity was tangled in weed and discarded netting. It shined incandescently, like the inside of an oyster shell. I knelt, removing the dried detritus of eelgrass from its surface, only to be startled away. I fell backwards, rocks digging painfully into the heels of my palms.

There was *someone* staring back at me through the glinting surface. She looked frightened, and well—frightening.

I leaned forward cautiously. Was she trapped inside this object? The being on the other side moved exactly as I did.

I blinked slowly as I grew to understand.

She was *me*. The woman staring with black eyes and swaths of dark hair was *me*.

I had never peered into something so clear as this to behold my nature. I stilled before it, crossing my legs beneath my body. My hands stretched out to touch the surface, saltwater leaving tracks across my visage. I leaned in closer still, breath obscuring my view in hazy circles. One hand reached up to my cheek, feeling the taught skin there. A smattering of dark speckles traveled across the pale bridge of my nose to my temples. Eyes dark like a seal's, fathomless and fearful to behold, fringed with heavy, salt crusted lashes. Angular cheekbones seemed to force my mouth into a downward arc.

I felt a stinging sensation in my eyes. A heat rose up in me. The thing looking back at me grew splotched as saltwater leaked down my face in large droplets. I watched as tears began slipping down my chin, blotting the rocks beneath me in inky splashes. I had never spied another being who looked as I did.

My stomach twisted like an eel caught in its killer's jaws. I was reminded again that I was alone; a creature with one purpose, one thing to live for.

Was it enough?

An image of a man, blurred with age in my memory, passed behind my eyes. *I wasn't enough, then.*

I sat in front of the reflective surface for I don't know how long. I turned my face in different directions, examining every angle of my being. I felt I was searching for something, but I wasn't sure what it was. I tried to pull the reflective object towards me, but it was large and cumbersome. I almost dropped it completely—something in me warned that it could break—so I forced it back upright and made sure to leave it in place.

At some point I stood and began to examine my body as a whole. I let my coat fall to the ground in a pile at my feet. Broad shoulders, lean limbs for swimming, large hands, calloused and knotted from use. Powerful. A being made for functionality—for vengeance.

A rustling in the trees above snared my attention.

A flush crept to my face as I realized how long I had been engrossed in this endeavor. I looked up at the cliff face towards the sound. A strange, dark creature stood on four legs, with a long snout and deep red eyes that looked down into mine. I'd never seen anything like it before. The beast's presence shook me from my reverie. The creature appeared to me like an omen of darkness to come. I dropped into a crouch and grabbed my coat before racing back to the ocean. Just as I slid into my sealskin, my eyes strained for our rock. Horror gripped every cell in my body.

A boat.

In that instant I lost all agency. My body was given over to the demands of the sea and I became her hand.

Wrath and fury propelled me desperately through the ocean to my kin. Muscles burned and my lungs screamed from holding so much air for so long, but I could not stop. They were so far away from me, from my protection. What was not long before this, a welcoming, peaceful stretch of water, was now dark and void of life. The cold seemed to seep past my thick coat and into my bones. The emptiness of the sea flooded into my being, readying me for the killing that was waiting.

There was no thought within my head as I surged up from

the sea, next to the large rowboat the men had anchored. I tore my coat away, revealing my naked rage. They had knives and another kind of weapon that rang out like a wave breaking in a storm. I watched only a moment as a booming death knell rang out, watched numbly as one of my kin flopped to her side, a river of her heart's blood leaking out into the ocean.

Then I became death.

I ripped my dagger from my neck and bellowed my agony as I sprinted at the man with the weapon. He stood dumbfounded, unsure of how to react, even as my knife slid easily across his neck.

I left him, his blood mingling then with hers. He fell as I turned, searching for the others.

There were two more men.

One was hauling a limp pup over the side of his boat, his downy coat now smattered with brine and sticky blood. There was no death I could bestow upon this man that would match his crime. I leapt up into the vessel and grabbed his skull between my hands before hammering it down along the angled bow of the boat again, and again, until his hands went limp, and the dead pup flopped into the ocean. His first and last swim.

My fingers grew slick with blood as I continued smashing the murderer's head against his boat. Still unsatisfied, but aware of the last man standing, I dropped him. A wet thud sounded dully as he, too, slipped down into the water. I looked up, unsure of where the other had gone.

A wave crashed, and a fire blazed up in my shoulder. No— not a wave, but that damned weapon. I looked down when I felt stinging heat oozing over my chest.

Blood. *My* blood.

I spun to see the man, weapon still aimed squarely at me. I snarled, bared my teeth at him as I sprung back out of the boat, towards him. His eyes widened a moment, and then, another crash of sound and pain. I shrieked, agony tearing through my gut as I fell into the water. I clawed and fought to get back to the surface. The man's expression was cold as he continued peering down at me from the rock. Then a real wave crashed upon me, crimson and frothing, and everything went black.

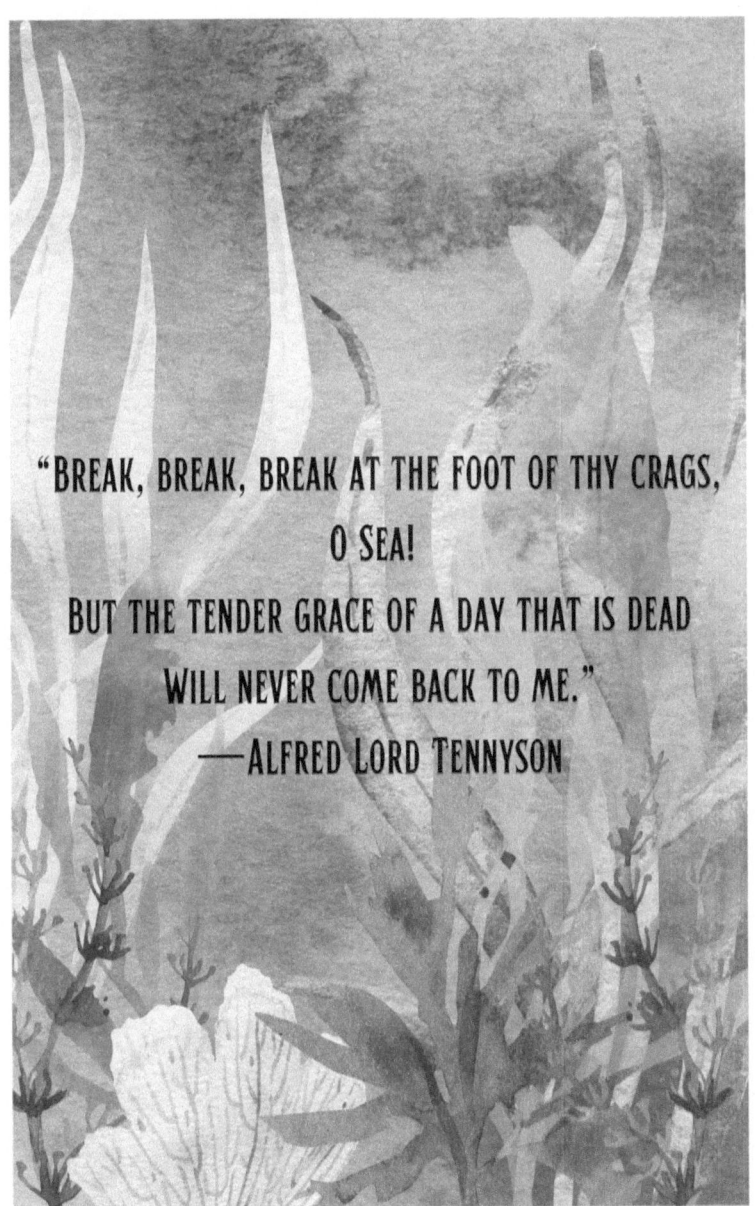

"BREAK, BREAK, BREAK AT THE FOOT OF THY CRAGS,
O SEA!
BUT THE TENDER GRACE OF A DAY THAT IS DEAD
WILL NEVER COME BACK TO ME."
—ALFRED LORD TENNYSON

Chapter Four

IONA

The sea pushed and pulled, abusing me for my failure. It ripped me up out of the depths so that I might steal a bit of air into my lungs before plunging me back into darkness. There was nothing but pain, rage, and the searing understanding that I had allowed death to enter our safe haven.

I let the ocean batter me. I welcomed it. Days, possibly weeks, or eons passed by. It did not matter. I was no better than a bit of flotsam, lost to the currents. I waited to be broken apart, unmade back into blood weed and sea foam.

I do not know when it happened, but my head stopped spinning. My fingers felt sand and silt. My cheek rested upon something warm, alive. I could still hear the sea, and water rushing towards it.

When I peeled my eyes open, I looked upon the same beast whose appearance startled me out of my shameful reverie that day on the beach. *Creathnach* tangled in its black mane, matching the color of its eyes perfectly—a deep red. The sight of the familiar seaweed after endless blackness was a strange comfort. I reached my hand to touch it and cried out in pain. I was alive enough to still feel something.

My head throbbed as I tried to move to look at my injuries. An angry wound radiated pain on my breast, and my stomach... I pulled away a dark cape that had somehow been draped over me to find that a portion, all too large, had been gouged out of my side. Whatever that weapon was, it had broken my body the way a shark's jaws cut jaggedly into the flesh of seals. I reached tentative fingers down, and when they glanced across my flayed flesh, the pain and shock sent a roiling wave of nausea through me. The creature beside me huffed almost like a seal might, my eyes rolled back, and I hit the ground hard.

When I came to once again, I was draped in the same black cloak, astride the beast with red eyes. Its hide was black like mine in my seal form, but softer, finer. I mindlessly curled my fingers in its mane, unsure of where I was or where it was carrying me. It didn't matter.

"Are you awake then, *Anamchara*?"

My body went rigid. *That voice—where—?*

"It's strange, I know. But so are we."

I was startled completely and lost what remained of my balance. Slowly, I plummeted, sliding off the creature and ending in a painful heap of black fabric on the ground. I cried out, my wounds roaring, sending fresh fire through my body.

The beast halted immediately. "Should have waited t'introduce myself, I know that now. Not often that I can be in this state and find myself willing to converse, but it's not every day that one comes across another of the Unseen, now is it?"

The words rolling out from this *thing* could have been complete gibberish, what little I understood. For all I knew I was already dead, being carried to hell. I had no words of my own to speak. There was too much to process. Instead, a wretched cough escaped my throat while I struggled to stand.

"Here—let me help." The words were clearer now, and I looked up to see where the beast was, only to find a man, just taller than myself. I swallowed.

He was stunning in a way no human could ever be. Hair the color of dried sand hung about his shoulders. His eyes were deep set, kissed with lashes that curled upward. His lips were full, slightly parted as he reached a hand my way.

His palm outstretched towards me, and I hissed, reached my hand to my neck for my dagger, but froze as his mouth curved into a sideways smile.

His eyes flashed red, like the beast, but only for a moment before rippling into a shade of hazy blue. The man bowed, grin spreading ever wider. "Name's Cian, pleasure to meet you...?" His voice was as soft as the hide that had once covered him. When he spoke his name, his lips opened wide enough for me to take in the sight of slightly sharpened teeth. A predator then, like me.

I realized he asked for my name. I clenched my jaw, searching for the human word to match the seals' endearments towards me.

Cian's eyebrows raised.

My voice was raspy from disuse. "Iona. What *are* you, Cian?"

He curled his fingers into a fist, realizing I wasn't going anywhere with him until he gave me answers.

"It's not 'keen', is 'key-an'—means ancient. And in order to answer your question...I must first receive a gift. Our kind gives nothing for free."

Our kind?

I glowered up at him. I didn't need this. I just wanted to crawl into a hole and forget the world. To be left alone to rot in peace. "You carried me here, isn't that something? I've never given you anything, so why must I do so now?" The growl I had hoped to push into my words was more of a hiss, though dripping with anger. I doubted I had spoken so many words in decades.

Cian's smile grew devilish, making me even angrier. "Well, that's not entirely true. You've given me the absolute delight of a lifetime. I'd never seen a seal change to a woman, let alone a *very* naked woman. Now *that* is the kind of gift I won't soon forget."

My entire being was engulfed in flames, and not from my injuries this time. I didn't know why after baring my skin to so many others before, the knowledge of someone intentionally spying on me was enough to fill me with rage. I tried to stand on my own, now seething with physical pain *and* embarrassment.

"I have nothing to give you, so be on your way." I clutched my injured shoulder, no longer able to stomach the ache in my side when I tried rising.

Cian's face took an interesting expression then, like a seal pup whose sibling had stolen their bit of fish away. "You can't just sit here. What will you do without your coat?" His question slapped me across the face. I flopped over and vomited in the dirt.

My coat.

Heaven and earth, and all the hells below. My cloak was gone.

Cian knelt before me and wrapped my arms around his neck. "Oh no, that can't be good for your injuries. Come now, you can owe me." In a moment I was once again laying on the broad back of the massive creature he was apparently able to shift in and out of. "I know a place where we can get you fixed up right pretty, my darling."

My side felt damp and warm, my vision became blurred.

"Cian?"

"Mhm?"

"*What* are you?"

"The question is... what are *we*?"

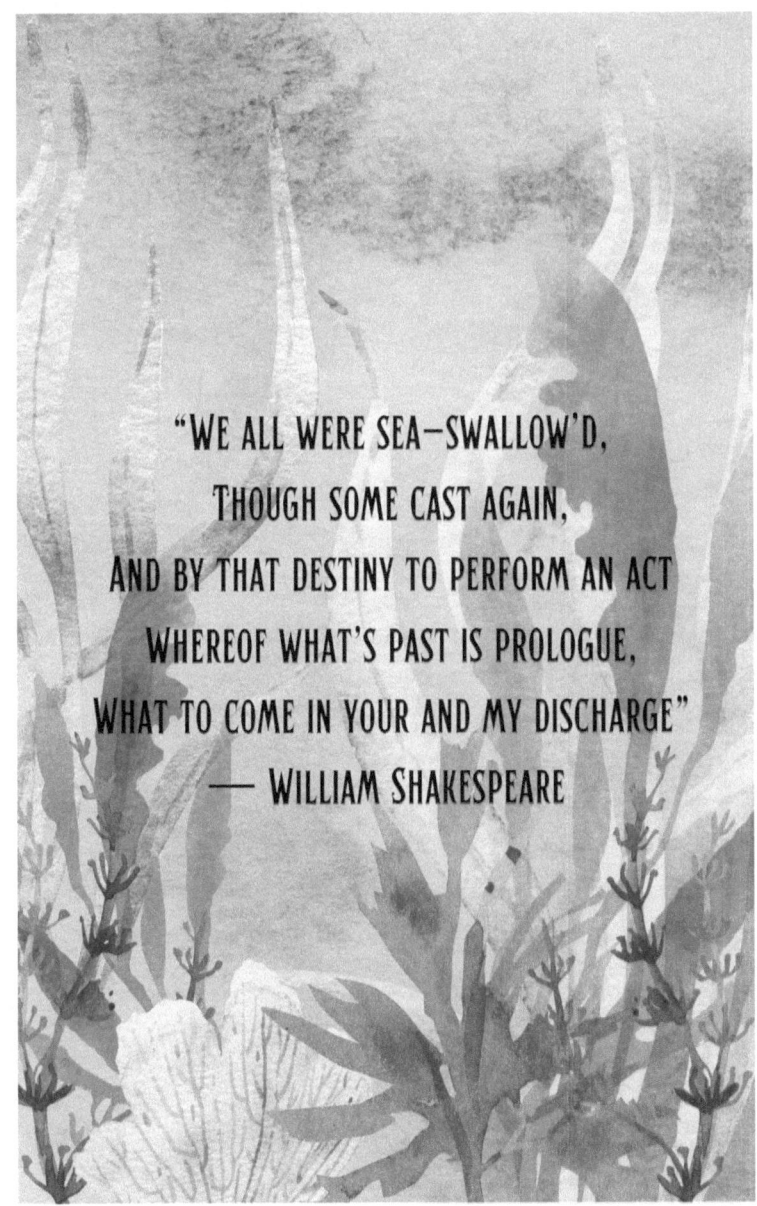

"We all were sea-swallow'd,
Though some cast again,
And by that destiny to perform an act
Whereof what's past is prologue,
What to come in your and my discharge"
— William Shakespeare

Chapter Five

CIAN

Iona had yet to wake after that last fainting spell. I dared not stop for fear that her injuries were serious enough to warrant her death. She felt warm against me, alive enough to hang on while I tried to remember the path to the witch's cabin. It had been so long since I'd cause to travel there. Perhaps she was gone or dead herself. I'd not bothered to check, and now I was cursing myself for it.

Riding with me was a treasure I thought to keep all to myself. Letting her die would feel too much like all the others I'd led to their watery marital beds. Right now, this experience so far had been an altogether different kind. New. Fresh. *Exciting*.

"Hold tight to me now, *mo mhuirnín*, we've got a steep climb ahead of us," I announced, hoping she was alive enough to do as I said.

Iona moaned, but she obeyed. Clammy arms snaked out around my neck as the incline increased. I was mighty grateful for the calm weather. The breeze rustled the low hanging branches of the rowan and hawthorn trees that lined the narrow pathway, filling my nose with Iona's scent. Ocean spray, cold, and blood. I hoped to help with that last. Another scent carried towards us in the wind: chimney smoke.

In a thicket of sun dappled saplings, barely upright enough to count as a house, was the *Cailleach's* dwelling. Thick moss clung to the sagging roof. A sorry excuse for a door was open, hanging crookedly from rusted hinges. Various vermin chirped and called from their hiding places in the grass and shrubs surrounding the hovel. There was an air of warning here, but I would not be deterred.

"Hello? *Seanmháthair*?" I used the human word for grandmother in hopes that the old hag would take kindly to me. Our past dealings had not been savory, to say the least. I stood silently, waiting for a reply.

Nothing.

Iona's arms slackened and she began sliding away. I shifted quickly enough into my human form, catching her before she fell to the ground. She was a dense sort of creature, all muscles and limbs. I tried to cradle her body in my arms, her head lolling over side to side as I awkwardly began to drag her into the Cailleach's home. Wouldn't she be so glad to see the pair of us when she arrived?

There was a small cot pushed into the corner of the darkened room. The windows were all shut and boarded up. The only light filtered in from cracks in the chinks between wood. It smelled of dried herbs and animal hides, though the room was mostly bare. I hefted the unconscious woman onto the bed, making sure her arms and legs all made it onto the small surface. Her limbs were quite long, and I had to bend them for her to fit somewhat properly on the cot. I found myself wondering what sort of place this Iona usually returned to for sleep, if she slept at all. My mind ceased all other questions when I noticed how the cape had fallen open, exposing her almost entirely.

I didn't feel an ounce of shame as I looked her over once more. I had to check her injuries, didn't I? Iona's skin was freckled, every single inch of her—all that I could see, anyway. She appeared to have been shot, at least twice. Her chest wound looked clean enough, but her side—or what was left of it—hurt to even look at. The bullet had passed through her in a way that ripped a chunk from her waist. The wound was weeping a mixture of blood and puss.

I'd never been injured so grievously, but I'd once supposed it would be no matter of healing. Things like us, we don't live and die as men. I thought we wouldn't be ill or hurt like them either, but I must have been wrong. I pulled the cloak over her body, not wishing to look at the gore any longer. I peered at her face.

A sheen of sweat coated her skin, beads of it slid down her throat to rest in the hollow between her collarbones. Her dark brows were gathered up over her closed eyes, her thin mouth parted slightly so that her breath came ragged and short. I inhaled, scenting her once more, and this time paired with blood and sea was that of death. Was my diversion coming to an end so abruptly? Where was that witch when I needed her?

"Come to my cottage with a dying girl? Has your river dried up then?" Her voice was rough as tree bark, biting, yet familiar. I turned from Iona to find the ancient hag holding a woven basket bursting with plants in one hand, pointing her cane accusingly towards me with the other. Her hair was a bird's nest of grey. I wouldn't be surprised if there was actually a little egg incubating within the tangles. The crone's face was weathered and scarred. One eye had gone completely milky. I'd heard some say she used that one to see into the souls of others. I thought maybe she'd just been kicked in the face by a horse. But then again—there were stranger things in this world.

I would know.

I bowed my head in respect, knowing a smile would not be enough to subdue the witch. "*Seanmháthair*, please. She is not my bride, but perhaps she is more. She was shot." I kept my head bowed low, curiosity welling inside me over my own word choice. *More*?

The Cailleach coughed and clucked her tongue as she tossed her basket aside and used her cane to propel her twisted body towards the cot.

"Don't try to butter me up with sweet nothings, I know I'm not your type. Get out of my way, beast. Leave my cottage. Leave me in peace to do my work." Her lip curled, clearly displeased with me.

I cleared my throat as I moved to stand. "Should I leave with...with her? Or will you...?" The old hag brought her cane down hard on my head without warning. I yelped in pain before scurrying away from the bed.

"Fool. Leave *her*. Get out."

I swallowed the smile that tried to grow across my mouth, nodded once and slipped out through the broken door.

Once outside though, I found myself incapable of going any further than a few steps from the threshold. I leaned in towards the entry, willing my ears to capture any sound coming from within so that I could learn what was to become of my newly discovered treasure laying near death on the cot. I heard several impressive curses, growled over and over again from the Cailleach as she inspected Iona's wounds.

Then there were the sounds of water, fire crackling, and a strong aroma of medicinal plants soon filled the air around me. I found myself pacing back and forth, gripping my hands into tight fists as I waited to be invited back. I hoped I would be invited back. I couldn't leave, and I couldn't wait much longer.

Why couldn't I leave? The creature inside was nothing to me after all, merely a curiosity I wished to know more about. I had a duty to fulfill, and it was not being accomplished standing here in this forest so far from where I ought to be.

Iona *did* owe me. She had been given my name, and my services. I could not let her go without receiving a fair and proper trade in return. It would be a disgrace upon my honor to do so. That was why I stayed—to get even. Yes.

And get even I would.

The witch began singing then, pulling me from my thoughts. She sang in the old tongue, one I hadn't heard since I was...newer in the world. She sang of stars and blood, the depths of the sea, and the sorrows of all living things. At the end of the song, I thought I heard a softer voice, weeping.

When the sun disappeared behind the hill, my patience went with it. I leaned in past the door frame, but the words on my tongue evaporated at the sight inside. The hag was brushing out Iona's hair, who sat cross legged in front of the fire. She was wearing a cottony looking shift that was a shade lighter than her skin. She hadn't died. I found myself feeling giddy at her aliveness.

Before the Cailleach could stop me, I stepped inside and joined the two of them at the now crowded hearth. Iona turned to me as the witch clucked her tongue in disapproval. Her face was red, eyes swollen, and tears raced down her face in large salty swaths.

I couldn't help but ask, "Why the tears? You're alive."

Iona shook her head and stared back into the fire. *Thwack.* That damned cane came crashing down on my back this time.

"Dolt. D'you not know what this lass is? D'you not know what she's lost? *Fool.*" The crone spit on the floor at my feet. I clenched my jaw, pursing my lips to keep cruel words from spilling out of me. She had done me a favor without payment. I couldn't go spouting out my rage and not expect to be banished from her good graces henceforth.

Iona spoke before we could argue. "I am nothing without my coat. I am this—*this.*" She held her hands in front of her face, turning them over and back again, as though she'd never seen them before. "You should have just left me there. Let the sea have me." She looked so small then, as she readjusted to pull her legs up under her chin, wrapping her arms around herself as if she was afraid she might come apart.

Iona's words rang in my head, a dull bell chiming. Again, why *hadn't* I left her? I'd led so many women to their deaths, why didn't I let this one go, the same as all the others?

I knew the answer. I just wasn't brave enough to give it life.

Not yet.

"HER LIPS WERE RED,
HER LOOKS WERE FREE,
HER LOCKS WERE YELLOW AS GOLD:
HER SKIN WAS WHITE AS LEPROSY,
THE NIGHTMARE LIFE—IN—DEATH WAS SHE,
WHO THICKS MAN'S BLOOD WITH COLD."
— SAMUEL TAYLOR COLERIDGE

Chapter Six

IONA

The old woman was not what I expected to see when I awoke. I expected not to wake at all, and when I heard her song, ancient like me and full of welling sadness, I knew I was alive. Her words sank into my bones, reminded me of my flock, now abandoned and fewer than before. They were helpless out there on their own, if any had survived—and it was *my* fault. I remembered that I was without my coat, and the heartbreak rushed back to me. I curled over on my side and wept.

Maybe it was because I was made of the sea, but my tears were incessant. They soaked the cloak hanging about my neck, the sheets beneath me, down to the straw bedding. The woman made a shushing sound and began rubbing my back much like I had done for the seal pups to help them sleep, and instead of soothing my heart, I remembered the pup whose coat was matted with blood and cried all the more.

"Hush now ducky, hush. What has happened to you so that I might know more to keep you well?"

I shook my head, tried to open my mouth to let the story

break free from me, but those words would not come. Instead, I stared at her, and she stared back. The one eye pale green, and the other milky like a pearl. After a long moment of seeing one another, she looked away, shaking her head. "Selkie?" I did not know that word. My brows knitted together, waiting for more. "Seal woman? Where is your coat?"

She knew.

Sobs racked my body, muscles taught with agony and my tears.

I swallowed once, then said, "Gone. I lost it. I lost them all." The woman patted my back again, shushing sounds whispered out from her.

"Come, sit by the fire, Selkie. Let's warm those bones and set you to rights."

I sat upright, suddenly quite aware of my injuries, or better stated, the lack of pain radiating out from them. My hands found the wound on my chest, now wrapped in gauzy fabric from under my arm and over my shoulder. My waist was wrapped as well, but it barely pained me at all. I pressed down on it to test my limits, only to be impressed with how dull the ache had grown.

"Here love, put this on ye, or that lecherous beast outside will surely not be able to contain himself." She must be referring to the creature who'd decided to bring me here. *Cian.*

"Thank you." I took the parcel from her gnarled hands, surprised at the object's softness. "How did you—?" I searched her face, wonder washing over my deep sorrow, curious at how I was so easily back on my feet after such terrible pain had racked my body. I'd seen creatures slowly waste away from much smaller injuries, and I could not understand how I had been spared.

"Tch—You think you are the only creature in the world with magic? No, my dear. You are not as alone as ye might think." She smiled and I saw her teeth, browned and tiny in her gums. Why had I never considered there were more things in existence than myself, the sea and those horrid men? The answer was simple enough: it had never mattered before. The woman helped me pull the cloth down over my head, tying two strings together at the base of my neck. Then she ushered me to the woven rug on the floor. Before I set myself down, I was horrified to see flames leaping out into her home. I turned back, clinging to her shoulders in fear.

The woman's voice was gentle as she said, "No dear, this fire will not harm ye, only warm you, and cook us dinner." She rubbed my arms as she guided me to sit. "Shhh, there's a good lass, just set yourself down right there now. Good girl." She pulled a small stool from the end of the cot and sat behind me. Pulled the length of my hair into her hands. "What lovely hair ye have. I should have loved hair like this for my own when I was a young woman, but I have always had this ragged mess to contend with." I didn't quite understand what she was going on about, but her voice, gravelly and worn, was a comfort. As she ran fingers and something else with teeth through my hair, the tears began anew. This time they silently slipped down my face, one after another. Tears for my kin. For my failure. For my coat.

Not long after finding the fire was actually quite enjoyable, all the while still managing to cry, Cian rushed in through the door. I'd half thought he would've left me here to return to his own dealings, whatever they might be. I spilled my guts to the woman, and then to Cian, when he'd foolishly asked, caring about little else but my aching heart. After a while of stunned silence, he sat silently behind us on the cot. I supposed he was mesmerized by the flames like I was, but maybe not. Maybe he had fires of his own, in his own home.

The crone grumbled, "Well, after your surprise disruption this afternoon, my dinner plans have been postponed a bit. I need to go check my traps. I'll be back in a wink." She looked fiercely in Cian's direction then growled, "*Don't* do anything stupid, beast." With that, she snatched up a threadbare cape from the chair by the door, tossed it around her shoulders and hobbled out with a basket and stick in hand. Cian clasped both hands behind his head and leaned back against the wall, then noticed me watching him. His mannerisms were languid; there was an ease to his presence that reflected its very absence in me. He tilted his head forward, the blue in his eyes dark like the ocean, threatening to drag me under once more.

There were so many questions filling my skull, I couldn't choose one to ask first, but it didn't matter, for Cian beat me to it. "Are you healed then? Did the witch fix your wounds?" His voice reminded me of the soft sand beneath the kelp forests, smooth and cool. I nodded once, pulling the garment I wore to the side so he could see the wrap on my shoulder. He inspected the old woman's work. "Does it...hurt?" Cian's eyes burned then, a deep ruby as his brows went low over the bridge of his nose.

I readjusted, feeling a lingering soreness in my bones. "Some. Not like before. Before I felt like I was inside this fire." I held my hand out to the flames, tentatively waiting to see if it would burn the way my belly had earlier today. It only felt hot, like the sun. Cian's gaze followed the length of my arm into the fire.

He asked, "Who shot you?" I cocked my head, slowly understanding that *shot* must mean what that man had done to me.

"Men came for my kin. *Shot* them. *I* came for the men, and they shot *me*." Rage bubbled in my gut, begging to be released.

Cian loosed a long breath before he spoke again. "Your family? There's more like you?"

I shook my head once. "There are none like me. My kin are true seals. I am only their protector, nothing more. Well—I *was*. Now I am simply nothing." Tears rushed down from my eyes, relentlessly this time. The story was simple enough to speak, but the pain that erupted from each word would cut me again and again for eternity. Cian crawled off the bed, and down to the floor beside me. He took my hands in his, pulling me too close to him for comfort. His humanity instinctively made me go rigid, but he barely seemed to notice.

Hazy eyes that were blue once again and fringed with pale lashes bored into mine, he breathed with a kind of excitement that unsettled me. "You say you are only a thing without your coat? Well then, let us get it back for you. Where did you last have it? Maybe it is as simple as going back to the beginning of this tale." Cian licked his lips, and I couldn't help but see him as a hungry seal, eager to hunt.

I pulled my hands free of his grip, turning back to the fire. "I left it on the rock where my flock lived. I cannot swim that distance in this form. It may as well be on the other side of the world."

Cian laughed then, and it was velvety to my ears—like being caressed by the sea itself. I balked at his cruelty. Before I could chastise him for his carelessness he said, "You can't, but *I* can." I couldn't help the arch of my brow. Neither this human form nor the gargantuan creature he shifted into appeared particularly equipped for the frigid sea. He cocked his head. "Oh, don't believe me, then? Well, *Miss Selkie*, prepare to be amazed as I reveal to ye my true nature—*tá mé Each-Uisce*." The phrase *water-horse* pushed my eyebrows even higher.

Once again Cian took my hand and gripped it so tightly, I could not pull away before he leaned ever closer and planted his lips to the back of it. "You and I, we're more alike than you know." I felt his breath, warm against my skin. Before I could ask what in heaven's name Cian was saying, the old woman returned to the shack, banging loudly on the threshold with her stick. I ripped my hand back from Cian, forcing at least an inch of distance between us.

"You there, beast—come help me skin these hares." She held out her hand. Clutched in her fist were two furred creatures, held by long ears, bodies limp. *Hares.*

My mouth went dry, and a lump formed in my throat. "You're going to eat them?" Heat sprang into my face when my voice sounded, a mere squeak escaping my lips. Never had I eaten a creature with soft fur. It had always been clams and fish and urchin that filled my belly. Cian turned to me, grinning now like a thresher shark, ready to take a bite out of my flesh if I wasn't fast enough.

"Never had rabbit stew, Iona? What sorts of things do seal women eat, after all? Pray tell, I find my curiosity brimming over the edge."

The look in his eyes sent a curl of irritation through my body. My eyes narrowed at his good spirits. What right had he to be so jovial? To behave so utterly nonplussed while my world was crumbling? Perhaps I should illustrate my strength. "I thought you knew what *seal women* ate—men who displease us."

Cian's cheeks rounded with his smile; he didn't back down. "Oh, 'tis a good thing I'm not wholly man then, isn't it?"

"I'd make an exception for you." I gave him a clear view of my canines and Cian's face tinged scarlet, all the way out to his slightly pointed ears. The old woman cleared her throat, halting any further discussion about my diet. Cian's lips quirked upwards for a mere moment before the pure blackness of my mood seemed to finally sink in.

"These hares won't skin themselves. Come now, I am owed for my services after all. It would be a pity to force you out into the dark woods at this hour." I knew her words should frighten me; put some sort of caution into my bones. But I was hollow. Nothing could upend such an empty vessel.

"And now my spirit twists
Out of my breast,
My spirit
Out in the waterways,
Over the whale's path
It soars widely through all the corners of the
world—
It comes back to me
Eager and unsalted;
The lone—flier screams,
Urges onto the whale—road
The unresisting heart
Across the waves of the sea."
— The Seafarer

Chapter Seven

CIAN

The seal woman had gone even more pale when I brought the skinned hares back to the *cailleach's* table. "Folk eat these quite often, Iona, it's nothing unnatural. I guarantee you will not die, nor are you committing some kind of evil by eating them." I thought perhaps she might have a tender heart for the helpless vermin, and it seemed I was right. The wrinkles in her brow eased albeit only somewhat, but I felt a small swelling of pride within me, knowing I had comforted her. There was a fragility to her that contradicted her physicality. Iona was small and yet immense in a fashion that held me captivated. She shifted her position so she could look me square in the eye.

Her black gaze was open and raw. She said, "I've only ever eaten things from the sea. And never anything that looked so..." I watched her neck as she swallowed down her next words. I wanted to kneel beside Iona, to push her braid over her shoulder, but the hag eyed me in a way that spelled murder should I come any closer to the Selkie. I thought about her seal family. Remembered seeing small wriggling pups way out on the

47

distant rocks of the coastline. I wondered if she was thinking of them, too.

I couldn't help myself but to study her as we ate. Clearly, she had not been around humankind long enough to learn their manners as I had. Iona appeared to like the stew, at least well enough to eat a bowl of it. She'd refused a spoon, instead holding the bowl up to her mouth. She'd burned her tongue at first, unaware that food could be so heated by the fire. She used her hands the way a brute would instead of the delicate ladies with whom I consorted. Iona was innocent in some ways, but one look into her dark eyes and I realized quite swiftly that she seemed as old as I was, if not older. There was a sea of too many things hiding behind those eyes, and I wanted to know them all. She was a puzzle, one I wished desperately to solve.

I knew one thing was certain. I wasn't ready to go back to my cottage beneath my *abhainn* just yet. I had time enough to court my next bride. I could hold off a little longer. I would help Iona and then resume my endless pursuit of love. Something in me had stirred to life, something separate from the unyielding drive to wed women to the water and I needed to see it through. Surely, I could stray for a while yet.

A tiny spark of it had ignited in my chest when I'd found Iona bleeding and broken at the flowing waters marking the mouth of my *abhainn*. Never had I wanted to do more than what I had been created for. Never had a current stronger than my own will pushed me onward the way she had. It was obvious this dark eyed woman was the very same who stood before the shipwrecked mirror below me just a few days prior.

After the quiet meal, Iona silently laid her body down at length across from the now smoldering fire. I took up a place behind her on the small wooden stool, leaning forward, elbows resting on my knees as I listened to the seal woman's breathing. Long freckled legs bare of any concealment stole my attention completely until the *cailleach* raised her cane in threat when she noticed where my gaze had strayed. "You'll not touch her, fiend. Not under my roof."

I frowned at the crone. "You've no need to fear for her. She and I, we're—"

She scoffed at me, said, "I know what you think—you think the lass is yours because you found her? Like she's a jewel to be ferreted away for yourself? She's just a prize you—" The witch stopped when she saw my changed countenance.

My voice rumbled out of me. "*Cailleach*. I did not wish to bring ill into your...*home*, but I will not suffer you to belittle me, to berate me as though I was a petulant child. I am older than the hill upon which your hovel rests. Choose your next words wisely."

The room darkened, and the air grew damp like death with my ire. The old hag shuddered, albeit only momentarily before sealing her wrinkled lips shut tight. I shook my head, pleased enough at her changed demeanor, yet I allowed myself to simmer while she stared at the sleeping Iona.

The Selkie's face was gilded in the firelight, obscuring the freckles on her skin. Even in slumber, she looked pained; eyebrows steepled and eyelids pinched closed, like she was bracing herself from the wind. I'd not known pain like this. To see it etched so plainly across someone's face, well—it was novel.

The hag picked at her teeth with a discarded bone before she tossed it into the fire. It hissed and bubbled in the flames. "*She* is not like you, *Each-Uisce*. *She* is a bringer of balance. A friend to the sea. *You* are a demon, a bringer of death. Your natures are night and day from each other. Do not mistake her for those of your ilk."

I stared into the witch's milky eye, wishing to stab it out of her head. Damn her for knowing me in ways no other did. I let her words slide over me like a winter current, willed my consciousness to forget them. For beneath her statement was a far less appealing one. One that I had forgotten many times before now.

I was alone.

It had never bothered me before. The aloneness was always a fleeting emotion, gone away the instant I found another pretty young woman to court, which was often enough that it had never truly occurred to me that even whilst holding fine hands between my own and whispering sweet nothings, I was still alone in my nature. A secret hidden from the world.

I would not allow the old shrew to make me feel inferior, so I pushed those thoughts down, deep down. "Aye. But we Unseen must band together every now and again, or what fun would the world be?" The witch's only response was to stare right back into my eyes, not once blinking. A prickling sensation skittered up the back of my neck. Painful memories, old aches, dreams, or better called nightmares, danced in my mind and I remembered why I decided to avoid this place long ago. "We'll be on our way at first light."

"Oh? And where will ye be taking her, then?" The *cailleach's* voice took on a weary tone. She must've realized she was powerless to stop me from having what I desired. The hag had nothing to fear of me, not this night.

My eyes returned to Iona's figure. "Wherever she wants to go, I s'pose."

"And what if she wants nothing more to do with ye, then what?" She stood up slowly, joints creaking audibly as she hobbled around Iona to add a bit of peat to the fire. A deep frown marred my face. I hadn't considered Iona would choose to leave me. No one had ever chosen to leave *me* before. I had always done the leaving, when my time with my brides ended. "That's what I thought. You can't make this one choose you, *Each-Uisce*. Her will is stronger than your tricks." Gritting my teeth, I stood abruptly from the stool, nearly butting my head against the sunken thatching.

I could not bear her soul-seeing another moment. It was too much. "Enough, *Cailleach*—I leave her in your care until morning." The door was two steps away, fresh air and peace awaited me outside.

"Where'd you think you're off to?" Her stare very nearly scalded my back. Much as I loathed the hag's company, it was a part of the ancient covenants we lived by that a favor begets a favor. Healing Iona as she had meant that I needed to find a way to repay her. It would not do well to leave this place without balancing the scales. That way, I would never need to see her again.

"Don't you worry your little head, *Seanmháthair*. I will return before dawn."

"WHERE THE SEA MEETS THE MOON—BLANCHED LAND,
LISTEN! YOU HEAR THE GRATING ROAR
OF PEBBLES WHICH THE WAVES DRAW BACK, AND
FLING,
AT THEIR RETURN, UP THE HIGH STRAND,
BEGIN, AND CEASE, AND THEN AGAIN BEGIN,
WITH TREMULOUS CADENCE SLOW, AND BRING
THE ETERNAL NOTE OF SADNESS IN."
— MATTHEW ARNOLD

Chapter Eight

IONA

I slept like a stone, not dreaming even for a moment. I woke in the dark, to the monotonous hum of the old woman's snores. The fire had weakened in the night, and now looked more like a cache of jasper glinting from some unseen light below. Someone had draped me in a warm bundle that smelled like smoke and something sour. It was heavy upon me, suffocating like the waves that had almost killed me.

I frantically began pushing it away before I could think more deeply on my actions. I twisted in order to remove the blanket from my legs, and my side injury flared to life again, sending a flash of pain up through my innards and to the base of my spine. I arched back, sucking in air. How long would it take for the pain to subside? Or would it live within me always? An eternal reminder of my shameful failure, as if I could ever forget.

I couldn't stop the cursed images from resurfacing in my mind. I could see our rock, dark and strange. Awash with tide and blood. I could hear the seals crying out in panic, fleeing as fast as they could from the men who preyed upon them. So helpless, so innocent. My fingers twitched, reaching up for my dagger that was no longer strung around my neck.

The room felt suddenly stifling. Laying in the darkness only prolonged my suffering. As silently as I could, I rose from the floor. The clothing I wore slid down my legs, shielding them from the night air. The presence of the foreign garment was more stinging than if I were merely naked in the cold. It held little warmth, unlike that of my precious coat. My second skin. I sent a silent prayer out into the darkness of the cottage.

Please help me find my coat.

The crone lay sleeping in her tiny cot, entirely undisturbed in her snoring slumber, Cian was nowhere to be seen in the cramped room. There was no salt breeze, no waves lapping at my feet. I was trapped. My head felt light, as though I'd held my breath for too long. Each step I took toward the door was unsure, knees wobbling, one hand pressing against my injured side. Though the wound was mostly sealed, it still felt as if one wrong move might cause me to expel my guts. I needed air, I needed space—and I needed it *now*.

The stars winked down at me from a black sky, which was merely a circle above the witch's hut. Spindly trees crowded around me, reaching up to the heavens. I'd never been so closed in, so far from the sea. I dug my toes into the earth, longing to feel water, or even barnacles beneath my feet, only to wriggle them into the dewy soil.

"You look like a ghost in not but that shift. Are you cold? Or do Selkies always stay warm?" Cian emerged from the copse of trees like a specter himself. His eyes, flashing red once more, were the only thing visible in the dark of the forest until he stepped forward into the starlight. He stood straight, arms full of—something.

He had a proud brow over a straight, if not slightly large, nose. His mouth was twisted to the side, as if he were about to smile or maybe snarl. His hair curled around his shoulders, shining a faint silver in the night. It was as if all color had run from him, except those crimson eyes, glowing as he looked me over. The hungry shark, preparing to snatch up a fish. A chill ran down my spine.

Cian approached the cottage, allowing me to better see what he held. In his arms were an assortment of plants, some dripping wet. In a blink, his eyes turned back into that unnamable shade of blue. " 'Tis payment for her work mending you. Nothing is given freely, surely even you know that." Cian arched a pale brow as he peered into my face, searching for understanding. I nodded, though I'd never had any kind of interaction that would warrant repayment. Cian cleared his throat and continued, "She's old and can't get to all the places where the best medicinal plants grow. I figured with this much, your debt is repaid."

My debt? If I was wearing my seal skin, my hackles would have raised. "But wasn't it you who decided to bring me here?" I tapped my finger to my chin, feigning ignorance. "I believe it was *you* who carried me all this way, and it was *you* who asked the woman to see to me. I just held on. Isn't that right? Clearly, she did all this mending for *you*." I gestured up and down my battered body to illustrate my meaning.

Cian's brow furrowed, lips curving down into a pucker. "That may be true, but *I* received nothing from this visit. Tell me Iona, are you displeased that I went out of my way to do your bidding for you?"

My fingers curled into fists, balling the gown's fabric up into my palms. Heat bloomed in my cheeks. "I am *displeased* that you would force all of this upon me, and then treat me as though you were doing me a service. I asked to be left alone. I asked for none of this." Ice coated my words. All of the misery I'd felt surged out of me, aiming for the being standing before me. I was no one's responsibility. I owed Cian nothing.

A muscle in Cian's jaw flexed as he looked away, nodding his head. "You are one hard hearted woman. Lord, help me." He fixed his eyes upon my face as he stepped towards me, his gaze an attempt to burn me.

Then he said, "But you understand this, Iona. Understand this well. There are rules. Covenants, and for you—I have bent a great deal of them. Gratitude is all I ask. And gratitude is what I shall have. From you." Cian glowered at me, shoulders hunched up towards his ears.

Somehow, I had gone from standing with an arm wrapped around my side, a safe distance away from the *Each-Uisce*—to standing so close to him I was practically pressing my forehead against his. I must have instinctively closed the gap to go in for the kill. My eyes narrowed as I returned his stare, knuckles white with rage bunched in my gown.

My voice shook in a tenor that surprised me. I'd never had cause to use my voice in such a manner. "I will give it when it is earned, and not a second sooner." My breath heaved out of my chest. I watched as his jaw ticked again, nostrils flaring in agitation. Cian broke our stare down first, backing away and then ducking silently into the old woman's hovel. He reappeared moments later with a large wad of black fabric.

He shoved a smaller portion of it into my arms, before stalking away from me back through the meadow. "Your temporary coat, Miss Selkie. Put it on. You may follow me, or you may stay here." Cian's words were clipped and charged with ire as he called back to me. He didn't offer a single look at me as he continued towards the trees.

I held the swath of material out, considering its shape and texture before reluctantly draping it around my shoulders. It was too thin, too long, too strange against my skin, made it cry out in agony over the wrongness of it. It was all wrong, incalculably so.

Cian said he could take me back to my rock. I'd have to be a fool to let him walk away from me now. I'd have to swallow my pride for a few days and deal with his insufferable ego, his posturing and strange attitudes, but it would be worth every single moment if in the end I could have my coat. I would happily endure much worse trials to have my second skin back. And not only my coat, no, retribution as well. My vengeance. To take the life of that man.

I looked back into the cottage and whispered a farewell from the threshold. Inside the witch stirred, "Do not be trusting him so easily my dear, he is a beast in disguise. A lovely monster, and nothin' more."

I said nothing, knowing already that Cian was more than he seemed. When I turned back towards the clearing, he had all but disappeared in the woods. But the sky was growing lighter above us, stars turning out one by one in fluttering flashes, and I was able to make out his form well enough after my eyes adjusted.

"Wait—Cian, wait." I heaved a breath out as I tried to get his attention. We'd been walking only a few miles when I realized I would never be able to catch up with him moving so quickly. I still felt stiff and weak from my injuries. The wounds on my body may have healed considerably, but the deep ache that resonated throughout my skeleton was not something I could easily ignore for long. Every step sent shots of unpleasant pangs up and out of my shoulder and side. The uneven terrain did nothing for my still unsteady legs, either.

Cian hadn't said a word since we'd left the cottage. Instead, he silently glared backwards at me every so often, I supposed to check and see that I was still following him. For the most part I was busy staring down at the earth in order to keep from tripping over a rock or root. I was less than graceful as I fought to keep up with Cian. When I glanced up, the outline of his figure had become entirely too small. The distance between us had grown in the hours that we'd been traveling. Now he turned, suddenly aware of my slowing pace.

Cian raised an eyebrow as he sauntered back towards me while I inspected a rotting log to sit upon. Beads of water slid down from my scalp to my jawline before I swiped them away.

When I looked up, Cian was kneeling before me—all too close. His eyes looked into mine, and where I expected to see frustration, there was merely curiosity. Cian's face was alight, like there was a star shining out from behind his eyes. "Are you unwell, *Anamchara*?" His large hand moved to my forehead, but I ducked away, muscles taught with fear.

My voice was a harsh whisper, "Don't." Cian's hand hung in the air, as though he were frozen. The expression on his face became unreadable.

He said gently, "I'll not ever touch you in anger, or with malicious intent. I swear it." The words seemed carefully stated, as though he were thinking of the millions of loopholes and workarounds within this promise. I remembered how he had spoken of bent rules earlier... mistrust filled me, twisted in my stomach like an eel.

I straightened. "You'll never touch me without my permission. I swear it." What was it about this—this *creature*—that filled me with such animosity? Without hesitation, I bared my teeth. A warning. Cian rolled his tongue in his mouth, no doubt swallowing a litany of curses. I had to wonder, why bother at all with the likes of me? There was nothing he could be gaining from this endeavor, and I was making sure of that.

The brute cleared his throat before standing. "We'll rest a bit, then I promise to walk at a more suitable pace for you. *Mo mhuirnín*." He turned away from me to stare upwards, hands on his hips. I leaned back, trying to relax my fatigued muscles. Birds chirped from the treetops, and smaller creatures scurried unseen in the thick undergrowth around us. Sunlight had been fleeting since it rose, with dark clouds moving in a rush across the sky.

The world smelled of earth. So much earth, and not a hint of spindrift or salt air. There was never a time in my life that I had remained in my human form for as long as this. I turned a hand over, holding it up to my face so I could inspect the lines and wrinkles I hadn't ever bothered to take stock of before now. My palm was crossed with the finest lines that deepened when I pulled my fingers in to form a fist. From the corner of my eye, I saw Cian's own hand twitching at his side and irritation flared in me, over his insistence at calling me names other than the one I had given him.

"Stop with the endearments. You hardly know me, you've no right to claim I'm your *darling*." Cian sighed heavily, pushing a hand through his curls before holding both palms out in offering to me. I could not decipher the expression in his eyes. Was he amused or pained?

" 'Tis common enough for menfolk to call lasses by that name, at least lasses who are unattached. There's nothing more to it. Shall I refrain from doing so?" Cian revealed a row of sharpened teeth while he grinned. "I've also been quite fond of the other following terms of endearment; *A Rún, Anamchara, A Chuid*—"

I balked at that last word. "*My portion*? What am I—a meal?" Cian's responding expression turned my flesh to fire. Eels coiled in my stomach, enticing and terrifying all at once.

A different kind of heat soared through my veins when he all but purred, "Sometimes, Iona, a woman can be many things." He licked his lips and I swear upon heaven and earth and all the hells below that his eyes truly glowed just then. I stood abruptly, wishing to leave this turn of conversation behind us. I fumbled for something to say, anything at all that might clear the heavy feeling in the air between us.

I squeaked, nearly dying of shame while I spouted, "How

long until we return to the shore?" As I hurried through the brush away from Cian, I thought I heard a low chuckle bubble out from behind me.

"Two days, *A Chuid*. Not long. Not long at all." The smile in his words sent fury rolling up and down my spine. Two days was an eternity with Cian. I reminded myself once again that it would be well worth the pain.

After trudging through the forest for the entirety of the day, stopping occasionally to rest and find a bit of fresh water to drink, Cian stood at the mouth of a cave and announced that was where we would bed down for the night. I watched as he scuttled around, searching for bits of twigs and clods of moss, creating a neat pile in the cave entrance.

He stopped mid-crouch and said, "You could make yourself useful, go and find some dried bits of wood for kindling." Then he noted my furrowed brow, and added, "You know, to make the fire? Fire needs food, and it likes to eat dry things. Now go." He winked at me as I seethed.

I had never been told what to do by any other creature. How dare this one think he had the right? I was my own being, with my own will, not some underling to do Cian's bidding. I bit the inside of my cheeks to halt the harsh retort in my head from coming out of my mouth. I relented—asking myself why it was so hard to do positively anything once he asked it of me? Cian was going out of his way to help me. I was being a stubborn fool. There was just something about his knowing smugness that had crawled under my skin and refused to leave me.

I couldn't help myself as I said, "You know Cian, just because I don't know how everything works here, doesn't mean I'm an idiot. If you stepped one foot in my domain, you would need *me* to show you the way of things." Cian's lips curled into a wicked smile, teeth glinting in the evening light.

"We shall see, now won't we?" He stepped towards me and said, "Pip pip, Miss Selkie, the fire won't light itself and night is falling." Cian made to shoo me off before turning away completely, effectively dismissing me.

I scrambled into the underbrush, crawling on all fours to hurriedly collect as many crumbling dry bits of brush as my arms could carry, scraping my knees and getting wrapped up in a tangle of the finest, stickiest substance that was hanging between two branches, almost completely invisible until it was stuck to my face.

Several moments later, I stood before Cian, covered in scratches from my knees down, my hair a nest of tangles and weeds. But my arms were full of foliage, and I was quite pleased with myself.

Cian assessed me, eyes raking down my figure and then up at the bundle of twigs and leaves in my arms. He was on his knees, his chin tilted towards the sky, his teeth glinting from beneath his full lips as he grinned then said, "Well done, you. Now I will show you the ancient magic of starting a fire." Cian motioned me to come over to the pile he had organized into a stack of debris.

Crouching low beside him, he motioned with his hands to stay quiet, so I clamped my mouth shut. Cian took two stones and brought one crashing down over the other, again and again until lightning bright sparks cascaded in a flurry onto the kindling. He leaned in and breathed, ever so gently, and right before my eyes—fire.

It *was* a kind of magic, beautiful and sudden, like the crest of a wave. I couldn't help the smile that spread across my face. Cian noticed too, leaned closer to me, but thought better of himself before he allowed his shoulder to graze mine.

Wonder took a hold of me, holding me prisoner as I asked, "Can you do other magic, Cian?" I found myself edging towards him, our noses once again coming close enough that if one of us surrendered another inch they would touch. Cian grinned at me, his brow arched in a way that made my stomach coil again.

"Shall I show you?"

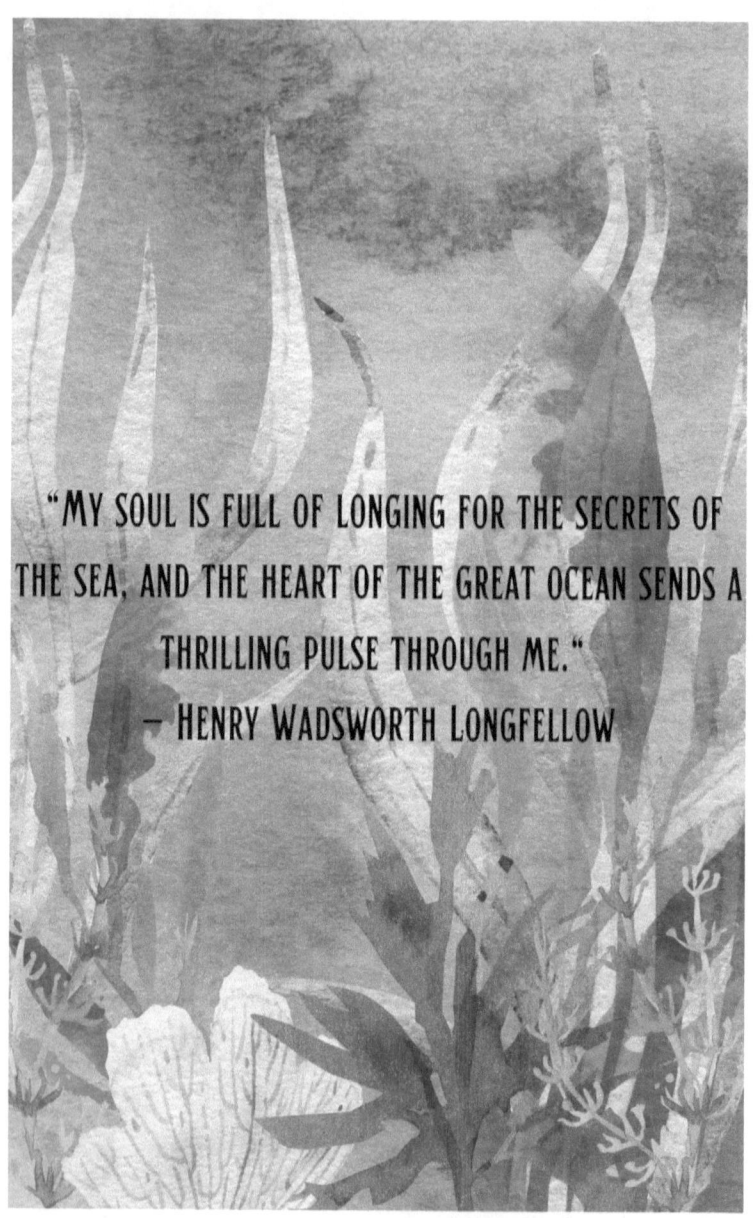

"My soul is full of longing for the secrets of the sea, and the heart of the great ocean sends a thrilling pulse through me."
— Henry Wadsworth Longfellow

Chapter Nine

CIAN

Iona's eyes peered into mine. Her irises were so dark they were like two black caverns, endless and ancient, yet innocent of so much. The closeness of her sent an old familiar thrill up and down my spine. If I had spied her in the streets of town I would have walked past, not thinking her a likely companion in the least. Though here I was, yearning to touch her. I wanted to pull her to me, to run a thumb along her sharp jawline. The need of her nearly overwhelmed me, but Iona could not be treated as a mere mortal woman.

It would be a black mark upon my existence to involve a kindred Unseen in my own affairs. She was a woman, yes—but she was so much more. If I'd let myself go about unfettered by rules and reason this deliciously interesting adventure would come to a close all too soon, and I would be back where I began —staring at the mouth of my *abhainn* with an insatiable desire for whatever it was I was feeling now.

Magic, yes, she'd asked to see my magic. No Unseen creature was completely alike, though many had similar gifts, at least as far as I could tell in my many years of life. My fingers curled around a small stone at my feet. I held it up between our faces. Iona's eyes darted between my gaze and my hand, waiting.

I closed my fist, then opened it to reveal the new treasure within. Iona gasped, a small, wonderful sound that made my chest tighten. Confusion welled within me—was this purely instinct or was there more to it?

Her hand went immediately to the blue sapphire that shined softly against the fire. She turned the gem in her hand over and over, marveling at its beauty. "But, how? Is the stone transformed, or did you trade it somehow?" She snatched my wrist, tugging my shirt sleeve up my arm to search for the stone before turning her demanding stare back on me.

I laughed, pulling my arm free of her. "Tis Glamour. The stone is still there, it is merely that your eyes have been deceived. Many of our kind can cast Glamours." Iona opened her mouth to speak, then frowned, her gaze sliding back to the fire. She pressed the magicked rock into my palm.

The lass held out the hem of her black cape and asked, "Then you couldn't make this cloak into my Selkie skin, could you?" Her voice was flat, resigned. I tossed the glamoured gem her way, smiling as she caught it with hardly a glance.

She mumbled as she continued to inspect the stone. "It doesn't feel like a rock. It doesn't even smell like a rock anymore. But it's false?" Iona's sadness weighed upon me, an uncomfortable sort of feeling that settled along my skin. I tried to shrug away the unpleasant sensation.

I shook my head once. "I cannot make you a Selkie coat, nor can I make you a seal. I can only trick others so they might see you as one. But even then, it would not be what you wanted. It would not be real." Iona said nothing, instead dropping the sapphire into the fire before resting her chin between her upturned palms. Something about the gesture made me clear my throat, swallow down the knot forming there.

"I said I would take ye to get your coat back, and that's what I'll do. I'll not go back on my promise, Iona." The only acknowledgment she gave was a solitary nod. Stifling silence filled the air. Hardly anything stirred in the woods, except she and I. The dire solemnity of it all felt like a millstone hung round my neck. I couldn't bear it any longer.

"I can, however, make you look like a fine lady in waiting, or perhaps you'd like to appear as a queen of the ocean?" The Selkie's head turned slowly towards me, thick eyebrows drawn low over her black eyes in suspicion. I held out a hand to her. "Come, stand, I shall adorn you in all the jewels befitting one as rare and fine as you." Iona's look was utterly dubious, but she stood and turned towards me. Curiosity would be this one's downfall. I rubbed my hands together as my mind conjured up an image of loveliness. I stepped towards Iona. "I must touch you in order to lay my Glamour. It's like a net, you see?" She nodded her consent, waiting silently, wonder plain on her face.

I let my hands trail lightly down her shoulders. In their wake, the palest green silk cascaded into wide bells, leaving her shoulders bare save for a thin line of pearls. I held her hands a moment, leaving behind emeralds and opals and diamond rings on each finger. Iona's mouth fell open as I continued. I touched her waist for the briefest of moments to create a flurry of diaphanous skirts, falling past her feet, in the palest shades of cream and seafoam. She stared into my face as I gingerly placed my palm against her collarbone. I'd be a liar if I didn't say I was pleased at the sight of raised skin when I lifted my hand to reveal a strand of pearls. Lastly, I combed my fingers through her dark tresses, smoothing her tangled hair into a braid. I left behind a towering crown of bleached coral and silver *creathnach*. I stepped back to appraise my work, lacing my fingers together behind my back as I took in the Glamoured woman in front of me.

Iona looked down and around herself, marveling at the jewels on her hands before running them down the length of her new gown. She reached up to gently touch the crown I placed upon her head. I bowed low before her, wrapping an arm around the front of my waist, peering up at her.

"My Queen, you look positively exquisite." Iona let out a sound that could have been a giggle as she turned around, her skirts swirling in a circle.

"Is this what women wear? How on earth do they manage?" She lifted the skirts and tried her hand at walking around the fire. I hadn't thought to give her shoes, and now I was glad of it. Though she looked lovely, she moved like a prisoner, trussed up and ready to be tried.

"I don't think I'd make it twenty paces in this!" Iona looked back at me from across the flames and there in her face was a hint of pleasure. Her cheeks were rosy for the first time, and a light glimmered in her fathomless eyes. Iona's voice had a new lilt to it, *intriguing*. "It is beautiful though. I especially like this." She took the crown off of her head to admire it more closely.

I felt a strange desire growing inside, a powerful urge to give her more. More than a swathed-up illusion or fleeting happiness, but there was little else I could offer her, here in the woods. I asked her, "What would please you to wear? Tell me and I can make it so." She looked up from the crown and eyed me up and down without pretense.

"I want to wear what you're wearing." Her request instantly put me on my knees. I bellowed with laughter. A woman in breeches? Oh, she was *not* of man, this confirmed it. I felt her glare even with my eyes closed from delight. "What is the matter with you? Is your apparel only meant for *Each-Uisces* as my coat is meant for Selkies?" When I opened my eyes I watched a flush crawl up her neck, staining her face red.

I tried to steady my voice, shaking my head while trying to explain it all. "No, no—forgive me, *Anamchara*. *Women* wear gowns and skirts. It is not virtuous to reveal the shape of your figure so outwardly. You'll be called a trollope, or worse." Iona balked, the ire visibly growing within her.

Her change in demeanor was so swift I nearly fell back to my knees. Her voice was a low growl as she said, "Forgive me, but was I not stark naked the first time you saw me?" She stepped nearer to me now, and it was my turn to flush at the recollection of our first encounter. "And have I not been naked each and every time I've chosen to walk on two legs since I first swam up from the depths of the sea?" She stepped even closer, and my eyes dipped to her neckline, where I at once cursed and thanked myself for creating a gown with such a low bodice. Her chest was heaving, and a lump was forming in my throat. Iona seemed determined to ruin the moment. She continued, "I am above such *human* notions. I will abide by my own standards, thank you very much." I nodded, feeling quite conflicted about our current agreement. Every motivation for my continued presence in this hellion's life began fading away as her eyes bored into mine. "Give me breeches, and a shirt."

Iona held her arms out, waiting for me to Glamour her once more. I was a creature of darkness, death, alluring down to the fiber of my being, and here was this woman, this spirit, who felt not a single ounce of shame at berating me. At commanding me. I didn't know whether to be excited or enraged. I clucked my tongue, looking into the woods a moment to gather my thoughts before I stepped in close to the seething she-devil before me. *Very well*. She could be the demanding and unyielding queen of the deep, and I could be *Each-Uisce*; a beast.

I squared my shoulders. This time I was not as delicate in my caresses. I held Iona's gaze as my hands wrapped firmly around her waistline. Her eyes widened, a scowl deepening across her mouth. I knelt before her and dragged my hands down her thighs to the backs of her calves, erasing the gown and replacing it with black fabric that hugged her curves.

Her face became a red flame while I maintained simpering eye contact. I brought my hands back to her waist and up, up, underneath her breasts to leave a cinched half-bodice in place. She gasped, lips curling into a snarl. I leaned in close, releasing a breath near Iona's ear as I let my hands wander up her back and over her arms, leaving behind white sleeves, loose until they met her wrists and buttoned in cuffs.

Iona's dark eyes were full of heat. Her lips parted, a likely threat on her tongue. *So close*—she was so close. My hands stayed locked around her wrists. Iona tried to pull her hands away, but I held tight, instead forcing her even closer to me. Her hips pressed against mine. I wrapped my arm around her, pulling her against me in a tight embrace. She started closing her eyes as I leaned in closer. In an instant, she was wrenching free of me. I gaped after Iona as she stepped out of my reach, abruptly turning away.

"*I said*, never touch me without my consent." Her words split me open from stomach to sternum. Clearly, she felt differently. I could see it plain in her eyes.

I bit my tongue; after all, she *had* said those words. I scrubbed my hands over my face, trying to find a bit of clarity, but alas. I stopped dead, eyelids fluttering in pure delight, freely appreciating Iona's backside. It became abundantly clear why it was forbidden for women to dress in such a manner. There was *little* left to the imagination. The length of her legs was jaw dropping. Heat rose to my face. I forced myself to look away, to think of anything other than the sensual, infuriating creature before me. Iona stood rigid like a pillar of stone, refusing to acknowledge my existence.

The night stretched on before us in silence. I'd walked to a nearby stream and caught some small trout for our meal. Iona snatched the pair I'd caught for her out of my hand and gobbled them down in an instant, not even bothering to clean or cook them. I'd eaten my fair share of uncooked meals, fish being no exception, but it had been many years since I had succumbed to my wilder instincts in such a way. After pondering it for several moments, I followed suit. The small fish slithered down my throat. It was efficient, and something about the act brought an ancient sliver of memory bubbling to the surface of my mind.

"Iona—how did you come to be? Can you remember?"

She settled on the other side of the fire, eyes permanently averted. She'd tucked her legs up, arms wrapped around them, head resting at an angle on her knees. Her thick braid was draped down the side of her arm, nearly touching the cave floor. Most of her face was cast in shadow, but I knew she'd heard me.

I waited in the dim light, for so long that I assumed she had chosen to ignore me once again. I threw a handful of sticks on the flames, but then she spoke. Her voice was low, mournful. "I was born out of blood and death. The sea brought me to life to serve her." It sounded like the words to an old song, familiar—yet secret.

"Did it hurt?" The question fell from my mouth before I could think what I meant. Being born out of death did sound painful.

She sighed and looked at me again. "There is very little in my life that has not hurt. What joys I once reveled in have been taken. The memory is forever tainted, no matter what comes next." A life of pain was something I'd not contemplated. Life simply *was*. There was duty, drive, and desire, but what of pain? I feared that Iona had opened a door I wished to keep closed.

Iona said, voice hollow, "What of you Cian, how did you begin?"

I rubbed a hand through my hair, resting it against the back of my neck. I found myself hating the question.

"I don't know. I remember seeing the moon, and then..." I piqued her interest. Iona's head rose from her knees.

She said, "That's it? You don't remember anything more?"

I sighed, searching my memories for a bit of *anything more*.

"That's it. It was many nights after when... I...the night I took my first—I learned my purpose." My toes curled up in my boots. Why had I kept my truth hidden? We were kindred spirits, were we not?

"And what is that? Your purpose?" A black brow arched on her pale forehead, her hand curling around her braid. Another lump had formed in my throat, and I coughed, trying to clear it.

"My purpose—well. Take a bride and give her over to the river. That is my purpose. For eternity. Choose a maiden, pure and lovely, and let her consent to be taken. Married to me and the rushing waters of time."

Iona's eyes searched me, trying to glean whatever she could from my face. I wasn't sure what she was seeing, but I feared it all the same.

"What does it mean to *take a bride*?" The open curiosity upon her face was amusing and unsettling. I did not like where this conversation was going.

"When two beings take to one another, they promise themselves to each other. To stay faithful and love the other until death takes them." Iona's cheeks turned crimson as her mind made the connection.

"You mean *mate*? You have more than one?" Her head was cocked over to the side, innocent in a way that burned me. I supposed she would know about mates and the mysteries of life in congruence with the creatures of the sea. Her blush faded as more questions popped into her head. "Where do they all live?"

A fine sheen of sweat coated the back of my neck. I didn't want her to know what became of my many brides. But I could not lie.

"They don't." I stared into her eyes, willing the truth to be laid bare without words. Her eyes widened only a fraction before she schooled her countenance. "Are you frightened, *A Chuid*? Afraid I'll take you next?" I couldn't help the cruel use of the nickname, *my portion*. It was a dare, a test to see how brave, how bold this Selkie was. Could she stomach accepting help from a beast like me?

"No. I am neither thing you claim to search for in a mate." I watched as a tightness overtook her, something hidden beneath the surface, too far below for me to understand.

It chapped me something fierce that Iona did not think herself compatible with me. She may be none of those things, true, but Iona was *more*. "And what of you, Miss Selkie? Pray tell, what is your purpose?" I leaned over, allowing an air of calm to smooth over the edges of this conversation. She stared into the flames, the orange light casting her skin in gold.

Whatever light that shone in her eyes was extinguished. A flame, guttered in the night. Iona held out a hand to the fire as she spoke, every word sending a strange sort of ache into the heart of me. "Without my coat, I have none. Without my coat, there is no purpose to my existence."

I watched melancholy dripping off the creature on the other side of the fire and I remembered my oath to her. To find her coat. Would it erase this pain? "Are those men still alive? Did you take your vengeance?" My questions were a staccato, righteous fury punching through every single word. Iona stared at me through the lapping flames.

"There is at least one man still alive. When I was shot, I was unable to... "

A plan began to unfurl, a new fern in the spring.

"Could you identify him?" My pulse quickened when she nodded.

"I'll never forget his face. He's the one who did this to me."
She brushed a palm against her injured side. Anger filled me to
my core.

"Iona, I'll make you another promise. Not only will we find
your coat, but we'll find the man who dared cross you, and we
will make him pay."

Iona shook her head. "No. *I* will make him pay." It was then
in the dying light of this fire that I realized before me was not
just a Selkie nor a magical creature, but a killer—old and relentless, just as I was.

Iona spoke again, pulling me from my thoughts. "And what
of your payment, then? What do you want in return, *Each-
Uisce*?" Her mouth was set in a firm line. She'd do whatever I
asked of her, I could sense it. This was a boon, one I could not
take so lightly. I reigned in my impulses and smiled at her.

"Iona my dear, don't you worry. When the time comes, I
shall tell you what is owed. For now, rest. Our journey has only
just begun." Her expression grew weary, but she nodded nonetheless. "Perhaps I'll just ask to see you naked again."

I shrugged, poking at the fire with a stick. She scowled at
me, throwing a rock near my head. I grinned as it whizzed past
my ear. "Och, now I'm going to seriously consider it! What a
timeless gift that would be. I could revisit you anytime I should
like in my memories." More rocks were tossed my way, but—
and perhaps I imagined it—with a touch less animosity.

"Go to sleep, you fiend. I'm tired of your chatter."

I scoffed at her rebuttal, though she was right. I *was* a fiend.
I tossed another bunch of sticks into the fire before laying back
against the earth. I cushioned my head with my hands and
stared up into the endless dark. I was not the least bit tired. It

wasn't in my nature to rest often. I stole a glance at Iona. She was staring back at me, an unnamable expression painted her face.

"What is it, *Anamchara*? It was only a jest. I'll not dishonor you with such a bawdy request."

Her voice was barely audible over the crackling embers. She said, "Thank you. For not leaving me to die. If it had been the other way around, I don't know if I would have." Shame was etched into her eyes. Iona thought she was crueler than I?

I chuckled, a cold empty sound. "Do not thank me yet. As I've said, we have a long journey ahead of us. There is time still for error."

Iona didn't speak again as I watched her turn away, curling into a ball on her side.

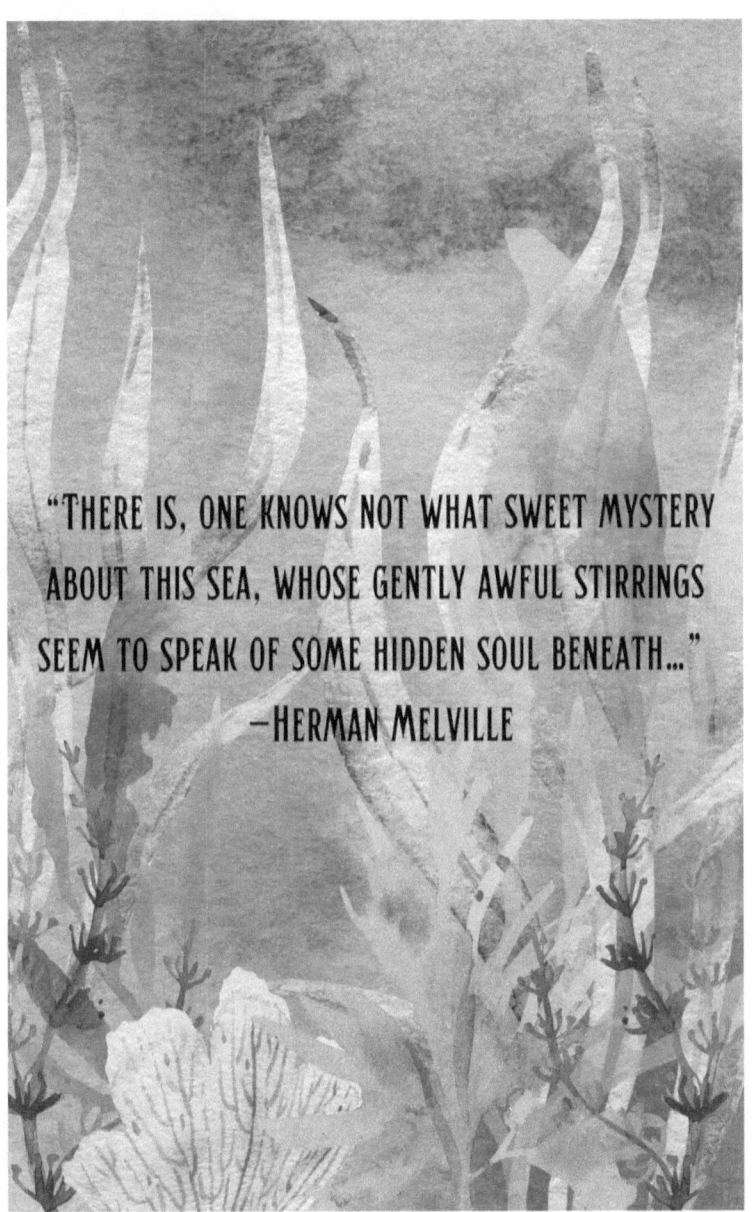

"THERE IS, ONE KNOWS NOT WHAT SWEET MYSTERY ABOUT THIS SEA, WHOSE GENTLY AWFUL STIRRINGS SEEM TO SPEAK OF SOME HIDDEN SOUL BENEATH..."
—HERMAN MELVILLE

Chapter Ten

IONA

I dreamt of the sea. Waves barreled over me as I watched a young pup, just out of arm's reach, and so helpless and fragile against the battering storm. Another wave came crashing down, smothering all hope of rescue. I awoke, newly heartbroken in a puddle of my own sweat, or tears—it was impossible to tell. My hands were clenched into tight fists, buried against my aching side. I shifted position away from the dampened earth beneath me when a song filled my ears.

The soft melody drifted in from the mouth of the cave. It was reminiscent of one I'd heard drifting out to sea from the men's ships. It was cadenced and fluttering over the air. A lone gull, soaring through unseen peaks and troughs in the wind. I moved as quietly as I could, curiosity nagging relentlessly at my spirit.

Cian was sitting with his back to me, barely visible in the darkness. He held a slender reed to his lips, fingers tapping and lifting in time with the melody. His shoulders rose and fell during the brief pauses in song. I realized his breath was needed to make this music. Something about it made me want to peel open my lips and sing the lullaby I would sometimes sing to my kin. I shifted my weight onto my other leg and his music ceased.

Without turning he spoke, "You were crying out in your sleep. I did not know whether to wake you or not." His voice was so gentle. I shuffled closer to Cian, oddly less wary of his proximity. Our growing familiarity with each other was beginning to wear on my defenses. There was a strange hunch in his spine that made him look small, forlorn. There was a moment when my hand reached for him, fingers uncurling and stretching, but I resisted.

"Do you not sleep, Cian?" My voice was a whisper, so thin I wondered if he heard me at all. A deep silence followed. All the world hushed as if waiting for his answer.

I began to move closer to the dying fire but froze when Cian said, "I do not sleep often. When I do, I always dream of her." My brows rose high, curiosity piqued. Cian was such a mystery to me. I felt like a novice around him, untried and naive to everything around me, including Cian.

I had to ask. "Of who?"

His body twisted towards me, neck craning so he could peer into my eyes. Was he able to see me better than I could see him? What other talents did this creature possess? It was impossible to tell what his expression held, or if he was even feeling anything at all, and not because of the darkness. He wore a mask of smooth indifference. It was false, yes, but impenetrable, nonetheless.

Cian's head bobbed as he answered, "My first bride." He turned away, and I stared after him. My heart turned into a stone, sinking down into the depths. I did not understand why, but his words, his voice, made me ache. I'd always felt alone, separate from the flock I watched over, and further removed from the humans who made my life so difficult. There was never a moment when I felt that I belonged with another, while Cian had belonged to so many.

"You should try to rest more, Iona, you are still not yet well." Cian's voice was tinged with wariness, and even though a cutting retort lay upon my tongue, I swallowed it down and went back to my place where I slept for the rest of the night.

The sun was high above us as we breached the edge of the forest. I had seen more trees in the last two days than in my entire lifetime. My skin was dry, and the clothing Cian had Glamoured was tight, hugging my body in a way that was foreign and invasive. With each step I grew closer and closer to simply ripping the garments away and continuing naked.

Large billowing clouds rushed past the sun, casting fleeting shadows over us. Between bouts of heavy mist and blowing wind, there were moments of tranquility when thoughts of slaughtered seals and guns almost slipped from my mind, but then my side would ache, or my tunic would brush my skin, and the absence of my coat crushed the air from my lungs.

After another day of walking, my injuries throbbed fiercely, radiating out from my shoulder and stomach in rolling waves of pain. I fought against it, breathing through my teeth, allowing my agony to fuel my momentum. Cian seemed completely unaware of my misery, but perhaps he was giving me space. It was difficult to be sure. He sauntered along, hands idly grazing against tall grasses and dangling tree branches. Occasionally his voice trailed back to me, a rumbling hum—singing a song that didn't have any words at all. His nonchalance began to grate on me. Cian's world seemed blissful, and I hated him for it.

Considering the state I was in only a few days ago, it was apparent the old woman had done a marvelous job of healing me. If it weren't for her, or Cian's actions, I would likely be nothing more than flotsam floating out in the sea for the fish to feast upon. The image of my corpse, rotten and bloated, made my skin pebble and my stomach churn. Best not to dwell on such darkness. I was here, and I had a purpose: to retrieve my coat.

And to have my vengeance.

Cian's excited voice leapt through my ears, stymying all thought. "*Anamchara*, Look! There it is, my *abhainn*. Can you see it through the trees?" His long arm reached out in front of us, finger pointing down the hill. I saw a river, its waters a dark green serpent rushing in between clusters of trees. There was something about the river that seemed...*alive.* Anything was possible. Perhaps somehow the very water itself contained a life force like the sea.

"It is very beautiful," I said, and Cian grinned my way as I followed the water with my eyes. It traveled southward, where it was soon hidden behind a great many human structures. My body grew rigid. I could see people walking to and fro between the buildings. There were animals of all shapes and sizes, the likes of which I had never seen. Some were pulling contraptions in open fields that were peppered nearby. Just being in Cian's near-human presence was enough to set my teeth on edge. It had taken days for me to grow accustomed to him. Humans were vile, exploitative, evil. I inhaled, wishing to open my lungs, to let more air in.

"Cian—we aren't going down there, are we?" Somehow my hand betrayed me. I watched as my fingers curled around his forearm. I gulped in another mouthful of air at the taut muscles beneath my fingers. I dropped my hand when he smiled, that predatory look once more painted across his face. Those sharpened teeth made me shudder, made my stomach flutter and my pulse raced ever faster.

Cian considered me, long and hard, his blue eyes piercing my defenses. "*A chuid,* don't fret. I shall keep you safe from any who would wish to harm you. The crowds will be behind us in a few short hours. The sea lies beyond it. We shall reach it before midday tomorrow. If we keep our pace."

Anger scorched my insides. Cian thought me *afraid*? "I do not need your protection. I simply have no wish to consort with humans in any way. Is there no other path we may take?" Cian's eyes rolled around, his jaw muscles ticked, and he turned to me, his red irises piercing.

"What will you do if we go around the humans, and you miss your chance to have your vengeance on the man who tried to murder you? Sometimes Iona, you must do what is necessary, not just what you wish." He pushed his slender fingers through his hair before planting a hand on his hip. A bull seal challenging a would-be contender.

I would not back down. "Are you so eager to walk among them? We do not belong there, Cian. We are beings made with higher purpose. Or have you forgotten that in your obsession with courting womenfolk?" The darkness on his face told me I had gone too far. I clamped my mouth shut, cheeks burning with indignation. Cian stepped towards me, hands reaching out to either side of my face, as though he wished to take my head and throttle me.

His hands remained hovering there, his voice a harsh whisper. "Do not pretend to know me, *Selkie*." His breath was hot against my face. "Do not belittle my existence in your fits of grandeur. I am as old as these hills and shall remain even after they crumble. Pray you remember that."

We stood there, toe to toe in silence for I don't know how long, exchanging angry breaths and seething stares. When I could bear it no longer, I looked to our feet, noticing my bare skin next to his boot in the grass.

My voice was a rasp. "Let's go then."

I turned, numbly traveling down the steep ravine before us. I stumbled on a rock hidden beneath weeds. My body lurched forward, but a strong hand gripped my bicep, pulling me upright.

I looked over my shoulder to see Cian grimacing. "You are going to hurt yourself moving so quickly. Walk beside me, *mo mhuirnín*, I will show you the path." He held my arm a moment longer, waiting for some kind of acknowledgement from me, so I nodded while pulling my limb free of him. The hidden trail Cian followed was only slightly less arduous. I had to keep my eyes on the ground to avoid stones and ruts hidden in the long grasses. It took us the better part of the afternoon to make our way safely down the hill.

I looked out into the distance. Seeing humans sent warning bells ringing in my ears. "I've never seen so many... people. Like this. What is it called?" My limited experiences with humankind held little information to be gleaned about their lives. I'd seen small structures scattered across the distant coastline, but not like this. It seemed more creatures than just myself craved togetherness.

Cian took my hand, and I did not protest as he helped me cross a deep crag in the earth, too wide for me to traverse without falling on the other side. "It is called a village. Folk live and work in groups and support each other through business. 'Tis a sort of give and take, if you understand my meaning."

"Are they all kin?" It would be a very large family, but my flock sometimes numbered in the high thirties when the sea was bountiful and predators were few.

Cian shook his head, a smirk flashing across his face. "No, not all but some are. Most families share a home." I pondered this concept a moment as we made our way through a cluster of ash trees.

"What makes a human family? My kin are a mixture of relations—mates, pups, elders, cousins..."

Cian nodded and responded, "It is much the same here. When children become adults, they leave to find their—*mates* —and make a new home with them." The word *mate* elicited a strange expression from Cian. My brows quirked up at his change of tone. Curious.

"And what of your kin, Cian? What makes a family to your kind?" It was then I realized he was still holding my hand because he dropped it abruptly. I felt the air rush through the gaps between my fingers, my palm suddenly cool in the breeze.

"My only family is the river." The statement was hollow, though his voice was light. I'd always had the companionship of the seals. It was not the same as having another to talk with, as I was growing to learn with Cian. But to be so isolated? There were many nights when comfort was being wrapped up in a huddle of warm flesh as my kin massed around one another to keep the winter chill at bay. Those memories filled my heart and mind, made me ache to be among them again.

Cian had never known what that feeling was like. He was truly a solitary creature in a way I couldn't fathom. We walked in thoughtful silence. Fields of grass spread out before us, swaying in the wind. To our right was a muddy path, rutted and packed from wear. To our left a fair stretch away I could still hear the hush of Cian's *abhainn*.

He looked over to me, his head nodding in that direction. "We should stop at my cottage, to prepare you to enter the realm of man."

The riverbank was littered with black stones, smooth and round from eons of water caressing them into shape. The water itself was a slow churning emerald. When I looked closer, I could see more black stones before the bottom dropped away into darkness. A part of me had feared to see water again. What if I could no longer bear its weight on my skin? What if I was unable to swim without the magic of my coat?

When I laid my eyes upon Cian's river, smelled the fresh water as it eddied in pools before making its way down towards the ocean that was out of sight, all my doubts subsided. Without any further thought, I pulled off my clothes, throwing them behind me before I leapt into the current.

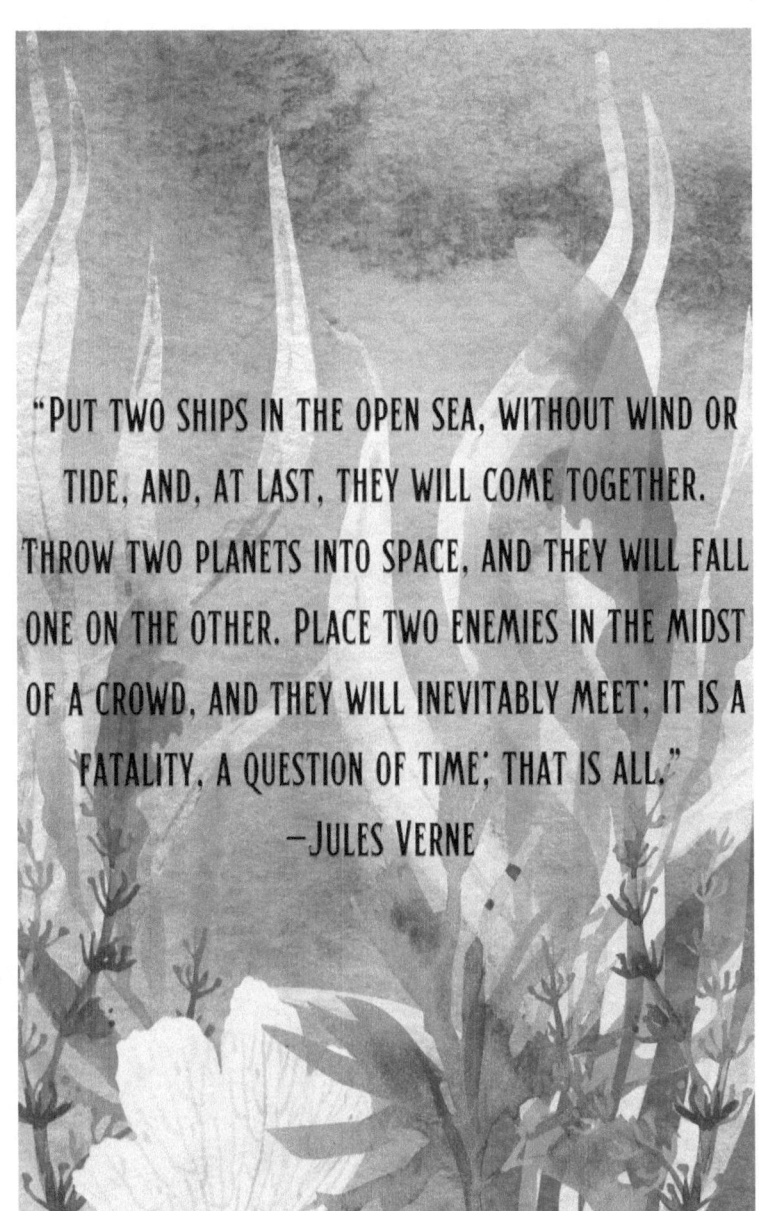

"Put two ships in the open sea, without wind or tide, and, at last, they will come together. Throw two planets into space, and they will fall one on the other. Place two enemies in the midst of a crowd, and they will inevitably meet; it is a fatality, a question of time; that is all."
—Jules Verne

Chapter Eleven

CIAN

I stared slack jawed as the seal woman stripped down to her skin in the blink of an eye, then unceremoniously dove into my river. My heart hammered in my chest as I followed suit, albeit still in my clothing. I did not need to shed my garments as she did—I could keep myself dry with my Glamour. I waded into the water, waiting for the Selkie to reemerge.

In a moment her head shot from the surface, water splashing around her. Black hair slick against her skull, freckled skin gleamed beneath the late afternoon sun. The look on her face stole the very breath from me. There was a wide, toothy grin splitting her expression open. Unfettered joy shined through those obsidian eyes.

I shouted at her, feeling overwhelmed and playful all at once, "Are you cold, Miss Selkie? Or does the water not bother you?"

Iona licked her lips and wrinkled her nose. "I forgot it's not salt water. No—no, the cold doesn't bother me. It is only that swimming is so clumsy with these *human* arms and legs." She bobbed up and down while trying to keep her place in the moving waters.

She looked graceful enough to me. "Where is your cottage, Cian?" Iona spun in a circle surveying the shore on both sides. The river was sheltered by ancient fir trees and alders, extending for miles on either side of the banks. But there was nothing, save natural beauty all around us.

I swam closer to her. A keen pleasure I'd not known began filling me from my toes up to my head. Never had a lass willingly, *knowingly* entered my river in this manner. Only the belief in the dream of romance and love-eternal did they join me here.

"My cottage is not on the river... it's *in* the river. Can you hold your breath?" I raised an eyebrow, daring her to see for herself.

Iona nodded but a frown marred her earlier expression of happiness. "Not as long as I could with my coat. When I have my coat, I scarcely need to breathe at all."

Electricity wound its way through my body like a bolt of lightning. *Interesting.* "Well, perhaps you can hold it long enough to see my home. Would you like to try?" I felt her wariness growing, as she looked me over. *Ah*, remembering she was with another predator. I regretted telling her of my dealings then. There was nothing I could say that would prove my intentions honest. Only my actions would.

"If it pleases you, I'll wait here. You can go on your own without fear of my drowning your pretty little head." Iona scowled, then without another word, sucked in a mouthful of air and ducked under the water. I waited patiently, treading water silently for several long moments. A lone crow sailed overhead, its call a rasping alarm. I watched the shadows and sunlight play on the creature's glossy feathers as I savored the light feeling inside my breast.

Then Iona emerged, gasping and laughing all at once. A delicious sound. "It's a whole cottage! Just like the ones in the human village! How did it get there? Cian! Did you build it?" I had never considered my dwelling to be anything extraordinary, but of course someone with as little experience with magic as Iona would be in awe over it. I laughed, full and rich as it echoed across the river. The Selkie's eyes narrowed at me, suspicious of my joviality.

She looked almost concerned before she asked, "Are you going to tell me that underwater cottages are *not* magic?" She waited expectantly as I scanned her face. She had a bit of *creathnach* tangled in her hair. She must have been able to get all the way down to the threshold then. No mortal woman had the strength to survive in those depths on just one lungful of air. I reached out and plucked the *creathnach* away, shaking my head. This time she did not shy away from my touch.

My heart once again began thundering in my chest. "My cottage is the only one below the river. 'Tis indeed magic. Would you like to go inside, and see the rest for yourself?" I didn't wait for her reply. I slid beneath the surface and shifted into my true form. A horse, unlike any other. I kicked down towards my home at the bottom of my *abhainn*.

I turned in the water to see if she followed me. Iona's face was smoothed over in concentration, unbothered by my transformation. She reached out and took hold of my mane, allowing me to pull her along. A bolt of panic spurred me down faster. It would not do at all to have Iona drown when she had just placed so much trust in me. I kicked harder, rushing to my door. Columns of milky green water weed swayed forward and backward on either side of the threshold, gently tugged by the current. The thatched roof and black river stones made the walls of my cottage come into clear view and then the wooden door.

From inside, a solitary light glowed through a small window. I looked back to Iona once more. Her cheeks were full, bubbles streaming from her nose. She was almost out of air. I pushed my door in and pulled the Selkie through it with me. Iona fell to the floor, soaking my rugs as she sputtered and coughed. The door sealed shut behind us.

Reverting from *Each-Uisce* to my two-legged form was swift enough. There was little space for a giant horse *and* a woman in my living room. Between gasping coughs Iona asked, "How is it possible that there is air to breathe so far beneath the surface?"

I knelt, pulling her up to a sitting position and checking her expression for any hint of fear or pain. Her eyes held nothing but fascination. "Magic, *mo mhuirnín*. I am able to keep my home dry and welcoming because of my magic." I peered around the room, remembering the day the river gifted my cottage to me.

"You are the first being to visit my home. What do you think?" Strange that I would want her opinion considering she had hardly any concept of what a home could be. It was true, she was the only other creature who had dared venture into such a dangerous place. She was the only one who *could*.

Iona looked confused. "The women you...*wed*...never make it inside?" I didn't know what to say, so I ignored her, instead watching as Iona stood, pressing a hand gingerly to the patch on her side. It was this moment I recalled that she was still injured, and very much naked.

Her eyes caught my stare, and I watched as she too remembered that she stood before me completely bare. Scarlet dyed her skin from head to toe. My own face grew warm, pulse skyrocketing. She was glistening, beads of water trailed down her freckled stomach—lower. I shook my head, trying to clear the fog that muted all coherent thought. I walked to my room, where I swiped a blanket that lay across my bed. I tossed it to her without a second glance.

"Thank you." When I looked back at her, Iona had pulled the blanket around her shoulders, not bothering to dry herself. Beads of water continued to course down her legs to pool on the floor around her. I nodded silently, swallowing the lump in my throat. She turned around and began to wander through the small space. She touched the whitewashed walls and the velvet chairs, the table's surface, all so gently and without comment. After leaving ample time for Iona to say something—*anything* —I could take the silence no longer.

"Well? Does it suit me?" At this point I'd gone to sit in the chair nearest the hearth, still watching her take a turn through my home. Iona shrugged and glanced at me.

"I would hardly know what suits you, *Each-Uisce*. Or any other being who lives inside a home. It seems a fine enough place. Though…" She stopped herself. I wondered if she had begun to think twice about sparing me from her cutting words. There had been less bite to her the last day or so.

"Though what? Speak your mind, *Anamchara*. You'll not offend me."

Iona stared at me hard, unblinking. "It seems as though *no one* lives here. It is very pleasing to look at, yet—it does not feel like it is *yours*."

My heart twisted inside me. I lived here. Seldom, yes, but it had been the only place where I spent my time when I was not out fulfilling my destiny. My duties as *Each-Uisce* often took me away for weeks on end while I discovered and courted my intendeds. It was no fault of my own that this place held little of me within its walls. Try as I might, any reply I would have given died on my tongue. They all felt like excuses. Iona seemed to sense that I was dumbstruck.

She shrugged again, angling her head in a way that reminded me of the seals she lived among. "What do I know of homes? I live out on a massive rock in the raging sea."

I nodded, wishing terribly to change the subject. "Now, let's strategize. We need to go through the village in order to make our way to the coast as quickly as possible. Yes, there is a chance we may encounter the walking dead man who wronged you, but in order for that encounter to be fruitful we must proceed with caution. The breeches will have to go."

Iona glared at me, mouth open and ready to tear into me again, but I held a hand up to stop her tirade. "*For now*. When we exit the village, you shall have your pants back. I swear it." She gritted her teeth but agreed. "Humanfolk have some... *strange* customs that we must follow if we are to go unnoticed."

Iona immediately began to argue. "I am not going to hide from these—"

I cut her off quickly. "Iona, *A Chuid*, unless you wish to start an uproar and be hunted for the rest of your days, you will need to do as I say. Will you trust me?"

The creature looked as if she was about to start snarling, a wild animal wearing a woman's skin. Her allure was maddening. Something about her lack of pretense, her bold fury—I was held fast by her, and it troubled me. Iona came to sit in the chair opposite me, pulling her slender legs up under the blanket she still held around her shoulders. A solitary drop of water slid from the column of her neck and stopped in the hollow space between her collarbones. I watched as her pulse sent the skin there fluttering ever so slightly. She fidgeted under my gaze as she spoke.

"You have given me no reason so far to doubt you, and so I will trust you." There was a tenderness in her words that stung me, as if Iona were baring her wounds to me, allowing me to see all the places she had been hurt. I also sensed a warning. This being was not one to be crossed.

"Good. The people of this village have not seen me come and go, so I will be a stranger to them. I learned long ago not to find my brides too near my river." I knew this next part would upset her. I was torn between giddy excitement and pain over the oncoming rejection. I cleared my throat, then said, "We must act as husband and wife—*mates*—to avoid any unwelcome attention. Should anyone speak to us, or question us, we will say we are just traveling through. Can you do this?" Iona's black eyes bored into mine.

I braced myself for her reply.

"Why must I be your *wife*? Why can't I be your sister or your cousin?" Ah, there was so much she did not understand about this world. Her words were not as cruel as I had feared. Frail relief found its way in my heart.

"Because *Anamchara*, an unattached woman is vulnerable to unwanted attention. 'Tis not that I think you to be incapable of protecting yourself, but more that I should like to avoid making a scene should some buffoon think himself worthy of your affection."

Iona considered my words then begrudgingly nodded before raising a thick brow in questioning. "And just how do we make people believe I am your wife?"

My lips curled up in a smile that turned her cheeks crimson as I leaned in closer to her. I was growing quite attached to those rosy changes in her complexion.

"Just leave that to me, Miss Selkie. None on Earth shall doubt that you are my beloved." Iona's eyebrow stayed raised, awaiting my instructions with visible skepticism. I studied her countenance, unable to look away from her for any length of time. There was a weariness about her that I wanted to smooth away. "There is plenty of time for us to plan, but first, you must rest."

Iona's eyes widened, black pools that threatened to swallow me up. "There is *no* time, Cian. I cannot be away from my flock any longer. They are defenseless without me... if any of them are still alive." Her shoulders rose up under her ears, and I could all but feel the tension roiling around her.

I sighed, leaning back against my chair. "You will be of no use to your seals if you are weak and injured. You must regain your strength. This is a safe place. I swear it. Rest for the evening. We will begin again tomorrow."

Iona frowned and studied the floor, considering my words. "Very well. But I do not know how to idle. At least show me how to disguise my true nature from the humans. What must I change to...avoid making *a scene.* " She scowled as the new phrase fell from her mouth.

I ran a hand through my hair as I tried to explain. "First, most ladies are not…fierce as you. They do not make eye contact as readily as you, nor do they challenge everything that is said. A difficult feat for you, I know."

Iona practically barked with laughter. "So, I'm to stare at the ground silently? That is easily done. What else?"

It was my turn to laugh next. Iona balked at the noise, baring her lovely teeth. "You doubt me, and that is all I need to prove you wrong. *What else?*"

"But can you do so knowing that to all the world around us you are my wife? My *mate?*" Her nostrils flared as I grinned at her. A tendon in her neck fluttered and she leaned towards me, daring me to continue. "Further, can you manage to not rip me limb from limb when I act my part to keep you safe from lecherous men?"

She sighed, staring past me. "I'm weary of your games, Cian. Speak openly."

I would do more than that. I rose from my chair and knelt before her. She did not move a single muscle. Her eyes found mine. Narrowed, expecting.

I reached up, tucking a strand of hair behind her ear. "Husbands like to dote on their wives." Iona's throat bobbed. "They like to hold hands." My fingers danced across the back of her hand still gripping the blanket. "Husbands caress. And kiss. May I?" I leaned into her further, grazing my nose against hers then down to the edge of her jaw. Iona was rooted to the spot, mine for the taking. She was so close, her skin still damp. I longed to taste the river that lingered on her flesh. But I stopped myself. Iona was above me, beyond my world. It was sinful to treat her so.

I pulled away, rising in a rush. I was desperate to breath air unscented with brine. "Very good. You make a quite convincing *bean cheíle*. Now, it's time to rest. Come. I'll show you your room." Iona's face gave no hint that she too suffered from our close proximity, but she remained silent as she followed behind me. My bedroom was adorned with the usual trappings of any mortal's space. A bed, a hearth, a table, a set of drawers. When I turned around, Iona was already nearing the bed.

Her eyes devoured the room, taking in every corner. "So much space." I was glad she didn't voice the rest of her thoughts. I knew well enough what she thought of me. I turned towards the dresser and tugged a shirt out from the drawer, then laid it on the bed.

Iona saw the shirt and rolled her eyes. "Why the obsession with clothing? I'm not cold."

I sighed, shaking my head. "Humans and many Unseen alike prefer to be garbed. 'Tis considered lewd to go gallivanting about in only your skin. Though you might not see the need, there are others who..." I clamped my mouth shut, horrified at what I'd almost admitted.

Iona tilted her head and her mouth curved into a vicious smile. "Tempted, are you?"

My lips pursed and I nearly growled in frustration. "Get some sleep. Morning will come soon enough." I stomped back through the threshold and pulled the door shut behind me. I thought I heard a rumble of quiet laughter, but perhaps I'd imagined it.

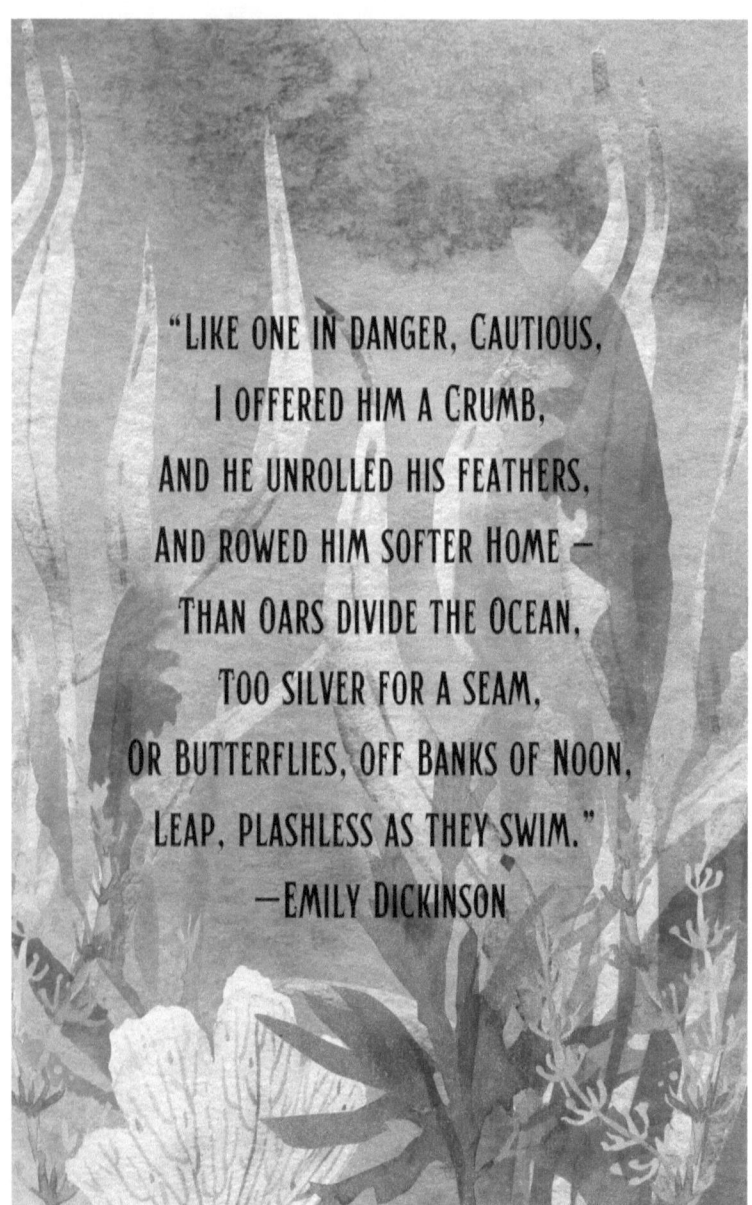

"LIKE ONE IN DANGER, CAUTIOUS,
I OFFERED HIM A CRUMB,
AND HE UNROLLED HIS FEATHERS,
AND ROWED HIM SOFTER HOME —
THAN OARS DIVIDE THE OCEAN,
TOO SILVER FOR A SEAM,
OR BUTTERFLIES, OFF BANKS OF NOON,
LEAP, PLASHLESS AS THEY SWIM."
—EMILY DICKINSON

Chapter Twelve

IONA

In the morning, Cian coached me on the ways that humans greet one another and how they go about their business in an effort to keep me from "making a scene" as he put it. When he was satisfied that I would not do that, we ascended from his cottage beneath the river. Cian turned into the beast I now knew to call a "horse", or something like it.

He grew four legs, muscled and lean, with a large torso. Hooves tapered outward at the end of his legs. He had a sturdy snout soft as velvet, paired with a strong neck. Cian's body was black as midnight—black as my own Selkie coat. His eyes changed once more—blood red. He allowed me to hang on to his mane, tangled with *creathnach*, as his powerful body propelled us upward. Pulling us up from the depths, where his home lay.

Cian's transformation did not startle me, but the creature he became was so large and imposing, he made the hair on the back of my neck stand on end. I could sense the raw power there, endless and unpredictable. There were many creatures much larger than he in the ocean, but he was something else.

When we reached the surface, Cian walked me to shore, still shaped as an *Each-Uisce*, and stood facing the other bank while I gathered my discarded clothing. His long tail swished impatiently as I began dressing.

I yanked at the breeches, trying to pull them over my soaking wet legs. Cian cleared his throat, and I looked up to see the male figure had returned, but his back remained towards me. "You needn't really get dressed, you know. I can Glamour you a gown, and none will be the wiser."

I had never been so aware of my own body in my entire life. Now, here I was, red as a flame, knowing that Cian was taking pleasure from my nakedness. What was even more maddening was the growing desire in the pit of my belly to damn all reason and claim Cian for myself. Every fiendish inch of him. I would be an absolute fool to travel down that path again. After the first time, I thought I'd learned my lesson. It would only cause me pain in the end.

I pulled my shirt down over my chest, which quickly became sodden. He turned before I granted him permission, spiking my anger. Cian's eyes poured over me. Still crimson, though his lashes and angled jaw somehow distracted from their unearthly nature. He was completely unashamed as he devoured my figure.

I tucked my shirt into my pants as I chided Cian. "I don't doubt that you would enjoy running your hands over my bare skin, but I think I'll manage just fine as I am now." The expression on Cian's face was that of a seal watching a gull fly off with his fish.

He huffed, then motioned me to come to him. "Alright then. I'll make you a fine garb that won't cause you to trip.

You'll look like my lovely little *bean chéile.*" I sighed involuntarily at the mention of being Cian's wife.

The old woman's warning echoed in my mind. *He's a beast in disguise.* But Cian had already told me of his dark destiny. I knew what he was, and in a way, I appreciated his honesty. There were still many questions I wanted to ask him. I found myself yearning to know him, and it surprised me.

I stood before him. There was a moment of eye contact, when his stare weighed me down, his gaze heavy lidded. The heat from the other night when he'd yanked me so close to him welled up once more, crying out for release. Cian pulled his bottom lip into his mouth, running sharp teeth along it. A fire rose up from my low belly, curling inside me as I watched the motion. Then he blinked hard, and the look vanished, the flame guttered.

He smacked his hands and rubbed them together vigorously. "My wife shall have the finest gown magic can afford." This time he worked swiftly, fingers hardly touching me at all as he left a trail of fabric behind each gesture. A long-sleeved linen gown with a deep green bodice soon covered my figure. He lay his hands gently on the crown of my head, leaving behind a braid that coiled around it. He knelt before me, eyes trained on my clothing. Cian pulled my right foot forward, and before I could protest, he eyed me, wrapping a hand around my heel. When he pulled away, my foot was thoroughly trapped in leather. I tried pathetically to wiggle my toes, feeling all too contained by yards of fabric. I immediately missed gliding bare through the ocean waves with nothing to hold me.

Soon. I'll have my coat back soon.

I ran my hands down the dress, the material nothing like my sealskin, but soft and light to the touch.

Cian stood before me and held out his hand, eyebrow raised in silent question. At some point along the way, I realized, his touch no longer repulsed me. Instead, I found myself in that moment, craving the connection. Perhaps it was because my heart was broken. I simply needed to feel the warmth of another being. I reached out, and he took the tips of my fingers in between his. He lifted his arm, pulling me around in a spin. My dress danced around my legs, a second behind my movement.

He grinned. "Och, pretty as a picture. The men will all be jealous of me with you on my arm."

I tugged my hand out of his and glared. "I'm not a *thing*, Cian. Remember that." He returned my glare before he rolled his shoulders and turned away. I watched as he began dusting off his sleeves and pants. It took me a moment to realize he wasn't simply cleaning off his clothing–he was creating Glamour for himself. The shirt and breeches that were drab and travel worn became crisp, the colors more vibrant. He shined his boots with a flick of his wrist and finished off by running both hands through his long, golden hair. He lifted them away to reveal his curls tied neatly at the nape of his neck with a black ribbon.

Cian turned round and bent at the waist, bowing low before me. His appearance made my toes curl up in my new shoes.

Heaven and earth and all the hells below.

His smile was alarmingly charming as he said, "And I am no prize myself. Face it, Iona, I am more suited to you than you'd like to admit." He smiled that predator's smile and began to walk away from the shore of his *abhainn* and towards the village, leaving me with a pounding heart as I stared after him.

When we made it to the worn path leading into the village, Cian slowed and walked beside me, his arm casually brushing against mine, hand tangling in my skirts. His proximity set me on edge. I couldn't predict what he would do next. Why had I so easily agreed to pretend to be a wife? I tried to recall Cian's teachings, but my mind was racing with our growing proximity to people. I couldn't very well blurt out my concerns now, not when we were quickly approaching the many humans milling about.

I should be more concerned with finding the man who would be the key to my redemption. I tried to clear my mind of Cian, to focus on my revenge, but every time I got close to finding my killing edge, Cian's hand would find my fingertips, or his shoulder would graze mine and—against my will—I would soften.

Twilight began pressing down on us more quickly than I wanted it to. We were supposed to be long gone from this place before the night descended. We would need to hurry to make that possible, but Cian's pace remained relaxed.

We walked through the first clusters of homes, all of which looked like Cian's but without the dark, smooth river stones. There was so much to take in, every single one of my senses abruptly fired to life. It was overwhelming, making me wish that I had my knife. I was strong enough to defend myself against anyone who sought out violence, but if those weapons that wrought such damage upon me and mine were to be used, I was defenseless. Humans filled the area, poured out of every doorway and alley. My heart pounded in my chest.

Cian must have sensed my heightened unease, for he wrapped those long fingers around mine and leaned in to murmur in my ear, "You are a vision in green, Iona. It brings out the bonny paleness of your skin." His way of soothing me, I supposed. I almost tugged my hand free of his, before I thought better of it. There were so many men and women walking about, casting curious glances our way. I did not want to *make a scene*. He knew it too.

His thumb ran over my knuckles, taunting me. He used our connected hands to pull me closer to him so that our sides were touching as we walked down the path. He purred, "I want all the world to revel in your otherworldliness, *Anamchara*."

My face burned from his compliments. "And you, *husband*, are a fiend. Do not forget yourself." I tried to make my voice sweet but failed miserably. Cian's lips twisted up, and I assumed he was stifling a laugh. This, whatever it was between us, was getting under my skin, filling all the cracks and crannies of my being with something new.

Cian's voice was silky and jovial. "I wouldn't dream of it, *A Chuid*. I'm enjoying traveling with my beautiful *bean chéile*, I just can't seem to keep my hands to myself." He was doing this on purpose, the teasing. I was sure of it. I was growing all too familiar with the feeling of my cheeks turning to fire because of this creature. He tugged on my hand, pulling me even closer, before he nuzzled my neck, lips grazing the thin flesh. The burning in my cheeks spread like wildfire. My body betrayed me, and I released a sigh.

My voice was hushed, radiating my frustration. "Cian, don't toy with me, I am *trying*, but I will not tolerate any more–"

Cian's jaw muscles ticked, and a dark look from him warned me to be quiet. A group of sour looking men ambled past us, each looking the both of us up and down. Sharks sizing up their prey. I ran my tongue along my canines, the sudden urge for violence welling up in me like a tidal wave. I turned and watched the men as they sauntered away. They may be sharks, but I was something much more fierce.

I felt Cian's hand travel up to my elbow, his breath against my ear. "Was he among them?" I shook my head, still staring at their backs.

I pushed my frustration aside, heaving another sigh to release the tension building inside me. "No, but I didn't like the looks of them."

Cian nodded, steering me back the other direction. "There are many men like that. 'Tis best to be on your guard. But do not be quick to cause a stir Iona, there are more of them than there are of us." The use of my name was pointed, a reminder in itself to take Cian's words seriously. I nodded my understanding. My moment would come. I would be ready.

"Would the lovely lady like a bouquet? I've got a bunch of dried roses right here that are perfect for you." A young man with a sack near bursting with flowers rounded the corner ahead of us, nearly scaring me out of my wits, though I would never admit it to Cian. No doubt he was already aware due to the new presence of my hand on his bicep. I refused to look at him, already knowing what sort of expression was painted across his arrogant face.

I could hear the smile in his voice as he responded to the boy, "Why, what a lovely bouquet. These roses bring out the best colors of my bonny wife." The boy nodded, a grin plastered on his face. I was quickly turning the same shade of red as the roses he held out to me. Once again, my voice failed me, leaving me to stand mute while the two men haggled for the price. Cian searched a pocket and produced a golden piece between his fingers. I didn't need to ask to know that it was probably a rock Glamoured to look like whatever it was the child wanted. The flower peddler snatched it out of Cian's hand, thrust the bouquet into my arms and went back the way he came, shouting his thanks over his shoulder.

Cian tugged one bloom out of the bundle and tucked it into my hair. "See lass? Not all humans exist to destroy. Some of them like to sell things." His fingers danced over the shell of my ear before he regained his gentle grip on my elbow. I fought the urge to lean into him, to allow myself to enjoy his affections. This was only an act. Nothing more.

Wasn't it?

I needed to distract myself from the heat racing through my body. "I suppose the children must wait to become killers until they are older."

Cian sighed as I investigated the plants in my arms, refusing to give him the pleasure of my eye contact. "Nothing gets past ye, *Anamchara*. Yes, traditionally, human children are what we would call *innocent*." I glared up at him, and thrust the bouquet into his chest, trying to get as close as I could to hitting him without *making a scene*. Cian just laughed, took the flowers up to his nose and inhaled. "Lovely."

We continued walking, our pace purposeful but not hurried until we reached a building that was a bit taller than the others. Through the windows I saw many people crammed inside, sitting around tables with food and drink before them. I glanced at Cian, my stomach dropping when I saw the look of giddy determination in his eyes. *Please no.*

Cian spoke my fears into existence. "Well my sweet, let me show you some of the joys mankind hath wrought upon the earth. It is time you learned something more of this world." I shook my head, panicked like a caught fish, but Cian was lightning fast. He linked his arm through mine and whisked me through the door.

I had no time to think or speak or claw my way to freedom. Before I knew it, we were inside the space. My eyes widened in terror that I could do nothing to diminish. We were walking into a den of villainous monsters, with nothing to defend ourselves save Cian's wit. *Heaven and earth and all the hells below.*

The interior of the place was dimly lit, a few small flames flickered on tabletops, and some hung from metal contraptions in the ceiling. There were seven or eight humans in the space, each conversing and dining on an assortment of items. The odor hanging in the air was an amalgamation of bodies and something similar to the stew we'd eaten at the old woman's home.

Instantly all eyes turned toward us, and a sheen of sweat gathered at the base of my neck. My terror shifted to a feeling of overwhelm. There were so many opportunities for chaos and conflict, each of them more awful to imagine than the next. I found myself staring into every person's eyes, gauging the level of violence I saw within them. My hands balled into fists, and I readied myself for a fight until Cian's voice boomed out from beside me. I looked wildly at him, trying to understand the kind of game he was playing.

"Is there room for two more? My wife and I are in need of refreshment before we continue on our way." I continued to gawk at him, but he was paying me no mind. The smile on his face was one I'd never seen before. It was golden and innocent. Like he was a being sent from above.

It was a *lie*.

I looked into the face of the man Cian was addressing. His expression was hazy. He looked almost half asleep. The man nodded, a soft grin growing on his face. He wiped his hands on his ruddy grey shirt and pointed to a vacant table in the back corner. Everyone else had resumed their conversations, forgetting us entirely. Cian softly patted my hand before he led us to the table.

I tugged at my skirts to offset my nerves wreaking havoc on me, trying to calm my raging heartbeat. "*What did you do?*" I hissed at him, and Cian grinned all the more foolishly. He raised his eyebrows, and those damned eyes of his shined like rubies. I needed to keep control, not swoon over this ridiculous fiend.

Cian replied, "What do you think? *Magic.* It allows me to come and go unnoticed. I can live the life of a man, with all the benefits of being an *Each-Uisce.*" He pulled a chair out for me and waited to seat himself until I sat. The man from behind the counter brought us two glasses filled with a dark liquid. Cian didn't waste a moment before taking a swig from his.

The drink left a pale line above his lip which he quickly licked away.

I pushed my glass away from me, bristling with rage. "What is so infinitely wonderful about this place? Why spend your hours here? What could you possibly gain from *this*?" I pointed at his glass, then gestured to the room at large. "I do not understand." I crossed my arms over my chest.

Cian's jaw shifted and a deep sigh exited his mouth before he leaned over the table. His nose was a hair's breadth from mine. "Because, *Anamchara*, you do not know loneliness as I do."

He very well might have slapped me with his words. The bitterness of it stung. *Loneliness*? Of course. Between his bouts of courting and pleasure seeking, he *was* more alone than I had ever been in all my life.

I watched him lean back against his chair from the corner of my eye. His eyes tracked my every movement, always studying me when he thought I wasn't aware. Neither one of us seemed to let the other out of sight. Was it curiosity or mistrust that held his attention? I knew which one drew me to him, though I was loath to admit it. He was callous and impulsive. Yet there was an undeniable gentleness beneath his arrogance, and it was beginning to sink its teeth into me. My eyes were fastened to his countenance now, despite the warring within myself. I wanted more of this feeling, more of this *togetherness*.

Cian's throat bobbed, as though he were disconcerted by the freely given attention. Was all his flirting and foolish play just an act? Was I no different than any other female he'd courted? My stomach soured at the thought.

Cian pushed my glass towards me and grunted. "Drink."

I sighed, then took up the vessel and sniffed it hesitantly. Its aroma was unfamiliar yet very pleasant to behold. I took a sip, then another. The drink was smooth as it slid down my throat. Its taste was reminiscent of the minerals found in the oyster shells my kin and I often cracked open so that we could feast upon what was inside. It was familiar, and it comforted me. I began taking deep drinks from my cup, not bothering to stop, until Cian noticed and put a heavy hand on my forearm.

"*A Chuid,* if you drink that too quickly you will find yourself altered in a way I doubt you would find pleasant." An amused smile curled his lips upward, made me want to lean forward and take them with mine.

My stomach pressed against the table as I inched closer to him. His eyes settled on my mouth, and I knew he wanted what I wanted, perhaps with as much intensity. His hand was still on my arm. So warm, so strong. He let out a breath, and my eyes strayed from his lips and down to his chest, which rose and fell in quick succession. The wanting was growing at a feverish pace, and I feared—no, I knew—it would lead me to ruin.

He whispered, and it was heavy with intent. "What is it about you? Iona, what magic do you possess that has entrapped me so wholly?" We were so close now, so very close. He reached up and took the tip of my chin with his thumb and forefinger. I held my breath, waiting. Cian's eyes were a deep ruby, full of desire. They began to close as he leaned into me, then—

A man rushed through the entrance, running into the humans standing at the tall counter near the door. His eyes were wild, panic stricken. "Have you seen her? Have you seen my daughter? She's been missing less than a fortnight. I've traveled up and down the shore searching. Her name is Diana, she's got eyes like the sky, blonde hair, bonny. She's my only daughter—eighteen, will be nineteen by the end of the season."

I twisted back to witness this turn of events. Cian went stock still in his seat.

The pieces began falling into place when Cian's eyes caught mine. The missing daughter was one of his brides. I started to stand, thinking of nothing more than to flee this place before the man noticed us. My chair scraped against the wood floor, and I froze.

The man turned his glare to our table.

I'd brought his attention directly to Cian.

The *Each-Uisce* looked befuddled as the man pointed a burly hand at him. "*You*. I know you. I've seen your face. With Diana. Where is she?"

And all hell broke loose.

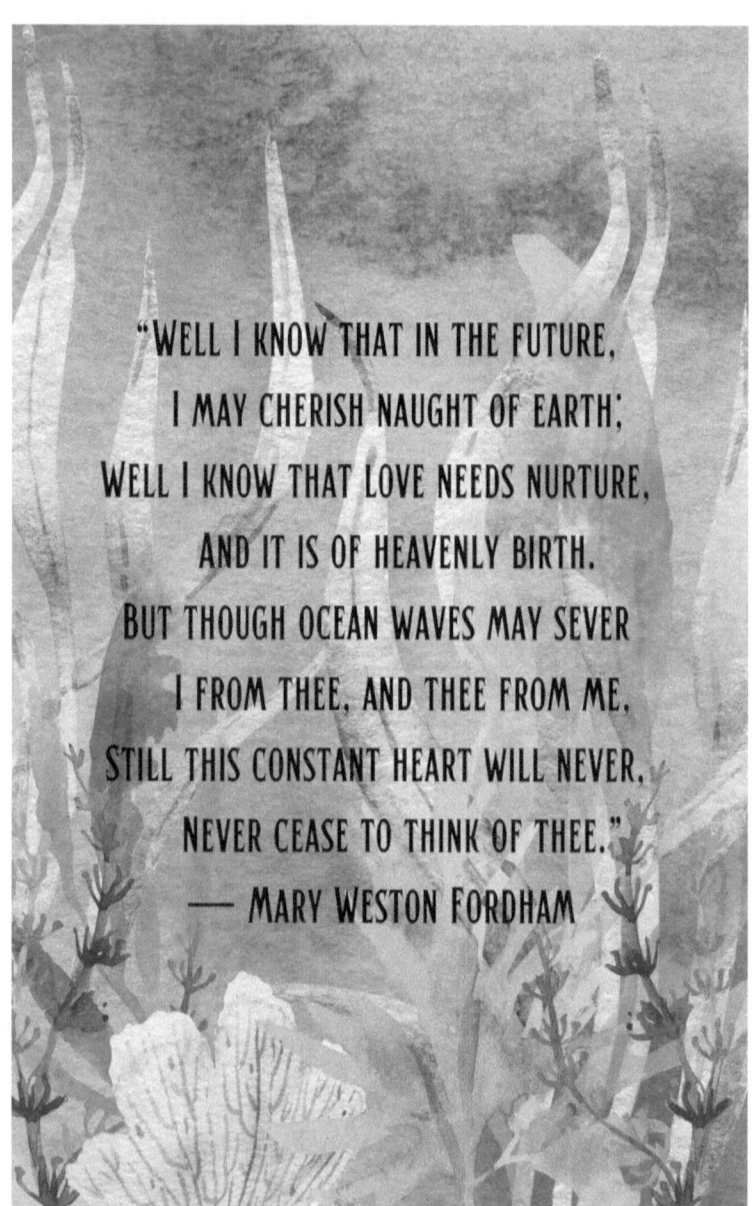

"WELL I KNOW THAT IN THE FUTURE,
I MAY CHERISH NAUGHT OF EARTH;
WELL I KNOW THAT LOVE NEEDS NURTURE,
AND IT IS OF HEAVENLY BIRTH.
BUT THOUGH OCEAN WAVES MAY SEVER
I FROM THEE, AND THEE FROM ME,
STILL THIS CONSTANT HEART WILL NEVER,
NEVER CEASE TO THINK OF THEE."
— MARY WESTON FORDHAM

Chapter Thirteen

IONA

Two things immediately became apparent. The first was that this man meant to kill Cian. The second, was that we were most decidedly cornered with the only means of escape blocked by several wary humans all slowly crowding around us. I looked to Cian, who appeared petrified, then at the men getting closer with each second. My eyes searched the room for anything that could be used to defend ourselves.

The angry father stumbled forward, his meaty hands gripping hard onto either side of Cian's shoulders, who still looked utterly confused. "You—you've taken my girl." His wild eyes searched the room. "This is no man! This is a demon! A beast from Hell!" The bartender's expression changed from the dreamy eyed look Cian had forced onto him to a now very alert, very raw one. The father shook Cian roughly, the force of which must have brought Cian out of his stupor.

Cian's voice was too light and jovial for such a turn of events, but he spoke nonetheless. "Gentlemen, let's not be so hasty with such angry accusations. As you can see—as you can see, I'm here with my wife, who is not your girl. There is no need to be so weary of us. We are just passing through. Let us be on our way and we will never trouble you again."

I recognized his tone for the same he had used with the barkeep earlier. The men around us continued to stare at Cian, and then they turned their glances to me.

Another man spoke this time, his pointer finger shoved in my face. "She's not of this world either, look at her, any man can see she's no lady, but an imp in disguise. Let us rid the village of these devils!"

Cian's jaw fell open, dumbfounded that his Glamour had no impact on these people. The man who still held fast to his shoulders let go long enough to grab a glass bottle from the table across from ours. Before I could move to defend Cian, he brought it crashing down over his head. The bottle shattered and Cian held consciousness long enough to cast a look my way that threatened to break my heart, then he fell to the floor.

No. The desire to protect this creature who had sworn himself to me surged out of me like a tidal wave. I had to act swiftly or else be lost to this sea of insanity. I would not let them take Cian from me. Not now.

I put both hands under the table then flipped it up and away from Cian and myself to create a sort of barrier from the men. It crashed down in front of us, sending some of the people backwards, afraid of the sudden sound. It bought us mere moments.

I crouched down to check Cian's injury. A thin stream of blood made its way down his temple, then his neck, where it stained his white shirt scarlet. Panic and rage gripped me wholly. My hand opened and closed on nothing, wishing there was a blade resting within my palm. It wasn't long before the barkeep began to heft the table out of his way, exposing us to the mob of humans.

In that second, I let out a heavy breath, pushing out all the fear and rage that was boiling beneath my skin. I filled my lungs anew and let out the only other gift I knew I had been given. My song.

There were no words any human would understand. It was as old as the sea itself. Older. It was a song of blood and pain, of love and endless longing. It was a song full of beautiful suffering. It was an endless song, with countless refrains and verses. I sang as though it was the only thing I knew how to do. My chest expanded and contracted with the flow of my melody. It was more than a woman's voice they heard; it was the song of the sea.

At first, the men stopped all motion and stood, completely awestruck. Then the barkeeper gently set the table down, and the other men slowly moved back to their perches as though in a trance. I continued to sing, power exuding from every line, as I pulled Cian's limp arm around my shoulder, and proceeded to drag him out of the tavern.

My body ached from everything I had gone through, but I would not leave the fool behind. I refused. Though he surely deserved his fate. I let my heart take wing from my body in my voice, my song. *Let the men be appeased. Let them leave us alone.* If I'd had my knife or some other means of destruction, perhaps this encounter would have been more exciting, but this was all I could manage.

I continued singing as I hauled Cian's mostly unconscious body down the path. Even when my throat grew raw from it, I did not stop. My shoulder and side flared in brilliant protest at his added weight, but I did not stop. I clenched my fists and willed my muscles to continue until I could find a safe place. Away from this terrible village.

Cian moaned incoherently several times during our trek. It was enough to know he was alive. Something in me held taut relaxed at the sound. A mere bottle had brought him so low. I wondered if he would wake in a state of embarrassment. I found the thought quite comforting. The idiot *should* be embarrassed. He brought us to that hell hole. Brought that attention to us, after all his warnings to me about *making a scene*. Ridiculous.

As I dragged his bulk along, I couldn't help but to inhale the scent of him. It was growing familiar, and that alone sent a terrifying thrill through me. The possibility of no longer being alone in this world was beginning to force itself into my mind, and I knew it would not leave me so easily. Nor did I want it to. Once I'd dreamt of a life that I could share with another, a life that was more than duty bound. I'd wanted to believe that dream had died when my heart had been broken, but it seemed I was wrong.

By the time we'd passed the remaining smattering of houses at the fringes of the village, my voice was merely a rasp, each word of my song less and less intelligible with every step. Finally, I came across a gathering of boulders and tall trees thick with broad leaves. I dragged Cian to a large, jagged rock covered in moss. I tried to let him down gently, but his head still managed to bob against the stone. I gave his injury a quick but thorough inspection. He had an angry gash cutting through his hair, but it was not very long.

He would survive.

Cian's face held a pained expression, and a great deal of blood had been smeared across his brow and eyes. I was no doubt covered in it as well. I tried to wipe it away from his skin, but it had dried to a crust. I'd need to find a stream to remove it. I pushed a clump of Cian's hair off his face, and watched his eyebrows pinch together as his head rolled to one side. He was a beautiful, pitiful creature. A wave of feral protectiveness swept me away, threatening to overtake any reason I had left in me. When I was younger in this world, I had felt an insatiable need to shepherd and care for every living soul around me. Now I felt it again. It mattered little what he was, only that we had somehow entrusted ourselves to each other.

His mouth parted and my name escaped, a hazy grumble on his lips, "Iona."

I ran a hand down his cheek. As angry as I wanted to be, I couldn't deny he needed attention. His skin was cool to the touch, like a stone chilled by the breeze. There would be words, but later. "Hush. I'm going to find water. We are safe here." I stood, and left Cian.

Not far from where he lay was a small brook. Clear water ran thin between stones covered in lichens and ferns, then pooled in tiers further down the creek. I took a moment to scrub Cian's dried blood from my fingers. It came away in flakes then disappeared in the water. I tore a strip of fabric from the hem of my dress and submerged it in the icy waters of the stream. The atmosphere was quiet. Full dark had descended and only creatures of the night were stirring. Soft rustling through the deadfall and trees was the only sound. We were alone.

When I returned, Cian had propped himself upright, his back rested against the boulder where I'd left him. His eyes were still shut tight, his hands clasped on his chest. A sentiment not far from the feelings I held for my kin began flooding my veins. How long could I deny myself the urges I wanted so badly to act upon? I watched him from the tree line before I moved nearer, watched his hands rising and falling with steady breaths. He did not open his eyes until I sat beside him.

He murmured, "My Glamour—it didn't work. I'd never needed to use it on so many at once. I'd never considered a limit to my ability."

I felt my eyes roll into the back of my head. "Hush now. Let me clean you up." I shot him a look that had his jaw clamping tight. I began to dab at the caked blood marring his perfect skin. It would not budge with a gentle hand, so I took his chin in one hand while I applied more pressure, scrubbing fiercely. Cian winced but did not speak. Nor did I.

Now that he was awake, I found my anger once more. The air grew thick with our unspoken words. I managed to remove the majority of gore from him, aside from what had dried in his hair.

"You'll need to go to the stream yourself if you want to wash it from your scalp. It doesn't look to be a deep wound, just one that bled plenty." I wiped my hands against my gown and tossed the soiled cloth aside.

Cian's voice was thick with disbelief. "No one has ever made me bleed. I wasn't even sure I could." His arrogance further kindled the banked coals of anger inside me. Everything bleeds, even I knew that. I frowned at him as he reached a tentative hand to investigate the gash in his head.

I seethed. "So you didn't think twice about bringing us to that place, because it had simply never occurred to you that *you could be* in danger?" I rose up on my knees, fingers clawing into the mossy earth. "Clearly, you have *never* known what pain and suffering is like, Cian, though you are quite adept at delivering it unto others, it seems." I couldn't help the snarl that peeled away from my mouth. Cian sat up straighter, balking at my words. His eyes flashed ruby, glowing brightly in the darkness. His anger now matched mine. I had struck a nerve.

"I was given a calling that I must obey. A calling I've ignored for *your* benefit I might add. Perhaps 'tis why my gifts have deserted me." His brows steepled over his eyes, hurt clouding his menacing expression.

I scoffed, leaning closer. "Oh yes, tricking defenseless women. Luring them with your empty promises of *love*. Lies. All of it. You are a deceiver. There is not an ounce of sorry in my bones for your lack of fortune." I dared him to challenge me, wanted him to fight back. Make me deny the feelings building inside my chest.

"And are you *so* blameless, Miss Selkie? How many innocent men's throats have you slit then fed to the sea, hmm?" Cian's voice was a velvet purr, full of scathing condescension.

The audacity of this lunatic.

I gaped at him a moment, before I growled, "There is no such thing as an innocent man—"

"But there are nothing *but* innocent women who fall prey to me?"

"That's not—"

"No. Iona, you see a beast before you. A creature of death, and it frightens you. But you need only look in a mirror, *Anam-chara*. You'll find another staring right back at you."

Frightened? How dare he. My mind raced as I put his insult

together. I'd only the vaguest understanding of what he meant until—that day on the beach, when I beheld my visage for the first time. He'd *seen* me taking my reflection in for so many hours. I flushed crimson. A *monster*. That's what he was calling me. Rage surged out of me, dark and cold like the sea in winter.

"You're a coward." I could taste the acid on my tongue.

"Unfeeling creature." Cian's nostrils flared as he scratched at his neck in agitation. He, too, was red in the face with passion. I chewed the inside of my cheek, wishing to inflict more hurt.

I leaned back, the balls of my feet pressing hard into the ground. I couldn't bear his look any longer. The fight began to leave me when I stood and turned away. I wrapped my arms around myself. A heavy weariness riddled my soul. A deeper ache devoured me. It was a pain worse than being shot and it ripped at my heart. A wound I'd not felt in ages. Not since I was much newer in this world.

The minutes stretched on with neither of us deigning to speak. Then I heard Cian rise and move towards me. Crickets sang out from somewhere in the trees. I watched my breath billow before me, wishing to go back in time, before we entered the village. Back to the river, when we swam together, simply two creatures caught up in the sheer joy of existence. I think I may have loved him then, as we twisted in the currents, and then again when we shared that peaceful moment in his cottage beneath the water.

Cian's voice smoldered in the chill air. "I know what I am, Iona. To call me a coward—it speaks to your ignorance of me. I was given a purpose, so very long ago, and I have served that purpose with diligence. As have you." His voice became rough, thick and sweet like the drink at the tavern. I felt the heat of his body as he moved even closer to me. If I stepped back an inch, I would feel the contours of his body against mine.

His breath caressed the nape of my neck, sending a river of fire down my spine. "Now, shall we succumb to our petty squabble, or shall we stop the pretense and act on our truest instincts?"

I spun around, his face mere inches from mine. His eyes devoured me slowly. Any anger that remained in my veins simmered away. In its wake was maddening lust. He was a beast, looking to me for satiation.

His hands went to my skirts where they gathered low on my waist. I felt the weight of them as he pulled at my dress. My skin felt flushed as my pulse hammered. Cian looked into my eyes, waiting. "Do I have your consent, *Anamchara?*"

I looked Cian up and down, appraising the creature before me. A being from another world altogether, and yet—so familiar, so enticing. Without words, I took Cian's hands in my own and brought them to my hips, stepping into his arms.

"You may touch me." I nodded while speaking the words, afraid my voice had run away completely. It was barely audible, but I knew he heard me. There was no laughter in his face as he pulled me ever closer to his body. He took a hand and tipped my chin up to his, held it there a moment while he considered me. I supposed he was thinking the same thing I was. I gasped when he brought his lips down to mine. His mouth pressed hard against mine, his tongue seeking entrance. My lips parted, and our tongues clashed. A war of claiming. Cian's hand moved from my face to my back, and down further to the curve below my waist. My fingers found his bound hair, and promptly freed it from its ribbon. I let it fall to the ground while entangling my fingers in his curls. Cian pushed against me and I pushed back, feeling every inch of the hardened shaft in his breeches. A moan broke from his mouth into mine, and he pulled away, biting my bottom lip before dragging his lips and teeth down the column of my neck, to my chest. I arched my back into him, hungry for more attention.

He glanced up at me, his expression dark and desperate, before he ran his hands over my torso, effectively erasing the gown and the breeches he had Glamoured for me. I was now back in the white shift I'd borrowed from the witch.

"It was torture seeing you in this, *mo mhuirnín*. All I wanted to do was take it off." I turned crimson at his words, but my body came alive. His fingers ran over my nipples, now visible through the shift, hardened with anticipation.

I breathed, "You can take it off *now*, Cian." His eyebrow raised a fraction before he slid his fingers down my thigh, then my calf, before he caught the hem and tugged it up, up and over my head. He tossed the shift aside then took in my body. Shivers danced across my skin, with the cold, with pleasure. Cian leaned into me, hungry for another kiss, but I stopped him. "It's my turn. Is this all a Glamour? Are you truly naked beneath your magic?" I pointed to his attire, wondering the best course of action. I could see clearly just how hungry he was for me.

"Tis. Shall I undress for you?"

I swallowed the lump in my throat.

"Can I take your Glamour off the way you take it from me?"

It was Cian's turn to swallow. Then he rasped, "Yes." He clenched his jaw and placed his hands over mine while I began running them across his chest and arms. Just as he said, Cian guided my fingers and together, we undid his magic. Each stroke of my hand beneath his left behind bare flesh, taut and beautiful in the night. When his shirt was gone, I gazed upon his features: sleek and strong with broad shoulders and a muscled torso. Oh, I wanted to claim every inch of him, and I would. I knelt before him, mimicking what he had done to me just a few nights past. I looked up at Cian, smiling *my* predatory smile. Then I ran my hands over his thighs and his backside, watching as his skin revealed itself to me. I stole a glance up at Cian once more before I took him between my lips.

Cian gasped, "Iona— *oh!*"

I continued to use my tongue and lips to elicit more wondrous sounds from Cian, who's hands held my head gently. He was salty and natural and everything I needed. My thighs were growing slick with longing, so I pulled away. I leaned back against the mossy earth, spreading my legs before Cian. There was a momentary pause as Cian's eyes poured over me again, then he laid down alongside me. I reached for him and stroked my hand up and down against him, eager for more. Cian leaned over me and nipped at my breasts with his lips, while his hand slipped between my legs.

"Have mercy on me, Iona—you are a dream. A dream." His lips found my earlobe while his fingertips pressed against me in a wave-like rhythm and soon my hips were moving with his hand. More—I wanted more. I pushed Cian onto his back, and threw a leg over his waist, pausing before I let him enter me.

I placed my hands on his chest and asked, "Is this what you want?" I searched Cian's expression, full of heat, and feral possession. His answer was to pull me down for a kiss with one hand while the other wrapped around my waist, bringing our bodies together. He held onto me a moment, despite my desire to wriggle against his body. "Are you alright, Cian?"

He huffed a laugh. "I think I'm s'posed to ask you that."

My lips found his. Slowly I kissed him as I let my hips glide up and down, feeling every inch of Cian within me. His hands traveled over my skin again and again, as though he were afraid to let any part go unexplored. We stared into each other's eyes as our bodies bucked and pushed against one another. His fingers went back to caressing my center, in time with my rocking hips. He knew what I wanted, what I craved so deeply.

Cian held my waist down against him and thrusted up into me. The intensity of his movement pushed me over the edge, and I collapsed on top of him, panting. He licked the sweat off my neck as I fought to catch my breath.

Cian held onto me as he moved me to the ground and repositioned himself between my legs. Something in our need grew heightened as he neared climax. Cian thrusted into me, fierce and full of urgency. I wrapped my legs around his waist and my fingers gripped his shoulders as we both held each other as tightly as we could. Cian's hips pushed against me, hard and fast, until he found his edge, then fell free from it.

He wrapped both arms around my body and nestled his face in the crook of my shoulder as we let our hearts slow. I could still scent the blood in his hair along with the dense night atmosphere. I gingerly reached up to touch his head. "Are you sure you're alright?"

Cian said nothing, instead nodding against my chest.

I felt his jaw move against my skin as he murmured, "You saved me. A life for a life." Confusion rippled through me. Cian must have sensed it, so he continued. "Before—you thanked me for rescuing you from the mouth of my river. You said you wouldn't have done the same for me. Well, you've proven yourself wrong."

"So now you owe *me*?" I twisted so that I could better see his reactions. He'd often spoken of maintaining balance, was this not a part of it?

His lips curled up devilishly. "*A Chuid,* saving a life is a sacred gesture. There is nothing in this world that could repay such kindness. But I am here anytime you may like a spot of company." The fiend winked at me, and I couldn't help myself as I pressed my lips against his.

"THE AWFUL SPIRITS OF THE DEEP
HOLD THEIR COMMUNION THERE;
AND THERE ARE THOSE FOR WHOM WE WEEP,
THE YOUNG, THE BRIGHT, THE FAIR.

CALMLY THE WEARIED SEAMEN REST
BENEATH THEIR OWN BLUE SEA.
THE OCEAN SOLITUDES ARE BLEST,
FOR THERE IS PURITY.

THE EARTH HAS GUILT, THE EARTH HAS CARE,
UNQUIET ARE ITS GRAVES;
BUT PEACEFUL SLEEP IS EVER THERE,
BENEATH THE DARK BLUE WAVES."
— NATHENIAL HAWTHORNE

Chapter Fourteen

CIAN

The gash in my head pained me fiercely, but it mattered little. I couldn't be bothered to care about anything other than the luminous being lying naked beside me. Iona's chest, dappled in freckles and starlight, rose and fell in steady breaths. Dark hair trailed down over her shoulders, fanning out around her head like a heavenly crown. I wanted badly to reach out and touch it, or to smooth the wrinkle between her brows, but I knew the slightest movement would wake her.

How did we get here? I'd tried so hard to keep her at arm's length, to treat her as the otherworldly thing she was, not a woman to be wooed and wedded. Despite my reservations, we'd become linked, she and I. It was a different sort of connection I didn't know I'd been craving—and it was growing stronger with every one of her breaths. This was so far from my life's usual turn of events. It frightened me, and that enticed me all the more. I would damn all consequences for this creature. Iona twisted on her side and nestled against my chest, nearly wrenching my heart from it in the process. I didn't want this to end. Her arm slid across my stomach protectively. Even in her sleep, she could not deny her instincts.

In a few small hours we would be walking into the sea, and Iona would find that precious piece of her being that had been so treacherously taken from her. I wanted to give her what she most desired. I promised I would help her find it. And yet, knowing the coat was her singular wish... it left a bitter taste on my tongue. I banished all further thought and wrapped an arm around her waist. I inhaled, wishing to savor every sense that could be attached to Iona. The lingering smell of salt filled my nose, and soon I was as deeply asleep as she.

"Cian. Cian, wake up." Iona's voice was quiet, a lullaby. Her fingers trailed the length of my jaw and down my neck to rest against my chest.

"Mhhmm, *Anamchara*, are you starving for my affection?" I cracked one eye to behold her dark eyed face peering down at me. She was wreathed in gilded sunlight, sending beams of gold through her black hair. I watched her eyes narrow, while her thin lips curled upward.

"I'm starving, in general, Cian, and if you aren't careful—I will make a meal out of you." She leaned over me and nipped sharply at my bottom lip. It was a call for play that sent my blood boiling. My hands gripped her arms, bringing her down onto my chest. Iona wrestled out of my grip easily enough, a wicked smile lighting her face. She eyed me up and down before making up her mind to whatever it was she wanted to say. "Please give me my pants back."

She raised her eyebrows as she stood. Iona held both arms out, allowing me an unobstructed view of her lean muscled body. She was a golden goddess blessing me with a vision of her loveliness. I mustn't ever forget this moment. I tried to sear it into my mind. Prayed silently that I would always have this image to revisit when I needed to see her again. Soon she would be just a memory anyway.

"I suppose I must. A promise is a promise." I stood slowly before realizing with an abundance of embarrassment that it might not work at all. Last night... it had been too long since my eyes had caught another's fancy. I'd never gone so long without searching out a lass for marriage. 'Spose the river was longing for more company.

I exhaled, summoning the gumption to cast my Glamour. There was a moment where I stood, hand poised above my legs, and there was nothing. But then, as if there had never been a magicless moment in my entire existence, I cast a black pair of breeches and a midnight blue tunic. I exhaled.

I thought maybe adorning myself in the colors of Iona's home might make her find me more pleasant. I was beginning to feel that lovesick pang inside my heart, along with the bitter fear of leaving and the inevitable end. I didn't want it to hurt the way I knew it would.

"Cian? I can always remain naked. I am not bothered as you are by nudity." Iona's words smoothed over my worries, pulling me into the present.

I stepped up towards the bare beauty, allowing my eyes to

drink up every inch of her. "Och, *A Chuid,* I am not bothered by *your* nudity, I am enamored by it. If it were merely you and I out in the world, I would simply refuse to ever lay a scrap of Glamour upon you, save for this." I ran my hands over the top of her head, leaving the coral crown behind. "My Queen."

Iona's black gaze nearly swallowed me whole, sending me spiraling down into wicked desire. She cocked her head as she watched me, a command more than an invitation. I knew I must obey. My lips found hers.

I pressed my hand to the back of her head, cradling it and pulling her into me. Iona's fingers clenched the folds of my tunic as she moaned against my mouth. I wanted to hear that sound and only that sound for eternity. Need drove my hands as they traveled to her breasts where her nipples hardened at my touch, then down between her legs. I could feel heat blooming where my fingers made contact.

"Cian," she breathed my name as her lips parted and her tongue found mine. I stroked my hand against her. Her body swayed in time with my movements. She hooked her arms around my neck pushing her hips down against my hand. I couldn't contain myself any longer. Iona gasped when I slipped a finger inside her. Then another.

"You feel so good, like silk." I moved my hand in time with Iona as she bucked and ground her body against the palm of my hand. My fingers were slick with her need. "That's it, *Anamchara,* let go, let go." Iona threw her head back, crying out. I held her in my arms while she caught her breath. I planted a tender kiss on the edge of her jaw.

"See? You must get dressed. If you go cavorting about naked, we will get little else accomplished." Iona's head hung against my chest, but I could feel her shoulders shaking with silent laughter.

"Very well, Give me my breeches, *Each-Uisce*." She grinned up at me, and the look was enough to confirm that I was indeed rubbing off on her. I let my fingers linger in some places longer than others while I cast my Glamour upon Iona. My gifts unfurled slowly enough to notice how the injuries on her shoulder and waist were fading. They were a pale pink, no more than fragile seams of flesh, now come together. Nearly healed completely.

A tiny ball of tension between my shoulders eased. Iona would heal from her misfortunes, she would carry on, and the seals would have their guardian again soon. The world would right itself once more. And I would return to my *abhainn,* to resume my duties as well.

I clothed Iona in fine breeches that felt like deer hide, and a black tunic, with silver kelp fronds stitched so they appeared to be curling up each arm. The dark colors made her look mysterious and formidable. A dangerous yet bonny thing.

"And what about this?" Iona motioned to the crown still resting on her brow.

"Is my gift unappreciated?"

The Selkie wrinkled her nose as she took it in her hands. "It is merely inconvenient. I do like it though. Perhaps I could find a safe place for it at my rock. Would it keep well enough out in the elements?" Her home. Where she was heading. Where she mightn't ever bother leaving again after the misadventures we'd been through.

I must have been frowning considerably for her to notice. She cleared her throat then said, "Cian? Will it survive the sea?"

I tried my best to shake the impending sense of dread filling my stomach, tried to forget that she would soon be gone from me. "We'll just have to see, now won't we? First things first—breakfast." I held out my hand, and Iona's fingers laced between mine. A feeling as natural as breathing. "How does trout sound?" I watched the Selkie's nostrils flare, no doubt trying to guess at what trout was. I stood a moment, gathering my bearings. She'd taken us to a mossy outcropping of ancient rocks, gathered by those long gone now.

The massive stones had been pushed upright in a circle, and we stood in the center of it. I'd come here often enough throughout my life. It was a place of solitude, where none but the natural beasts of the world came and went. Humans had strayed from this formation. Instead, they flocked to their settlements, leaving the woods to the Unseen, like me. A black bird sailed silently overhead, probably making its way home.

Iona's voice echoed in my ears. "You'll be wanting to wash that blood from your hair. Or perhaps you'll just Glamour it away?" I reached up to touch the fine crust that had cemented my curls against the side of my head. It stung considerably. Iona's eyes shone without pity. I supposed I deserved as much. I had been a fool to risk our safety in such a manner. I had wanted to prove to Iona that there could be more to life than duty, that frivolity could exist for things like us. It hadn't worked out the way I had thought, but I'd be a liar if I said I didn't enjoy how the night had ended.

I ran a hand through my hair, willing away the grime, but nothing came away. The dried blood remained. I'd never been made to bleed before. Perhaps one's own blood could not be magicked away. It was possible, I supposed.

Iona's voice was curious, lighthearted. "The creek will wash it clean for you. I'm guessing trout must be a kind of fish that lives in freshwater?"

While she spoke, a thought occurred to me. One I hadn't the mind to ask last night. "Iona—how did we escape the men? What happened?"

Her brow creased and she looked away. We continued walking towards the stream silently, while my thoughts spiraled endlessly around the possibilities that could have occurred.

Not long after we caught sight of the stream did Iona decide to speak. "I sang. I sang to the men, and they let us go."

The statement was so plain and yet unfathomable. She *what*? "You sang? And it beguiled the men?" I dropped her hand and placed a palm on my hip. "Then, you did what I could not. How does it work? You never told me you had your own magic." A knot began to form in the pit of my stomach. So many secrets. So many unknown things I may never learn.

Iona shrugged. "My song was given to me when I was made. It is my last line of defense, and it requires all my concentration. It cannot be performed under any circumstances save the most dire. I've never used it like that before." Iona peered at me through her thick lashes, waiting for more questions.

"I suppose I should be honored that I was the cause for the unveiling of your most precious gift. Thank you for singing us to safety. Such a noble thing to do for such an unsavory creature as myself. I shall forever wonder what possessed you to take such extreme measures."

Hurt flashed across her face, gone in an instant, but unmistakable. I wished I could bite my tongue for once in my life. Iona deserved better than my ilk.

"Is it such a shock that I should want to protect you?" Iona turned away and crouched over the brook.

Of course, it was the wrong thing to say. So calloused. I was a brute and a beast after all; no Glamour could make me into a gentleman. I rubbed at my eyes with my fingers before walking several paces downstream to wash with the water. Every moment with Iona was like grappling with eternity. Though we'd been joined as lovers, we were on opposite ends of the Earth, one running after the other, and I feared she would get away all too soon.

I sighed. *"Mo mhuirnín*, it is not that I am surprised at your willingness to help. It is that I am not deserving of such acts of kindness. Forgive me." I could not bear it if we parted on anything less than terms of love.

Iona's shoulders relaxed, the tension leaving her frame. "To me, there was no choice to be made. You are a fool, but you are *my* fool."

I would never be gladder of the slight than I was in that moment. I tried to catch her gaze, to see how deeply she truly meant her words, but she was too focused on the task at hand. No other being existed who could tease me and make me love her all the more for it.

Iona's hands splashed deftly into the water, and in mere moments she had caught several small trout. When she turned around her triumphant grin nearly knocked me over. A beautiful, strange creature she was.

Iona waited for me to hold out my hand, then placed two fish on my palm. "I caught you a meal. This is what the seals do for the ones they deem inept." Her grin turned fiendish as my mouth dropped open in dismay.

Inept?

She tilted her head back and dangled a trout over her mouth by its tail but paused before ingesting the creature. "Maybe I shall take you hunting when we reach the sea. Would you like that? When I find my coat you and I can swim unbothered."

I nodded silently, too overcome by her kindness to form words of my own. She grinned, pleased by my response before swallowing the fish whole.

It didn't take long to gulp down the rest of the trout, especially when I realized how famished I was. I found myself staring into the brook after my last fish had been eaten, still hungry for another. Iona would not allow us to linger any longer than necessary.

She chided me while reminding me that there were plenty of fish to be caught out in the ocean. "I promise, I will feed you all that you could want. There are so many delicious things to be found beneath the waves." Her smile was sharp, alive with hope. The Selkie was eager to return to her home.

The day was heaven sent. Sunlight glittered across the hills, warming everything it touched. Tiny white and purple flowers dotted our path, swaying slightly in the faint breeze. Iona pushed ahead, asking questions of every little thing she spied. Her curiosity was abundant. Overwhelming, even.

I couldn't stop the sigh that escaped my mouth when yet another query came from Iona's lips.

"What makes this hole? Is it man-made?" She'd found a badger's den and stuck her head nearly entirely inside. Panic spurred me on to grab hold of her arm, but she yanked free of me. Iona looked over her shoulder, a sour expression on her face. She was a maddening thing.

I tried to warn her. "Iona don't—the beast that made that hole is not friendly in the least. It will bite your nose off as soon as it scents your presence." A dubious brow was raised at me, before she resumed sticking her face where it didn't belong. She took a deep inhale, and I wondered again what other tricks she was hiding up her pretty little sleeves.

She remained crouched, waiting. It was clear there would be nothing to pull her away from the den. There was an echoed scratching, snorts and snarls rising up from the darkness, and then a stout, angry head lurched out. The badger's eyes were mere slits while its lips curled up in warning. Burly shoulders propelled its body out of its hole, but it stopped mid stride.

The banded black and white face stared up into Iona's. The two black-eyed beings silently considered one another. Never had I spent a single one of my days communing with the lower creatures scouring the earth. I'd always thought my time was more valuable than that. Iona clearly had a differing viewpoint on the matter.

I found myself muttering some rather impolite words while simultaneously kneeling down next to the seal woman. My movement startled the beast only momentarily, before it seemed to understand that I was simply another animal. Separate from the world of man, though try as I might at blending in amongst them. Here was where I truly belonged. The badger sniffed at me, and then glanced back to Iona, who nodded, and then the creature turned and slowly made its way back into the darkness.

"That is the company I prefer to keep." Iona stood, wiping her hands against her breeches.

I could bear her condescension for only so long. "Iona, *A chuid*, have you ever kept company with humans? It would seem you are at least somewhat...*acquainted*, but your rigid viewpoint begs the question." Her dark eyes narrowed, confusion whirling in them. I continued probing. "Iona, what happened?"

She sucked on a tooth, brooding over her imminent response. "Once. Yes. For a time."

It was my turn to burn with curiosity. "Yes, and? What happened?"

Iona turned away, wandering up the hill before us.

I could barely hear her voice as it rolled down the slope to me. "He said he loved me. Then he did love me. Then he left me. And I never saw him again."

Agony tore at me. I, who had never been left, never wanted for love, had also never known this kind of pain. Her distrust and malice finally melded into place.

Iona had been abandoned. And soon she was going to abandon me.

"Would you tell me? The story of your love?" Dark curiosity nipped at me, and I couldn't help myself but to ask.

Iona continued facing away from me, but she stopped in her tracks. "Just this once. And only because I've never once told any living soul. Maybe the telling will heal me."

"When I was... *newer* in the world, I would often watch the shores day in and day out, as I was keen on learning all I could of the many creatures I saw skittering about on the land. The drive in me to protect was so wild and voracious that I often thought perhaps I was meant to be the steward of every living thing within my domain." As if she sensed the mirth rolling off of me, she paused. "I know, I was more... back then."

I cocked my head, confused at her statement.

"Iona, since I've known you, you've been more than I could ever want for in all of existence. Being young is not a crime. It is merely an inconvenience."

She nearly turned her head my way but thought better of it. I spied her ear turning a raspberry pink.

"Well—as I said, I watched the shores. I would often walk upon the beach, searching for anything that captured my curiosity. One day, while I was lying beneath the sun, warming my body, a man approached me."

Iona knelt to pick up a stone. She cradled it in her hand as she continued, "He'd assumed I'd been shipwrecked, immediately trying to cover me in his coat. Like I said, I was younger, and so naive. I thought he seemed kind. I knew then, in the very moment he and I locked eyes, that I would claim him for my own."

Iona glanced back at me, her eyes distant with memories before looking away. "Turns out, he thought the same thing. He convinced me to return to the beach, and I did, many times. Until our talks turned to embraces and kisses, then... more. I wanted more, but he only wanted my flesh." She hurled the rock as hard as she could, and we both watched it bounce once before disappearing in the brush.

Iona sighed. "Cian—in the end, I was an object of fascination to be used and discarded. A quest and nothing more. I didn't know that at the time."

She started walking again, and I tripped trying to keep up with her pace. "What happened?"

Finally, she turned and looked me in the face so plainly it hurt.

"I thought I would be his protector, his lover, his *bride*. I wanted to go home with him, stay with him, and leave my kin. He said he would take me. He swore on his life that he would love me forever." I reached my hand out to hers, managing to entangle our fingers. I wanted to give her comfort, to let her know things were different. This was different.

A flash of electricity shot from her hand into mine as she continued. "I believed him, and it cost me. He promised me and then I woke up on the beach, alone. I never saw him again." Iona tilted her head back, looking up into the sky. Her eyes were open windows into the black night. The vastness within them set the hairs on the back of my neck to raise. An echo sounded in my mind of the multitudes of nuptials I had rushed through. The women I'd wedded to the river, and never saw again.

The witch had been right when she said Iona brought balance and I only chaos. I hated her for it. I'd never even thought to consider my role in this world, and the darkness that my existence was forever shrouded in. Iona's story weighed heavy on my chest. It threatened to crush my heart.

Iona nodded my way. "Now tell me. Tell me about your first bride."

I scrubbed a hand through my hair cursing myself for ever mentioning her. Iona had given me her tale of sorrow, and I must return the favor. It would be unscrupulous of me to leave her empty handed. I sighed heavily. I'd never intentionally conjured her back into my thoughts. In fact, I tried stubbornly to deny her existence.

"She loved me at first sight, and I her. There was so much desire in me, for us, that my instincts came to life. And then, I killed her." I swallowed hard to alleviate the painful lump in my throat. There was nothing more to it. Nothing more to say. I was a beast. Iona was an angel. We were night and day.

Iona's eyes did not hold any contempt for me, only a sad understanding lingered in her gaze. I blinked away the ache, turning my stare to the horizon, wishing to forget all we had just shared.

"In that shoreless ocean,
at thy silently listening smile my songs
would swell in melodies,
free as waves, free from all bondage of
words.

Is the time not come yet?
Are there works still to do?
Lo, the evening has come down upon the
shore
and in the fading light the seabirds come
flying to their nests.

Who knows when the chains will be off,
and the boat, like the last glimmer of
sunset,
vanish into the night."
—Rabindranath Tagore

Chapter Fifteen

CIAN

The ocean first greeted us with her scent. Briny and rich. Then, as we walked closer to the shore, we heard her. Iona gripped my hand tightly when she first recognized the constant roar for what it was. "Cian, we've made it! Hurry. Hurry!"

I laughed, heartily enjoying her newfound enthusiasm. Soon she was dragging me along behind her.

Her white knuckled grip held me fast to her. When we crested the beach, Iona held both hands up on her brow, shielding her eyes from the sun so that she could survey the seas. "Cian! There! There—do you see it? The rock. Come, come!" She was already sprinting down the beach tugging her clothing off in a flurry as I tried to make out the distant black outcropping of rocks. It was going to be a long journey.

I half ran, half slid down the steep embankment after Iona, who was already neck deep in the surf. The waves crashed in black and green torrents against the shore, relentless, but Iona remained. She was a steady presence, ghostly and magnificent. Something weighed my legs down, slowing my pace to a near halt once my toes were planted in damp sand. I was fulfilling my oath, the promise I had sworn Iona.

So why, why on Earth was it so damned difficult to step one bit of myself into the water? We were beings of fate and fortune; it was our lot to be the keepers of balance, and therefore we must occasionally fall prey to its whims. I longed to turn back, to keep Iona for myself just a little longer, but one look into her beaming face and I knew what I must do.

I stepped into the tide, letting it gather around my calves, pulling me on as I slowly made my way to Iona. "Are you ready, *Anamchara?* Ready to find your coat?" I held out my arms to her, waiting for the last embrace, my last chance to hold the Selkie to me. Perhaps it would hurt less. Perhaps we would see one another again. My stomach soured. I knew better than to hope for a happy ending.

Iona grinned brighter than the sun itself as she took her hands in mine. They were strong but slender, powerful like she was. I willed my hands to remember this sensation. Remember the feel of her skin on mine. "I'm ready."

I tried to return her easy joy with my own, but it felt hollow, empty.

A chasm opened within me again, the same that had been my constant companion for so many years. Just another good-bye. There would be more, there were always more. It was fated and there was no escape. I never once pondered a life without the ceaseless taking of brides. Not until now.

I let my body change. Legs grew and elongated, a body once small was now wide and muscled. The man was gone and, in its place, a black horse. The version of myself that was real. Honest. A beast to ferry an angel.

Iona wrapped an arm around my neck as I began to swim. The waves splashed up against us. Salt water stung my eyes, and the air whipped my mane into my face. Out of the corner of my eye I saw Iona, enraptured over each sensation. She let out a feral cry, slapping the water with her free hand.

My pace was slow and dogged by the tides, but I did not stop, though I longed to do nothing more than to turn around and take Iona away with me. It was not long before she was swimming from my side occasionally to dive into the water ahead of us. She would disappear beneath the waves and come up after several long moments, and every time she resurfaced, she looked even more beautiful. A light shone behind her eyes that I'd never witnessed until now. It ached to see her this way.

A sleek, speckled seal came gliding through the waves to inspect us. It kept a great distance at first, choosing to peer at us with his snout just above the water line. Black eyes so like Iona's, gazing inquisitively at us. Iona shrieked when she saw the creature and immediately began pulling herself along towards it.

I called out, "Iona, is it one of your kin?" My voice was nearly drowned out by the sea. But Iona waved, head bobbing frantically. She wrapped her arms around the seal's body, and soon they were both slipping in and out of the water on their way to me. Unbridled jealousy bubbled up inside me. I wanted to be the one to carry Iona home. I wanted to be the reason her eyes shone so wonderfully.

The seal swam next to me, spinning onto its back as it floated away from me before turning around again, those dark eyes assessing me every second. Wondering what devilish thing I might be. Perhaps it sensed my true nature. Saw beyond the velvet hide and deep into my black soul. If there was a soul buried inside at all.

Iona had let go of the seal to claim her place at my side. The gesture eased my irritation considerably. I wanted her as close to me as I could get. Any distance between us at all was intolerable. "Shall we continue on then? Will the seal be our escort?" Iona nodded, a small wave lapping up into her face. Her tongue snaked out across her bottom lip. It sent chills down my spine. To be that salt water—if only.

Further into our journey, as the rock grew ever closer, we were flanked by seals on all sides. Each was a different sort of grey, some covered in a smattering of white freckles, and others were almost completely slate. They snorted and cleared their nostrils forcefully, sending plumes of mist into the air. The water churned with a mixture of seal bodies and swell.

Iona swam to greet each one, embracing the creature then pressing her forehead against theirs. Clicks and whistles rang out every time one of them resurfaced. It was a riotous event. There was exuberance here, clear and buoyant like the beasts flying through the waves. I allowed myself to slip beneath the surface and found many more creatures swimming just below us. They weaved in giant loops around me, always watching. I caught a glimpse of Iona's pale figure jetting alongside a seal, her lean legs kicking in powerful slashes through the water. I could watch her move for eternity. Something in my chest pinched, and I wished I no longer wanted to continue watching what would soon be lost to me.

The rock grew larger and larger until we were at its shore. A curved black peak hung above the majority of the rock, with jagged and steep edges on all sides. There were seal pups scattered about, barking and crying at Iona. I waited until she had both feet firmly planted on the ground before I reverted to my human state. Iona didn't speak when she saw the pups. She fell to her knees, arms open wide for them. They wasted no time and immediately began to hop towards her. Soon she was beneath a pile of fluffy white seals. She let out a giggle that could have killed me.

"Cian, come." A slender hand emerged from the furry mass. When I took it, she immediately tugged me down with her. Then I, too, became a target for the pups. They snuffled against my face and neck, and one rather rotund pup nearly crushed me with her weight as she clambered up into my lap.

Iona watched me as I ran a hand down one downy spine. "They like you."

I liked them, too. The round seal looked up into my face, her whiskers snuffling against my cheek when I leaned into her. I was almost struck unconscious by the powerful odor coming from her maw. Cute, but terribly smelly.

Iona gently ushered the pups out of her way as she stood and held her hand out to me again. She hoisted me up from the cuddly mob then began scouring every inch of the rock, clearly searching for her coat. I cleared my throat, suddenly feeling as though I may faint. I wasn't ready for this.

"*A Chuid,* what does your coat look like then?"

She didn't deign to look my way as she continued her search. "It's very much like your horse's hide. It's the deepest black you've ever seen. Like midnight during a new moon."

I ran a hand through my hair before turning away. We matched. *Just as well.*

Iona raced to the opposite side of the rock as a grey seal pup

146

began wiggling away from me, all the while turning his head back to watch me. His behavior struck me as odd, so I followed him to the edge of the rock. There was a large mass of stones littered down the side of the shore, and at the base of these stones was Iona's coat.

I knew the instant I saw it gleaming in the sun like obsidian. It had been crammed into a small groove that ran the length of the largest stone. The ocean licked at the coat gently, as though it were tenderly patting the seal skin. Keeping it safe until its owner returned. I knelt and pulled the fur out from its hiding place.

Iona's coat felt soft like the finest silk. It was dense and rich like night. It felt like Iona.

It felt like a sin to hold it in my hands.

I caressed the material with my fingers, imagining that it was the seal woman herself. This was it. I was going to call out to Iona, announcing that I had found her precious cloak. I was to be the hero of this story. She was going to run to me, pulling her treasure from my grasp, pulling away from me entirely as she put the cloak about her beautiful strong shoulders and transformed. She would dive from the rock and disappear from me forever.

I opened my mouth, lips forming her perfect, hideous name but—silence. Instead, I clenched my mouth shut, and cast a Glamour around Iona's coat, turning it into a handkerchief.

Iona's voice echoed off the rocks and waves. "Do you see it? I've looked everywhere else. It must be here." I shoved the cloth into my pocket. I swallowed once, willing the acid in my throat down.

The words burned as I said, "I'm afraid not, *Anamchara*. Are you sure there isn't somewhere else it might be?"

Iona did not respond. She ran down to where I stood, leaning over to look in the shallows around the rock. She tried to clamber into the ocean, caring little to avoid the sharp barnacles crusting the rock's edge, but I reached out to her and held her fast.

"Iona—it's not here. We've looked everywhere." She tried to leap from my arms, but I didn't dare let go.

"It has to be! Where else would it be? Cian, do you think— did the ocean take it from me?" Tears poured from her eyes and began sliding down her cheeks and neck. Her body shook with pent up emotion. I'd done this. I'd caused Iona pain. I couldn't very well pull the handkerchief from my pocket now. She'd never speak to me again. There had to be another way.

I could keep her a little longer, hold this beautiful creature for just a while more. I asked her, "What if the man who shot you took it? Do you think he saw you take it off?"

Iona grew still as she tried to recall that day's events.

"Yes. He saw. I remember he watched me climb from the sea. He's got my coat? Why?" Fury roared through her and my arms shook with her trembling. I tried to console her, tell her that we would find him, but I could not get a word out to formulate a new plan with her.

Iona ripped free from my hold and began to rage. She howled and tore at her hair. Fingers digging into her arms and face as she sobbed in agony. Iona had been so sure that she would be redeemed this day. And I had stolen that. I could not give up my farce now—no, I could salvage this.

I rushed after the Selkie, until I was able to once again pull her into an embrace. I tugged her arms down to her sides, holding her against my chest as tightly as possible. She wailed and snapped her teeth, but still I held. This would not be the end. This would not be goodbye.

"Iona—shh, Iona, we will find him. And as I swore before, we will end this." She stilled against me, and when I was certain she would remain calm I relinquished her. Iona looked into my eyes, searching for what, I'm sure I didn't want to know. She wrapped her arms around her naked waist, then sunk to the ground.

"I *will* kill him. I will kill them all."

I knew then that if Iona learned of my grave betrayal, I would meet the same fate. There was no time to consider my next steps, for in that very moment, a ship entered my periphery, and Iona's as well. She snarled, the woman gone entirely with only a ravenous beast left in her stead. She leapt into the sea, the ship directly ahead of her.

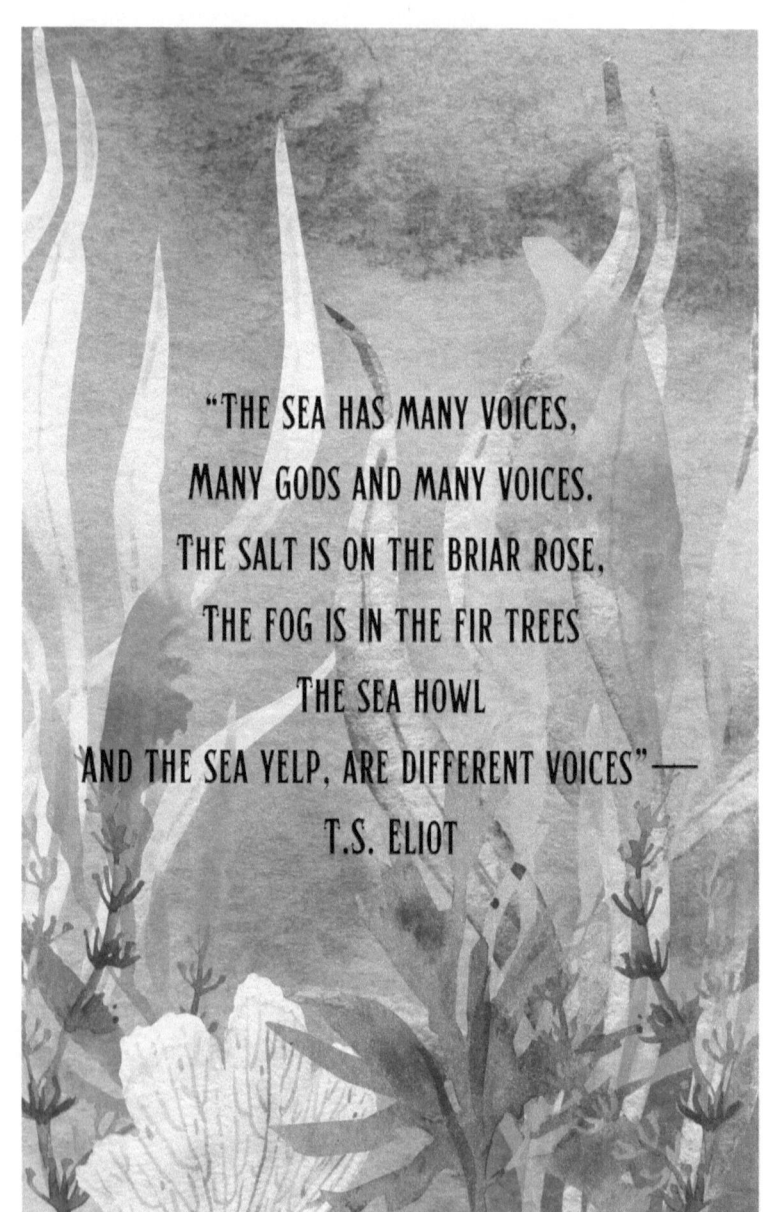

"THE SEA HAS MANY VOICES,
MANY GODS AND MANY VOICES.
THE SALT IS ON THE BRIAR ROSE,
THE FOG IS IN THE FIR TREES
THE SEA HOWL
AND THE SEA YELP, ARE DIFFERENT VOICES"—
T.S. ELIOT

Chapter Sixteen

IONA

My dreams of being whole again were dashed away so instantly I lost control. I had no future or past, only bottled-up rage that festered inside me. It erupted from my flesh in a poisonous rush. I clawed at my own skin to release the sense of agony I felt. Deep within myself, I knew there would be no reprieve from this pain. The only comfort I found was in Cian's brutal embrace. It was harsh and it was painful, but it was real. It was now.

He pulled me back into myself, allowing me to once again feel the air in my lungs and the stone beneath my feet. Cian's heart throbbed against my cheek, the timing of it almost as fast as my own. He'd proven himself true to me, and this I would not forget. His promises of vengeance soothed me, but again I was left with the knowledge that I was still only half of what I was meant to be. My coat was still lost to me.

That man had taken so much from me, killed and maimed and now he'd taken my coat. My life. It had all been so easy for him. What little he knew of the consequences. For now. When I found him, I would be sure he learned the full breadth of the damage he'd inflicted upon me.

The semblance of calm I'd regained in those brief moments with Cian was obliterated when I saw the same ship that had sundered my existence not but ten meters from me. Clearly, they had learned where my kin dwelled and were about to take full advantage of the easy prey. There would be no end to the cruel killing, to the taking. It grew closer, waves cresting out from its hull as it traveled towards us.

I would end this.

I would destroy the man who had tried to destroy me.

He was so close. *Revenge* was so close.

My honor would be forfeit if I did not act now.

I heard Cian call out to me only vaguely as my head ducked in and out of the blue-black ocean. I let my wrath carry my body across the water, each pull of my arms bringing me ever closer to my prey. Though my limbs were clumsy and weak against the current, I refused to let the ship escape. Justice called to me like a gull on the wind, and I chased after it with everything I had. There was only anger roaring in my ears when I reached the hull of the boat and hauled myself up and aboard silently. Cold and ancient rage fueled each step I took.

There were two men on deck, each one on opposite sides. To the right of me, on the railing, was a blade wrapped in leather. I pulled the slender knife out of its sheath and tossed the case to the side. It was most likely used to skin my beloved seals. Holding it in my palm gave me a surge of righteous fury. I inspected the blade for a moment, before I decided it was as good a tool as any to end these despicable creatures.

The sea became wrathful around me, waves cresting up,

threatening to flood the deck as I surged towards the man on the port side.

"Where is it?" I bellowed. He didn't even turn around as I came up behind him. I gripped the back of his collar in one hand while I pushed the pointed blade into his skin, and repeated. "Where. Is. It."

My fury turned me stupid, and without waiting for his reply, I pulled the knife across his stubbled neck, slicing his throat with the other. Blood cascaded down his front as he let out his last garbled breaths before he fell to the ground. I did not spare him a glance before I sprinted to the other side of the deck, where the second man stood coiling a massive rope.

There was no time for him to realize what was coming. I took his shoulder and ripped at him so that he faced me. I stared into his terrified eyes while I shoved the knife, still bloodied with the other man's gore, into his guts. I jerked the knife to the side and ripped it free of him. A small groan escaped his lungs before he, too, fell in a wet pile of his own innards.

The killing felt right. Natural. In this moment it was all I was and would ever be again. I embraced my true self. Coat or no coat, I would always be a weapon. My blood lust had not abated, for neither of these men was *the* man. He must be here somewhere. I would not be satisfied until I was certain all who were aboard were no longer breathing. I scanned the ship, seeking out my next victim. There was a small entrance leading down into the hull of the ship.

Before I left the main deck I stood still, listening for any signs of life. All I heard were the tiny gasps one makes when taking their final breaths. Soon the ocean would be the only sound.

I made my way for the ladder. I stalked downward into the darkness, the long blade in my hand quietly dripping blood as I paused for a moment. When I reached the bottom, a snoring sort of sound came from a swinging hammock. I moved towards it, wary of any nooks and crannies someone might hide in.

I peered down at the man asleep in the hammock and knew I had found my target. His face remained cold even in slumber. I sneered as I positioned the knife at his jugular. I pressed the end down into his flesh as I growled, "Where is my coat?" The words came out clipped between my gritted teeth.

The man's eyes snapped open when he felt the pressure of cold steel against his skin. He tried to swallow, but the blade wedged against his throat stopped him. His eyes rolled around, searching my face, no doubt thinking he might be trapped in his own nightmare made real.

I repeated myself and he garbled, "I don't know nothing about no coat. I'm just a hunter. I didn't take nothing, I swear. I swear." His arms had come up on the sides of his hammock, holding his palms out to me as if he was offering himself up. *Very well.*

"You stole my coat. My Sealskin. Where is it?" I bared my canines, snarling an inch away from his face. His expression was wild and confused, but I did not yield. Was it really so easy to forget a magical coat? Fury coated my tongue. "Tell me." I pushed the knife harder into his skin, his blood pearling up to the surface.

"I swear, I don't know. I swear—please, I swear, please don't kill me. Have mercy, please!"

My patience was at its end, and my soul needed to be

appeased. I screamed at the man as I looked deep into his soul-less eyes. I pushed my knife in as far as I could. He sputtered and coughed as a river of crimson flowed from his neck. I ripped it free, and a fountain of blood spurted out of his wound. The whites of his eyes shone with terror, and it sickened me. I did not want to see them anymore.

So, I stabbed them out.

I crawled back to the main deck, covered with blood and nothing else, and found Cian waiting with his back to me. He was looking out at the sea, both hands on his hips. He stood calm and collected, though I knew he was aware of the violence I had committed. He was right when he said we deserved each other. When I saw him, a strange wave of emptiness crested over me, sending me spiraling down into the darkness.

My voice rang out like a frantic whistle. "He was here. I killed him."

Cian whirled around, his eyes wide as though he were shocked at how easy it had been. He took in my appearance, searching over my body for any injuries. His gaze rested on my face, brimming with concern.

"What do you mean? He was on this ship? Truly?" I nodded silently, wringing my bloodied hands together. Cian's face held a hint of fear I didn't understand. Was he frightened of me?

"He denied having taken my coat. So, I stuck his knife in his throat, then his eyes. Will you help me search for it? It must be here somewhere. It has to be. Right, Cian?" A muscle twitched in his face, which had become curiously blank.

Cian began to move towards me on the ship, his arms outstretched as though he were going to restrain me again.

"Iona, do you think it's possible he traded it?" Bile rose up in me at the thought. Traded my coat away to some other despicable man? Like it was just some common good? I vomited across the deck, folding in half as I wretched. Cian knelt beside me, pulling my hair up away from my face.

"I promise this, you will have your coat again. On my honor as *Each-Uisce*. This is not the end, not yet." Cian's voice was muffled and distant.

When I finished, I wiped the back of my hand against my mouth and turned to see him. My vision grew dark. It was too much. There was too much loss; I was too broken and tired. I felt his arms go around my middle, and then I felt nothing.

There was water, lapping against my body, washing over my head and swirling in my ears. A breeze of ice licked at my nose, the salty air filling my lungs with every inhale. And then darkness.

I heard the chirping of seals as they splashed around in the dark. Where was I? Where were they? So close I sensed I could touch them if only I could move, but my body was unresponsive. My mind was the only piece of my being I could access. I knew I was being pulled along, for there was a surging motion of forward momentum, churning against the current. My body tugged about like a bit of kelp caught up in the riptide.

Something filled my hands, something sleek and reedy. They

were only vague sensations running through me. The ocean was no longer cradling me. Someone continued to pull me. Sand and rocks nipped at my toes, then tall grasses. I could not say how long it was until I was pulled into water once more. It was swift, rushing one way constantly, pulling me, begging me to go along with it, but I could not. I was held fast by strong arms that refused to let go. I pushed, as weak as I was, yearning for the water to drag me into the deep. It was time to go back to what I had been before. Back to the briny darkness. Back to nothingness.

"Iona, Iona, *Anamchara*, Hold your breath now. Now."

I did as the voice demanded, gulping down a lungful of air. Then down we went, under mountains of water, down and down. My lungs ached from holding air, my head spinning from lack of oxygen. Suddenly, a burst of force pushed me forward and then there was air filling me once again, clean and dry as it entered my body.

Cian murmured against my skin. "Shh now, love. I'll take care of ye. Shh." It did not matter now. I let go and sank into the blackness of my mind.

When I woke, I was in a bundle of the softest material I'd ever touched. It was warm and downy. I burrowed under the blankets until I was completely beneath the many layers. I never wanted to leave. There was no point in emerging. I would never find my coat. That monster had probably dropped it on the other side of the world. It might as well have been swallowed by the depths.

I would remain as a half-formed beast—a creature without purpose. I squeezed my eyes shut tight as I tried desperately to remember the last time I had been my seal self. It had been a beautiful day. My body had been strong and powerful. I was at peace with my nature. At peace with everything I had ever known. And then, it changed.

My kin were slaughtered, and I was mutilated, body and soul. The scars on my flesh would likely fade away into nothing, but the invisible scars would never be anything but raw and aching. My hands moved to the uneven bands of skin where I'd been shot. Already it was disappearing, the physical proof of my emotional turmoil.

A stirring from nearby startled me from my thoughts. I stilled my breathing, listening for any hint. A melody, faint and sorrowful, drifted in from under the door. It was Cian. He was playing his flute. The same song he'd played all those nights ago when we were only strangers. So much had been wrought and twisted up in me since then. There was pain and failure, and so much agony over it all. Cian was a beacon in the storm raging within me. The knowledge of his proximity eased the tension in my body.

I rolled over on my back, pushing the covers away from my head. Smooth clay walls washed in white, bleached wood carved furniture. I was back in Cian's underwater cottage, laying in the bed Cian seldom ever used. I buried my face in the cushion next to me, inhaling. It didn't even smell like him. The only aroma was a faint tinge of rain, and the smell of damp earth.

The music from his flute pushed its way into the room

through the walls. The song had shifted. It rose and fell, a cadence that was as much a part of me as my own coat. I couldn't help but smile when I recognized the tune as my own. It didn't have the same effect when Cian made it, but it was still beautiful, and it was still mine. I lay there, dozing in and out while he continued to play. I wanted to know how my song had become a part of him. I thought he had been totally unconscious during my attempt at rescue.

Cian saved me again. He saved me from death and despair.

Through the nothingness, in the deep void of my being, was a flash. A burst of color, the shade of blood and fury and Cian's beautiful eyes.

Cian.

He had promised he would find my coat. He'd made his word true to me before, what reason did I have to doubt him now? There may still be hope that my sealskin would be returned to me. That someday I would be whole again. My heart fluttered inside me like a stingray leaping up above the sea in jubilation. I took in another deep breath and my lungs were filled with renewed faith.

I believed in Cian. He and I would go to whatever end to reclaim what was stolen from me. Cian continued playing, his song soothing me further and soon I fell back to sleep.

"Iona. You must eat something, *tch, tch.* It's time for ye to wake." Cian purred into my ear, his knuckles grazing my cheekbone. My eyes were crusted with dried tears, making my vision blurred as I tried to open them. Cian was perched on the bed beside me, one hand braced against the side of my body while his hand made tracks up and down my cheek. Near him was a basket of what smelled like fish. Cian's face looked worn and weary. There was an agedness to him I had never noticed before. Fine lines edged around his pale blue eyes, his brow wrinkled with worry. I reached up to smooth those lines from his forehead, and when I touched his skin, all of the sorrow I saw was smoothed away into a mask of careful calm. Had I been the cause of his pain?

His voice was barely audible. "I've brought you the finest fare to be had from my humble *abhainn*. You'll soon feel right as rain having eaten from this river." Cian nudged the basket towards me so that I might peer into it. Trout of all shapes and colors were laid out. They were beautiful, their scales a myriad of iridescent greens and silvers and rusted reds.

Cian wrestled some pillows behind me so I could sit upright, leaning so close I could smell the river on him. Clean, ancient. He leaned back once he was certain I was comfortable. His face had shifted from concerned to relaxed in a matter of moments. I marveled briefly at my willingness to be helped. Cian had worn me down like a stone in the ocean. I was different than I was before.

Softer.

I wasn't certain it was an entirely bad thing.

I dipped my hand into the basket, selecting a smaller trout by its tail fin. Cian observed me with a thoughtful look in his eye, waiting. I swallowed it down in two gulps. The trout was earthy and free of any brine. I realized that I had been so preoccupied with my search that I had taken for granted my proximity to the ocean. I'd barely had a taste of her water on my tongue. Shame washed over me, turning my skin hot as I reached for another fish.

I was mid-bite when tears began to stream down my face.

My existence was always so singularly focused. There had never been so *much* for me to care about. And now that I was here, it was overwhelming.

My chest caved in, and tears surged out of me like a typhoon. Still, I kept eating, hoping to fill up the chasm inside me, gulping down one trout after another. I could hardly see through my tears, but Cian's expression darkened as he sat by my side. He said nothing, only running a hand down my back and through my hair as I ate.

When I'd eaten the last of the fish, I began to cry in earnest. Taking in great gulps of air while I moaned and wailed. My hands balled into fists as I held them firm against my eyes, rocking back and forth.

There was simply too much in me. Where there had been merely one purpose for eons, now there was more. It had taken losing my beloved coat, losing my kin, and finding Cian for me to realize. It did not matter if I ever found my sealskin, for I could never go back. It was all changed, and so was I.

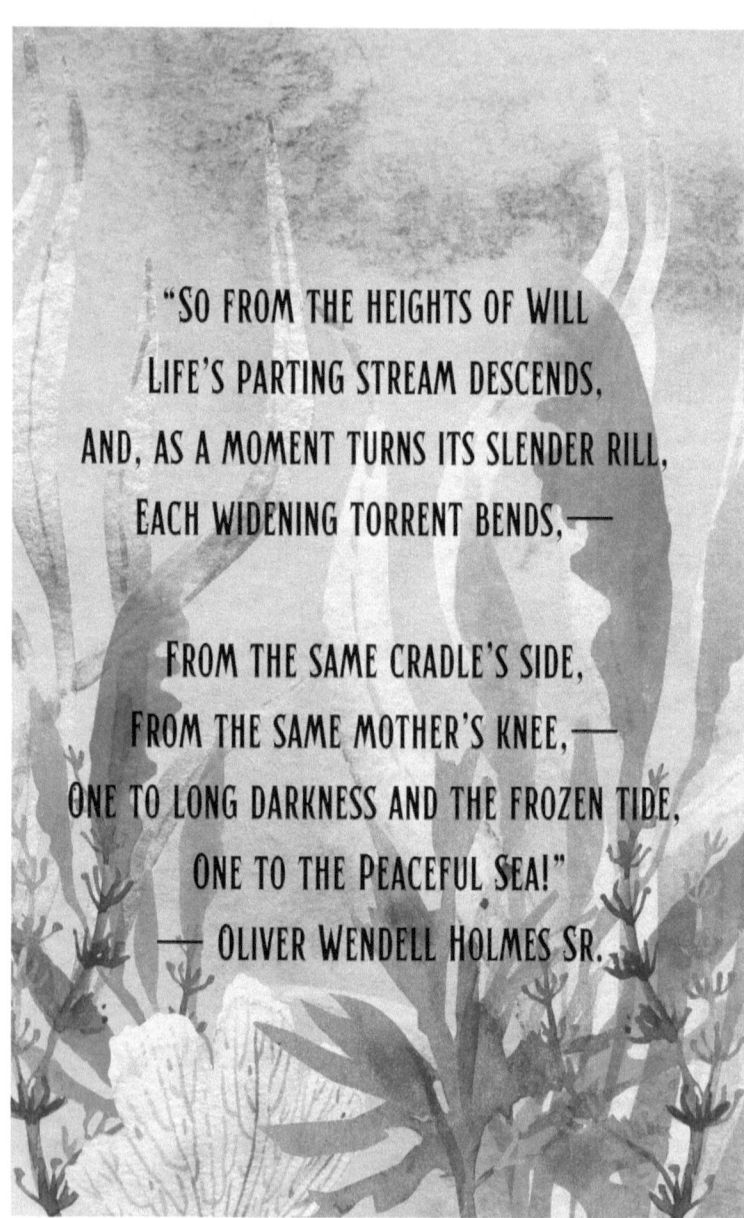

"So from the heights of Will
Life's parting stream descends,
And, as a moment turns its slender rill,
Each widening torrent bends,—

From the same cradle's side,
From the same mother's knee,—
One to long darkness and the frozen tide,
One to the Peaceful Sea!"

— Oliver Wendell Holmes Sr.

Chapter Seventeen

CIAN

I *was* a beast. There was no other word for it. The witch had been right about me. I coveted Iona, wanted so desperately to keep her for myself, and it turned me into a creature without conscience. I had acted out of sheer desire for the being beside me.

The magicked handkerchief in my pocket nearly burned to ashes against my skin. I had betrayed the only other creature who might have withstood all the darkness in the depths of my life. Now I was living on borrowed time. I would reveal my cowardice, and I knew without a doubt it would be the end of this.

If Iona wanted to claim my blood as repayment for my sin, then so be it. I would not fight against her. There must be a limit to my depravity. There was no going back now. What I had done was an act so vile, made all the worse for the love I held in my heart for Iona, who I had betrayed.

Yes. *Love.*

I'd felt it many times before, and would feel it many times after, but for Iona, it was a different sort of love. It was true, and it was raw. I loved her with the deepest tenderness. The most infuriating, excruciating kind of love I'd ever known. And I would lose her.

I felt I had lost her already, for there was no more honesty between us. I had tainted that. There were no words I could utter, no caress I could bestow upon the Selkie that would condone my treachery.

When she had lost her senses upon learning her coat was not to be found on that ship I watched in agony as she fell. I was a coward. The bitterest taste had come to coat my tongue, one I knew would only be gone when I had rid myself of my deceit. I had nowhere to take her, save my home, back the way we came. I hated myself all the more for stealing her from her kin after everything she had been through; but a lonely rock out in the surf was no place to rest and recover from such a heartbreak.

I needed to gather my thoughts and concoct a plan that may ease the blow. So, home we went. I'd never been struck so low, and to be here by my own hand was an irony that I could not ignore. She would leave me, and I deserved it. Oh, how I deserved to be left in the darkness after having wronged such a brilliant creature of light and nature.

I finally found a woman who could live with me below the river. A woman who would not drown nor grow old and wither away. A woman who was wild and ancient like me, but different and wholly herself.

No.

It was not lost on me that my deceit would be the cause of my heartache. It was a reckoning from my past. It had been building for years, with every bride I led down to her watery grave, away from those who loved her, away from her world of endless possibilities. To death. There was no end to the lengths of which I would journey. For only myself. My sanity. My magic. With every trick and Glamour I'd used to manipulate those around me into doing my bidding under the guise of magic, I'd lost bits of myself. Every time a woman gasped her last, and filled her lungs with river water, I'd lose a little bit more. Until all that remained was a ghost, haunting his home with residual feelings of love now long faded and forgotten to the world.

As Iona lay sleeping in my bed—the bed I longed to share with her but dared not—I hoped. First, I hoped that she would remain sleeping, so that I may never have to break her heart the way I knew I must; so that she may remain dreaming of a life where she was whole and loved and content. Then I hoped that she might decide to no longer seek her coat, choosing instead to stay with me here. Perhaps she would realize that she could still live a rich existence without her beloved coat. Perhaps she would realize that she loved me as deeply and truly as I did, and that she would choose me over her coat, and her kin.

I knew she'd never give over her life as easily as that. Would I? We were creatures of a singular design. Two parts of a coin, one light the other dark. We answered the deep unknowing calls within us, fated to our natures. I doubted either one of us had ever dared to dream beyond our destinies, for it was not in the nature of Unseen such as us.

Iona stirred in her sleep, and I began to resign myself. I could not torment her any further. I would be sure she was well enough to endure her journey home, but then I would reveal myself, and let her decide what to do about it. Though it set my teeth on edge, after seeing her display of power on the ship.

I knew whatever my fate, it would be what I deserved. I tried to make peace with it all, but there was no peace to be found. It stole the breath out of me. And I deserved it. I was wicked and devilish and cruel, a selfish fool who reached without thinking. I wanted Iona desperately, and I would always want her, even after she loathed and despised me.

I tried to swallow down my pathetic suffering. How far I had fallen. Fallen with my heart in my hands, ready to let it shatter into millions of pieces as we both crashed to the earth.

"Cian?" Iona's eyes were pinned to mine, watching intently like a predator. She wanted something, something I feared I would not be able to give. I cleared my throat, suddenly feeling stifled. I didn't want to give my emotions away.

"What's on your mind, *Mo mhuirnín*?" She shook her head, and reached her hand out to me, fingers stretching wide. Beckoning me to make contact. To connect our souls through our linked palms. I was afraid to accept, but my heart longed terribly to be one with Iona in whatever way possible. There would be no victory here. Only eternal pain and shame.

Her voice was hushed. "I've never known someone the way I know you. Is it pitiful that I've lived all these years and the one soul I know better than my own has only been in my life less than a month? Am I truly foolish?" She turned away from me, but I saw a silver tear stream down along her jawline. I slid my fingers through hers, marveling at the heat emanating from her palm. A heat I wished I could bottle and keep for the rest of time.

"You are not foolish. You are a rare jewel, who has no need of others. There is no cause for comparison, for you are incomparable." I couldn't help myself, as I leaned over her, and pushed my lips to her forehead. I held my lips against her flesh for as long as possible. Each moment spent was one closer to the last. I ached at the realization. She flushed beneath my touch, her strong hand tightening around mine.

Her eyes searched my face. "I'm grateful for your blatant affection. You fiend. But I am, aren't I? I've spent so many years cloistered at sea, believing I was merely an empty vessel for vengeance, but here I am, and I feel so entirely"—she pressed our joined hands against her breast, her heart beating in a stout rhythm inside her chest—"full."

I could not bear the look of her, so I did the only thing I could. I lay my head down on the bed beside her, forehead against the blankets. The shame inside me eclipsed any feelings of joy I might hold of her declaration. I wanted to weep. All the love in the world could not save me from myself. I was cursed. Damned.

My voice was muffled coming through the bedding as I responded, "Then we are both fools." *Fiend. Liar. Beast.* I felt the bed shifting beneath us as she turned on her side towards me. I didn't dare move to look at her expression. It would be the end of me.

"My coat is a part of who I am, Cian. Without it, I have felt more weak and afraid than I ever thought possible. I've doubted everything. I was lost and angry and ashamed of my fragility. I've realized there was an emptiness within me"—her fingers twitched between mine—"long before I'd lost my coat." Iona's voice was hushed and thick with emotion.

I didn't want to hear any more. I couldn't. It was a sin. It was cruel. I was a monster. A terrible, lying monster.

"Iona—please, you don't need t'say—"

She squeezed my hand even tighter, ignoring my plea.

"I was without passion, without a lick of fire inside me. I was empty except for the singular sense of duty to the seals. There was a void as deep as the sea, inside my chest."

I couldn't bear another moment. "*Anamchara*, hush, now, you don't know what you're—"

"Now I know, Cian. It's you. Before you pulled me from my death, I'd hardly known life. You saved me in more than one way that morning. How can I ever repay that debt?"

No.

No, I could not go on a moment more. Not like this. I released Iona's hand, snatching my fingers from her before stuffing them down into my pocket.

I flicked the magicked handkerchief once, twice, then it unfurled before her for what it truly was. Her beautiful midnight black sealskin. "The debt is mine to repay. Here. Take it."

Iona's eyes widened in utter shock as she reached both hands towards her coat. Fingers ran over the hide as her brows furrowed. She was about to understand my crime. I looked away, agony ripping at my guts.

"I don't understand. This is my coat?" The words were lilting and strange, as though she had too much drink in her.

"I was afraid. Iona, please. I was afraid if you found your coat I would never see you again." She stood from the bed in a violent flurry of blankets and seal hide. Before I could react, she had planted both hands on my chest and shoved me backward.

Her voice was harsh as it ripped out of her. "You deceived me?"

I would not look at her. I couldn't.

I responded through clenched teeth, "I deceived you."

Her hands balled into fists as she pounded against me. A torrent of rage battering my body. I deserved much worse.

Iona howled, "You swore to me you would help me, you *swore* it, Cian! Why?" My heart pounded in a jagged rhythm. It was all wrong. I caught her fists in my hands, holding them against me. I had to try. I didn't want this to be the end. I would do what I could to fight against the inevitable.

My voice was pleading, pitiful. "I swore, yes, I swore, and here it is—I have returned it to you." I tried to brandish her coat, to wrap it around her as if it were a gallantly won prize for a fair princess. Iona ducked away from me, eyes blazing at my connection with her precious hide.

"You lied! You let me think those men—those men I killed..." She choked on the last words, words I never imagined she would shy away from.

How strange this argument was becoming. How unlike Iona to pity man. Confusion clouded my thoughts. "They deserved their fate, do not feel pity for them."

She snarled at me, "You tricked me. How dare you? *Why*, Cian?" Her snarls turned to sobs as she continued to struggle against me. "I hate you for this. I hate you. You are no better than those men I slaughtered. I thought—I thought—"

Her face crumpled as a strangled cry escaped her lips. My chest cleaved open. Out of it poured my true feelings. There was nothing left to do.

I swallowed my own tears as I grappled for purchase of Iona's arms, her hands, any way I could touch her. One last time. "You thought I loved ye? I do. It is precisely why I hid your coat from you. I love you so much I wanted only to keep you for myself. Damning all consequences." The fire in her eyes guttered any small amount of hope I might have hidden away inside myself. She pried her hands free of me and pushed me so hard I fell on my backside. I stared up at her, waiting for the last of it.

Her chest heaved, anger seeping out of her. "*That* is not love. We do not torment those we love. You are cruel and unfeeling. I told you once, Cian. I am no *thing* to be trifled with." She knelt over me and slapped me hard. She waited for me to look back at her, hand still raised. Her eyes were black pits of pain. She slapped me again.

And again.

Her tears spilled down onto my face and chest, as she wept while berating me. My face ached from her punishing blows, but I did not try to escape. I would pay whatever penance she demanded. She slapped me once more then slumped to her side with her back facing me. I did not move for fear that any motion at all would send her away. I would gladly accept this torment for an eternity if it meant she would stay.

Iona's words rumbled out of her chest. "I should kill you, but you have returned my coat. And so, I will leave you to your solitary existence. I never want to see you again. Do not attempt to find me. Do you understand?" Her voice was rasping and bitter, like the shores of the river when the frost turns the shallows to ice. Each word was my death, over and over.

I watched her rise and gather her sealskin in her arms. She did not look back at me until she was at the threshold of the bedroom. When she did, her face was a well of sorrow, overflowing.

"Iona—I love you." I had to say those words one more time.

I had to be sure she heard them. It didn't matter what she felt towards me now, only that she knew the truth of my heart. Her eyes welled with fresh tears, as she bared her teeth in warning.

"You are a liar and a coward and a thief. Your words are empty."

I scrambled up after her as she stormed through the cottage, not sparing a single glance for me or anything else before she pried the door open. She didn't even bother putting her coat on before she entered the river and left me. I wanted to swim after her, to be sure she made it to the surface safely, but my shame held me rooted to the cottage floor. I put both hands against my heart, as though the pressure might stop the tremendous aching I felt.

Iona was gone. She left me.

And I deserved it.

"Unfathomable Sea! whose waves are years,
Ocean of Time, whose waters of deep woe
Are brackish with the salt of human tears!
Thou shoreless flood, which in thy ebb and
flow
Claspest the limits of mortality!

And sick of prey, yet howling on for more,
Vomitest thy wrecks on its inhospitable
shore;
Treacherous in calm, and terrible in storm,
Who shall put forth on thee,
Unfathomable Sea?"
—Percy Bysshe Shelley

Chapter Eighteen

IONA

I kicked and pushed my way up from the depths of Cian's cursed river like I was being chased by the devil himself. The only thought in my head was to get away, get away, get away from that— *fiend*. How the word had twisted and morphed into something loving and now, terrible. I didn't want to think anymore. I just wanted to get away. To escape from my feelings of endless shame and stupidity.

How could I have been so foolish? No. Cian was the one who'd ruined this. He'd chosen to deceive me. Didn't he understand what he was to me? Confusion and agony churned my guts.

When I breached the surface I gasped for air, my lungs heaving painfully. I ripped off the shirt Cian had clothed me in, letting it sink. I wanted to be rid of all evidence that he ever existed. Then I pulled my coat around my body. The hood curved over my brow, the arms cascading down past my fingertips. My sealskin and my body fused together.

The reunion with this part of my soul was tarnished. I had so longed to be made whole, to be completed once more, and now that I was... I refused to acknowledge the urging inside me that screamed out I was anything but. I wept as I swam downstream towards the sea.

The water was rough and thrashed against me, but it felt paltry compared to the desperate ache inside my chest. I'd been torn apart again, only now it was from within. The place I'd kept sacred for so many years was desecrated in a moment. Stones scraped against my belly in a shallow section of the river, clawing at my scars and begging to feel anything other than the hurt. Let it tear me to pieces. Anything to rid myself of this. My mind summoned Cian's face, his red eyes burning me with his deceitful gaze. They were burning pits of fire, and they were consuming me entirely. I swam even harder, pushing my muscles to pump and push me through the water as swiftly as I could.

Now that I had my coat back, I would never be so careless again. No, I would rather die than to be parted from it. I never wanted to walk on two legs or feel my fingers when they slid between those of another.

No.

I would be a fool to allow myself one moment to think of changing into a woman again. I was so helpless, so unsure of myself. And look where it led. I was a creature of the waves and the wind. A creature who dwelled in the dark waters of the deep. There were other beings who needed me. Those were innocent and pure and defenseless. My kin. They needed me, and they would never betray me. I swam with the river currents as they tugged me closer towards my true home. Away from *him*.

My heart was shattered into so many pieces there would

never be any hope of recovering all of them. The pain sent my mind spiraling into a myriad of dark places, memories, old hurts, lost love. My body twisted in the water as if I could maneuver through my torment. Fish flashed past me, and I scented the fear in them. The sensation of smell sent a shudder through my thoughts.

I scented the water again, and my mind went still. I honed my senses to experience the water as though I were merely a seal, not Selkie. Minuscule bubbles erupted from my nose, streaming out behind me. The water jetted against my skin, frigid and invigorating. It tasted briny. I jettisoned myself out of the water for a mere moment, testing my strength. Soon. Soon I would be back in the sea. I filled my lungs with breath, then submerged my body, shutting out all conscious thought.

Who could say how time moved. It ebbed and flowed. Pulling me out into the vastness of the ocean, where I hunted and swam and looked after my kin. The sun rose, and then it set. At night I stayed awake, ever vigilant that some hidden threat may come upon us unaware. Hours flaked away, one tiny shard at a time, until there was only the ocean, only the seals. And that was all that mattered.

My life once again revolved around the sea and my seals and the true purpose of my existence. I never allowed myself to look back. Not once. I needed to believe with all my being that *there was no* other reason for me to live. Even when the thought nearly put me to tears. I needed to forget why I had changed. Who had changed me.

At first, the pain was so piercing it was like I had another bullet planted in my breast.

Cian.

The traitorous fool had ruined everything. I spent so many hours cursing his duplicity. Had he been honest, had he only *just* given me my damn coat, so many things could be different. He was a fool—a wretched, miserable fool. I had loved him then, loved him in all the ways I'd sworn myself against. I would not allow myself to be so reckless ever again.

He was probably wiling away his days seducing young women and drowning them when he became bored of their company. How had I been so blind? So naive in my ways that I'd truly thought I'd found my mate. I should have known better, and my ignorance cost me so much more than I'd imagined.

I rarely slept, for when I did, I suffered. I would wake after dreaming of crimson eyes and sweet whispers of *Anamchara* while slender arms wrapped themselves around my back, and gently urgent kisses nipped at my neck. And I'd swear on heaven and earth and all the hells below that I could hear his song. I would weep until the sun rose, heart split anew.

And then, perhaps a little at a time, the images of those eyes and hands began to fade. When the wind blew, it was just the air, and not his melody come to visit. I forgot. There were so many things to divert my attention: the call of seabirds as they dove and soared after fish, seal pups shedding their furs and taking their first swims, and squalls that lasted days and days.

He never fully left me, but his memory grew dim and his voice all but faded away from me. My heart barely twinged inside my ribs anymore. My eyes no longer searched the shore for a dark horse.

The ocean washed me clean.

I didn't wait long to find another stone. Though I loathed my human form, it was necessary to keep my flock safe. I sharpened it to a fine point, then hung it round my neck. I knew there would be another boat full of wicked men who would try to harm my flock. They came, and I was waiting. Ready to destroy the life of every killer on board. Their deaths were satisfying enough.

I was a bringer of balance. I was born from death to protect life. I wrought vengeance upon those who threatened the balance. I had been loved. And I would never love again.

Life had become simple. Wake, protect, sleep. The moon swelled and shrank. The tides came and went. I existed in a circular rhythm that was neither sad nor happy. Nothing else mattered in the entire world. Beyond the waves and grey sky was a fathomless place that didn't concern me in the least, or that's what I thought.

Years passed, bleeding into one another, until the future became the present. On a late autumn evening, pewter bits of starlight eddied and swirled along the crags where I lay along the end of my rock. The sea was black, obscuring much of the world in its darkness. My kin had amassed on its shore, flopping clumsily on top of one another, in the midst of claiming their space for the night. Huffs and growls echoed in the air then blended with the quiet roar of the surf pounding against the cliffs in the near distance.

A pregnant moon hung above us, casting a pearly gleam on the backs of the seals as they drifted in and out of the waves, mine as well. I hadn't taken my coat off in many months—not since the last time I'd needed to get a good grip on my knife. It was my choice to remain in the form of a black seal. The part of me that was a woman was a foolish, unnecessary fraction that made my life too complicated. The part of me that was a seal was swift, powerful, and driven by ancient instinct. When I was a seal, I simply *was*. I kept myself shielded and hidden among my flock. I only ever revealed myself when there was no alternative. Something about my human skin sent me trembling, an alien sensation I loathed.

I rolled to my side, looking at the indigo shore. The sea broke along the jagged coastline, sending spray high up into the air. Millions of the smallest drops caught the evening light as they fell back into the ocean. Mesmerized, my eyes tracked the plumes of mist up to a high cliff farther up the shore.

A massive black creature stood as it pawed the air before stamping its great hoof into the earth repeatedly. The sky purpled behind the beast, and the ocean roared while it crashed against the rock face in a surge of violence. Something about the animal gnawed at me, a silent memory. Something I'd buried deep inside my mind.

The horse reared up on its hind legs, screaming out into the night air. The sound tore my heart out of my chest, flooded my head with pretty words and a handsome face with piercing red eyes. A beast I thought I would never see again. I stared in silent horror as the black stallion reared again, bellowing another horrifying scream before it ran straight off the edge of the cliff and barreled down into the waves below.

Cian.

"FOR THE MOON NEVER BEAMS, WITHOUT
BRINGING ME DREAMS
OF THE BEAUTIFUL ANNABEL LEE;
AND THE STARS NEVER RISE, BUT I FEEL THE
BRIGHT EYES
OF THE BEAUTIFUL ANNABEL LEE;
AND SO, ALL THE NIGHT-TIDE, I LIE DOWN BY
THE SIDE
OF MY DARLING—MY DARLING—MY LIFE
AND MY BRIDE,
IN HER SEPULCHRE THERE BY THE SEA—
IN HER TOMB BY THE SOUNDING SEA."
—EDGAR ALLEN POE

Chapter Nineteen

CIAN

My bride. Where is my bride? I've tried, oh how I've tried to find her. In the villages and towns. In the forests and in the fields. So many bonny lasses have loved me and followed me to my *abhainn*. Women with eyes of emeralds and the evening sky. Lovely pale skin and ample curves to linger on. Hair of spun gold and fiery crimson. All beauties, all called to me in some way.

So many have been wedded to the river. None are her. None are her.

The days bleed into sorrow and agony as I watch my lasses float away from me into the murky darkness, and yet feel nothing. Not a single fleeting ounce of love, of passion. The void is a yawning chasm. I fear it each day as I sense it growing larger. Each day the void takes more.

Where is my bride? The one with eyes black as ink. The woman with strong hands and a sour smile. She, with silken hair as deep as the sea. A crown of coral and shells shining upon her freckled brow. These brides, none of them are her. None of them are my *bean chéile*.

The river knows. The river knows they are not my bride. She takes them nonetheless, though she grows dissatisfied. Each woman I lead into her waters pleases her less and less. Until she is angry. She rages at me, urging me out again and again.

Find her. *Her.*

The bonny thing who swims without fear, who snarls and snaps like a feral beast. My bride with the wicked tongue that hurts then heals. None of them are her. She is gone. She is with the sea, and I cannot go to her. I swore I would not. I swore.

My *abhainn* will not release me. I must go on my own. I will never find my bride. She is gone. So I, too, will go.

"SHE STEALS TO THE WINDOW, AND LOOKS AT
THE SAND,
AND OVER THE SAND AT THE SEA;
AND HER EYES ARE SET IN A STARE;
AND ANON THERE BREAKS A SIGH,
AND ANON THERE DROPS A TEAR,
FROM A SORROW-CLOUDED EYE,
AND A HEART SORROW-LADEN,
A LONG, LONG SIGH;
FOR THE COLD STRANGE EYES OF A LITTLE
MERMAIDEN
AND THE GLEAM OF HER GOLDEN HAIR."
— MATTHEW ARNOLD

Chapter Twenty

IONA

Memory and instinct had me rushing into the water. My skyrocketing sense of urgency sent me speeding through the crashing waves as quickly as I could. I barely stopped for air in all the time it took me to make it to the cliffs. There was no time for me to ponder the insanity in my actions. This creature had betrayed me and yet I swam to save him. Damn him for that. Damn me, too.

The water foamed as it pounded against the walls of the rock face, shattering into rain as swells brought me up, up, up, then plummeting downwards. I tried to dive deep to avoid the rising and falling of the sea, but the rocks were jagged and massive. I needed to focus my senses to avoid being crushed against one of them.

My mind had only one thought running through it, again and again.

Where? Where?

I breached the surface to search for the sight of slender hooves or a black mane, but saw nothing. I dove down beneath the peaks and troughs of the waves when I was confronted with wild red eyes burning up at me from the inky depths. The ocean had become so black it was almost as if he were nothing more than those eyes. Those eyes that scorched me from the inside out with one glance. They threatened to consume me entirely.

His hooves churned the water beneath me to whirlpools as he raged upwards. I didn't have time to think or feel as he barreled forward, shoving his elongated snout hard into my stomach. The force of his impact sent me back up into the surface. When we breached, he continued to swim forward, pushing me with him. I struggled to maneuver away, his broad snout shoved deep between my ribs, relentless and insane.

Finally, I twisted away, diving as swiftly as I was able to gain some kind of distance between us. I tried to calm my racing heart, but my body ached with the impact too much for me to focus. My body propelled itself away until I was twenty lengths from him. We both broke through the waves. Cian's eyes were glowing in the dark as his thin legs pounded his hooves into the water. He must have spotted me, for he screamed again, and turned towards me.

I shrugged and my coat opened from hood to flipper, revealing the woman that had been hidden beneath my seal's hide. I pushed my hood away from my face before I shouted over the tumultuous surf, "Cian! Have you lost your mind?" Sea water slapped me across the face, filling my mouth with brine. I sputtered and shouted once more, "What is your purpose? I told you never to seek me."

The black horse quickly cut through the water, nearing where I had retreated. I searched the creature's face, longing for some sort of recognition. Some piece of Cian that was still *Cian*. His eyes were wild, glowing red like flames. His nostrils flared and he screamed again. There was nothing I recognized within him. I squeezed my eyes shut, then opened them, hoping that something, anything about the terrifying beast before me would spark understanding.

I slammed my hand on the water's surface. "What is it? What is the matter?"

Cian bellowed in a voice deep like winter, but with a bite that reminded me of burning embers. "My bride. *Bean chéile.* My bride." He surged towards me again, this time biting at me with snapping jaws.

I tried to swim backwards to escape from him, but his teeth snapped out and caught the cuff of my sleeve. Desperate to keep contact with my coat, I pulled it shut as high as I could go, then I held on for dear life as Cian began to drag me towards the shore.

It seemed he did not care whether I could breathe, for he held my body in a way that made me bob up and down beneath the sea. I gasped whenever we reached the surface, filling my lungs before being dragged below. I tried to kick and twist to free myself, but his teeth held fast to my coat, and it would not be torn from me again.

Cian screamed, a chilling, violent sound that made me want to wretch, and, though I loathed myself for it—yearned to see his human visage. Where was the being I had known? What had become of him? There was little time to ponder much else while being battered by his incessant pulling through the turgid sea.

Life had gone too long in my favor, it seemed. It was again my turn to be dealt another blow. My body scraped against sharp stones as I was pushed upstream, into the mouth of Cian's *abhainn* as he continued to drag me away from my world and into his once more. There wasn't any more time to think. I wriggled into position and wrapped my arms around Cian's neck as tightly as I could. My muscles strained from the pressure.

I bellowed, furious and afraid, "Cian! Enough! Enough of this madness. Release me, you bastard!" He did not. It was as though I was merely a sack of flesh to be ferried to wherever it pleased him most. I tried to dig my heels into the stones of the riverbed, stalling for time. It did little good. My feet, though calloused and tough, didn't stand a chance. They were sliced to ribbons while I pushed downwards with all the force in my legs. He still did not stop.

There was only one thing left to try.

I opened my mouth. I unleashed my voice. The words that poured from me were new, though the language was ancient. A melody I didn't know burst free of my lips. I sang of a horse and a seal. Two hands held fast in a sea of differences. I sang of kisses, and betrayal. I sang of love and wrath and death. With every word, the feelings I had buried in the bottom of my heart rose up to the surface, forcing me to see—see what I had chosen to erase from my memory. I was there, the moment Cian shook my coat free of his damned Glamour. Revealed himself a liar and a traitor. When I'd fled and he'd called those words.

Those that I rejected. Forced myself to ignore them entirely. *Liar.*

But I knew. Oh, I knew in my heart he was no liar. Merely a coward. Pathetic. And so why did I still want him?

Soon I was singing through my tears, and Cian, or the beast that had once been Cian, stopped raging. His snorting slowed, and then he was still. I continued to sing until he relaxed enough to unhinge his jaw and let my coat slide free of his mouth so that I could move away from him. I sang for him still, a little softer as I pulled his mighty head down towards my human one. The melody coiled around us, my voice radiating from nowhere and everywhere at once.

I was waist-deep in the river, but the water barely came up to lap Cian's chest. The beast's lips twitched as though nervous. His crimson eyes didn't roll wildly in their sockets. Instead, they peered intently into my own. I sang gently as I reached up and ran a hand down the front of his snout. The cuff of my coat sleeve rested against the backs of my fingers. Both his hide and mine were as deep and velvety as midnight. My coat was far superior in weight and texture, but the same, more or less. An old ache pulsed through me, from my chest down into my core. Without conscious choice I began singing Cian's name. It was a curse and a prayer, a promise that I wanted to hate myself for, but couldn't find the strength within.

The next verse began in a mixture of song and sob.

Cian, you fool, what has become of you?

The beast nudged its head firmly into my palm, demanding more affection. Now this behavior *was* entirely in line with the Cian I knew. I held the last note while trying to keep my eyes from rolling into the back of my skull.

"I still hate you, you know." I uttered those words without melody and Cian reared away, pulling his massive head from my hands in a start. I reached up, wrapping both hands around his snout, demanding he look at me.

What has happened to you? Speak to me.

Cian stared back into my eyes. This time, they were forlorn and confused. It broke me. The anger I held for him dissolved, and all that was left was the desire to help. Somehow, I knew I must be the cause of this change. Why else would he be so hell-bent on dragging me to his home?

"My bride." His voice echoed out around us, hardly coming from him at all. It disturbed me. What happened to his bride? Maybe he'd been cursed. The horse tugged his head downward as if confirming my fears, ears turned back in renewed agitation. Somehow, he'd been reduced to this animalistic state. He was neither man nor creature. He was lost to himself.

"*Bean chéile*. My bride." That voice was alien. It sent a coil of horror down my spine. *My* Cian was not here. This was something much darker. I looked around us, desperate for a sign as to what I should be doing. We were nowhere near the place in the river where Cian's cottage lay; that was still a great distance before us. There were no other creatures around. It was as if they had sensed Cian's unnatural state. All life had fled away from this strange wretch.

We were alone.

I hummed quietly while trying to puzzle out a plan.

I had no connections to the Unseen world, no way to learn of a cure for this curse. Cian had been the only other being like me that I'd ever met...unless—unless the old woman in the woods was still alive. I did not know if witches aged and died like humans, or if they remained, like us. I had no other choice.

I turned to look back at the sea, its roar still loud and alive in my ears. Our rock was a distant shadow in the night. At least for now the seals had the shroud of darkness for protection. There was no time to lose if I wanted to make haste and return before any ill could befall them. They were safe. For now.

I felt a broad smack against the length of my spine as Cian's head rammed into me. He snapped out his strange jaws and his teeth once again latched onto my coat. He started dragging me backwards again, farther into the river. I splashed about as I lost my footing and ducked down under the frothing current for a moment.

My patience was wearing thin. "Enough of that. Enough. Cian."

I yanked my coat free of his teeth and resumed singing while I regained my balance. This time the words were of my plan. There was no rhyme or pattern, but as long as I carried a tune, I believed I would be able to keep him from going wild again.

You and I will go to the Cailleach's dwelling,
Do you know the way?
Will you take us back there again?

I continued to sing wordlessly, dumbly hopeful for a sign that my Cian may still be inside this bulk of a water horse. Cian stamped a hoof into the river and sent a harsh rush of air out from between his lips. He lunged out for me, angling his body against mine and turning his head and neck into me so that I was pressed against his side. Cian knelt forward, bringing his massive shoulders down low so I could climb on top.

I dared not let my voice stop as I wrapped my fingers in his kelp mangled mane and hoisted myself upwards.

Please let this not end in my death.

Cian rose swiftly, startling me. I flopped forward and wrapped my arms around his neck in a panic as I tried to find my balance. My voice stalled in shock and Cian reared up on his haunches, nearly throwing me from him and into the river. I gulped in a lungful of air and hastily continued my singing. I sang a warning this time, furious and terrified of my lack of control.

If you throw me off your back
I will leave you to your beastly ways
And you will be stuck this way for eternity.

It did not sound particularly beautiful in my ears, but Cian settled and began gliding upriver. The night was full upon us, and the moon was a distant mirage, high above. The river reflected the light of the stars, and Cian's movement sent a stream of silver light out behind us. How strange we must appear to the moon. *Each-Uisce* and Selkie, journeying together. For what purpose?

A rise of old and festering pain bubbled up inside me. Why *was* I helping Cian? There had been no redemption for him. We had never mended what had been so terribly broken that day. So why, *why* would I do this for him? Why not let the fiend rot away? Leave him to his madness. Or simply kill him and be done with it. I wanted to throttle myself. I wanted to throttle him. But that was a lie.

I hated that even after so many years, and so much pain, I still held love in my heart for this demon. There was no lie I could tell myself to make it go away. It did not matter that he had wronged me now. What mattered was not his folly, but that I carried him with me. Despite his sins, I did not want to see him suffer. It was not my nature to be forgiving, and yet here I was.

Cian's strokes were relentless as he worked against the river to bring us closer to the *Cailleach*. It was there that I decided to sing him my truth. So much time had passed without Cian. Countless days of that empty chested feeling never truly fading away. I wanted to be done with it. I yearned for that fullness to take its place and never be gone from me again.

Cian, you fool. How could you betray me the way you did?

You knew, you knew, how much my coat meant to me.

You knew how much trust means to me.

You deceived me for your own selfish purposes.

You gave me so much and ripped it all from me when you lied.

I have been empty. I have been a tool, working mindlessly for so long,

and when I finally realized there could be more, you took it away.

Cian's ears flicked backwards and stayed that way while I continued to berate him in song.

And even through all of this, you, terrible, selfish, beast.

Even through the hurt and the distance and the years gone by.

I still love you. I love you. And you don't deserve it.

But still. I love you.

His head dipped down, as if he were bowing, or nodding in understanding. I didn't know if he was aware of my meaning, or if he was simply placated by my voice. A tension in my chest, taut for so long, sprung loose. I leaned forward and rested my cheek against Cian's warm neck as tears raced down my face. I sang with all the emotions I had longed to feel since the day I left him. I sang of my life and my duty, and my longing for connection. For Cian.

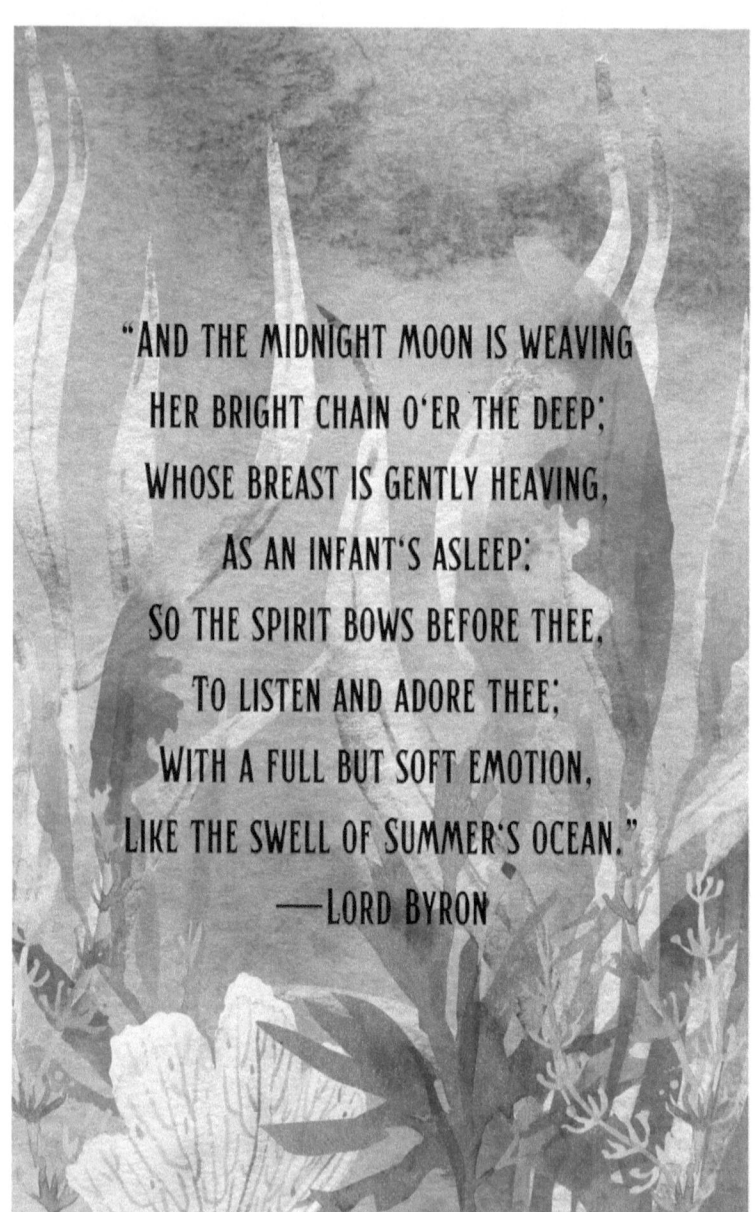

"AND THE MIDNIGHT MOON IS WEAVING
HER BRIGHT CHAIN O'ER THE DEEP;
WHOSE BREAST IS GENTLY HEAVING,
AS AN INFANT'S ASLEEP:
SO THE SPIRIT BOWS BEFORE THEE,
TO LISTEN AND ADORE THEE;
WITH A FULL BUT SOFT EMOTION,
LIKE THE SWELL OF SUMMER'S OCEAN."
—LORD BYRON

IONA

Cian brought us as far upriver as he could until the bed below the water grew small and began winding as it navigated through thickets and up jagged ravines that were too tight for Cian's massive frame to traverse. I learned that humming was enough to keep him soothed, and so I hummed while we climbed the steep hills through the forest back to the beginning of our story.

How strange it was that now our roles were reversed. I had been the hapless victim, needing rescue, and the old woman was the only one Cian knew could help me. And without my consent or agreement, brought me to her out of some strange compulsion born when he saw me at the mouth of his river.

A chill crept up my spine when I remembered how displeased the witch had been with Cian. There was no mistaking her behavior towards Cian was anything other than anger. I sent a silent wish into the sky that this was not all in vain, though I knew it was pathetic. Even if she *was* living, the *cailleach* may very well refuse to help him. I couldn't fault her for that. I was still somewhat stymied at my own change of course. Cian was not an easy creature to love, but neither was I.

I had no idea what I would do if she was gone. I prayed she was immortal like us. And that she hadn't decided to abandon her rickety old cottage. I could not sing and hum for an eternity and Cian could not go on this way.

The thought nearly knocked me off Cian's back, so quickly I concluded I *would* save him. Somehow. It was as sure as the need I held within myself to protect my kin. After years separated by heartache and tide, Cian was still as dear to me as one of my own. To save him was surely as much my destiny as it had been to save my seal family. It was a compulsion I was unable to deny.

I patted his side, curious if he was still somewhere inside, at least some part of him. He had once been able to speak while in this form, and it had been almost an entire day without him screaming, "*My bride*" with that unearthly voice of his.

Cian, are you in there?

Carrying a tune while talking was not easy, but I was growing more and more desperate for a sign that my Cian could be recovered.

It's me. Iona. Remember?

You used to call me Anamchara.

Soulmate

You knew we were fated to each other before I did.

But that's you, isn't it?

You called me darling and I called you fiend.

But we are both fiendish in our own ways.

Cian? Please, please—say anything.

His mighty black head swiveled back at me, his red eyes

wide and frightened. I didn't know what it meant. My heart cleaved in two. Cian could not go on this way. Trapped inside himself, no end in sight to his imprisonment. Eternal madness to be suffered in silence.

My muscles were beginning to fatigue as Cian continued forward mechanically. Maybe Cian could understand me—he just wasn't able to respond. He *must* know we were going to find a way to break his curse. I needed to believe that. I needed to know that I wasn't alone in this agonizing mystery.

My body ached from sitting in such a strange position for so long while Cian jostled me about as he trekked over the uneven earth, but there was no time for stopping. The song I had to keep humming became strange and dissonant in its tune. I dared not sleep for fear that my beastly friend would go mad when my voice ceased and the magic with it. My throat was raw from singing and humming for as many hours. It didn't matter; as long as sound continued to flow through my lips, I was able to keep Cian soothed.

We traveled through the burgeoning day, and then again into the miserable night. Finally, we crested a steep hill. My eyes strained in the dimming light to see the hovel, afraid it was merely a trick of the fading light, an illusion to drive me mad. I rasped out a new song, singing for her help.

"*Cailleach please, you must help me.
Help me break the curse of this beast.*

You helped me once—help me now."

My voice was so destroyed I feared she would not hear me. I allowed my body to slide over the side of Cian, and all but tumbled to the ground, all the while still singing. I needed to get to the door. Needed to find her there.

My legs felt as though they might permanently remain in a bow. My muscles screamed in agony when I tried to stand upright.

"*Please, Cailleach, are you home? I need to break the curse on Cian. Please.*"

My voice was nothing but a series of squeaks and rattles like a dolphin's call. I repeated myself, each word more painful than the last. Cian stomped his front hooves, growing more frantic with the fading of my voice. The witch's cottage looked just the same as it had those years past; still dilapidated and nearly overcome by the forest crowding around the lopsided walls. I could see dancing flames through the broken door. Then it flew open, and the witch appeared.

I did not know if she looked the same or not. I could hardly see her with the fire's glow lighting her from behind. She barely spared me a glance before hobbling towards Cian, stick in hand. Cian began to rear up, a leg kicking out in warning, but I warbled what little song I had remaining within me, bringing his hooves to the ground. He was right to fear her. Another hint of the being I knew before.

The old woman held something smoking in her hand. A smell that immediately made my head go fuzzy emanated from the smoldering bundle. She waved it around in front of Cian's face. His nostrils flared, and his eyes widened momentarily before they began to drift closed. My mouth dropped open in amazement when he knelt to the ground, all four legs tucked beneath him. Cian's eyes stayed closed as he rested his long face on the ground before him. He let out a low rumble, and then was still, save for the rising and falling of his body as he inhaled and exhaled.

The witch whipped around toward me and crowed as she pointed her cane toward my face. "Did I not tell ye he was a beast? Ye didn't listen, and now here you are. Fool. Just as much of a fool as this one." She brought her cane down over top of Cian's head but he was so lost to sleep that he didn't stir.

She made her way towards me. The smoking bundle blurred my vision and made my tongue feel thick. She waved her hand in front of me, heat from the fire curled up around my face. And then everything stopped.

I awoke to the smell of burning peat and mildew. My mind snapped back into place. When I peeled my eyes open, I could see the witch's backside, hunched over the fire as she stirred something in a black pot. I tried to leap up from where I was, already worried about Cian, but my body was stiff like a seasoned piece of driftwood.

"Oooooch." I moaned with pain. The old woman startled, turning around in a flurry of wispy hair and sour smelling skirts.

She sighed heavily. "You're awake then. Good. We haven't much time and there is much to say. What do you know of the *Each-Uisce?*" Her tongue darted out of her mouth to lick the end of the spoon she held in her hand. The *cailleach* grimaced before nodding and setting the spoon back in the pot. What did I know of Cian? Or what did I know of his kind? Were they one in the same?

"I know he has magic. And he takes brides then drowns

them in his river. He claimed that he was compelled by his nature to do so. He's also an arrogant, stubborn, charismatic ass." My cheeks flushed, and I clamped my mouth shut. There was more. But she didn't need to hear it.

The witch came to sit beside me, and I swore I heard her joints creak. "And do you know *how* he gets his magic?" She raised a bushy eyebrow, waiting for my reply. It never occurred to me that there must be a cost to Cian's abilities. He had spoken of covenants and rules...there was nothing like that for me. At least, not that I'd been aware of. But we were very different sorts of creatures.

I shook my head "No. I thought he was created with it."

The witch grunted. There was a long pause while she took me in. Her milky eye roved over my face, searching, before she spoke again.

"I had a daughter once. Did he tell you he knew her?" A lump grew in my throat. My mind conjured distant images of that angry man who recognized Cian for what he was. I swallowed, afraid of what I was about to hear. Cian's acquaintance was a death sentence for many women, that much I knew.

I didn't want to ask, but the need outweighed the discomfort. "Did he...was she—your daughter—his bride?"

The old woman stood and turned back towards the fire and her brew. I braced myself for her response. For an entire lifetime, I'd only ever considered killing the murderer before me, ending that wicked life. Never did I think of all the others tied to theirs. It was only ever about revenge, and the need to right an imbalance of life and death. I wondered if it had been the same for Cian. Whatever he had done, how much more terrible could it be than the acts that I'd personally committed?

The witch's voice became soft and thick with what could only be sadness. "She was his first. And they loved each other dearly. I was myself there when he promised himself to her. It was a beautiful day, and my daughter was alight with passion and affection for the beast. We did not know what he truly was. Nor did he. If I had been aware of his true nature, I wouldn't have thought twice about taking my daughter far away from his river, never to return again." She did not turn to look and see if I was listening. My mind raced trying to piece it all together as she told it. How did Cian not *know* what he was?

"He came to our village one day, told us he'd no family, and no past to recall. A handsome lad, friendly and charming. Too charming. We were all fooled." The old woman coughed, a ragged awful sound, before continuing.

"My daughter stole away in the night, but I followed her. I was worried she would be tainted before they were properly wed. I did not know he had asked her to elope with him." My heart thundered in my chest. I waited for the rest of it. For what I knew was going to be a tragedy.

"I lost them in the tangle of woods, but when I found them —it was too late. He was already leading her down into the middle of the river. I remember so clearly the look of pure elation on my girl's face. On his too.

"Then I watched him change. I tried to stop him. I called out waiting for her to break free of his hold, but she did not. She disappeared with him. I myself went into the river, and nearly drowned trying to retrieve her. I waited in the shallows for hours. As the dawn crept ahead, the beast surfaced. Only he was a man again. He saw me at the banks and fell to his knees as he wept."

A blade twisted in my gut. The betrayal, the sheer agony, must have torn them both to pieces. It was one I knew well enough, thanks to Cian. Why did it need to happen? If there was so much love and devotion, why destroy it all?

My mouth moved before I realized what it was going to say. "He wept?" I didn't understand why I asked the question. But I needed to hear her answer.

She finally turned around and stared me in the face, hers a grizzled mosaic of wrinkles and folds. There was a bitter twist to her lips when she said, "He *loved* her. He loves them all. He must, to remain as he is. The river gives and takes. It gives him life when he brings those he loves to it."

I knew the root of his suffering was hiding somewhere in her words, but I couldn't sniff it out. It had been too many days of hard travel with an unpredictable beast as my escort. I wished I could just ask him what he needed and have him answer me back.

"What is wrong with him then? Why has he become so... wild?"

The witch huffed and her eyes rolled up into her skull.

"Are ye really so naive, Selkie? Tell me. Why are you here? Why have you come to such great lengths to help the monster?"

Oh. My face burned with realization.

The hag answered for me. "Because you are in love with him. And tell me this, is he not in love with you?" Those words. He'd called out to me as I stormed away from him, frothing with pain and rage over his deception. He'd said those words. Said my name, like a spell on his lips. *Iona—I love you.* She pried me from my memories as she took my face between her gnarled hands, ancient fingers pressing dents into my cheeks.

She snarled, "I don't have time for this, nor does he—*Each-Uisce* cannot fall in love with another bride because he loves you. He will never be the same again unless he takes you beneath the river. You and he are not of the same ilk. He is a creature bound to darkness. Born for reasons far different from those that brought you into existence. He was cursed from the start, and there is no point in trying to make sense of it now." My stomach sank like a stone. Cian was trying to drown me?

I felt as if I was floating outside of my body. A bit of flotsam pushed between the currents. "Does that mean I must die in order for him to live?"

The witch was still holding my face, her one milky eye wide and unseeing.

"Perhaps. There is only one way to know." She dropped her hands away from my jaw, turning back to the fire. I watched her scoop a portion out of the pot and pour it into a clay bowl. *Perhaps?* What a small word so incongruous with the enormity of what it meant.

I was going to ask her to tell me what she thought, but she interrupted me before I could begin. "Here. Drink this. It will give you the strength to do what must be done." She handed me the bowl before going to peer out the front door.

"The beast is still drugged. You have some time to get that in your belly. Drink. Drink!" She pointed her stick at me, urging me to hurry. The liquid was molten hot, but it did not burn. It slid down my throat, sweeter than anything I've tasted. As I drained the bowl of every ounce of the liquid, the aches and stiffness in my limbs began to subside and the pain in my throat waned.

I paused long enough to ask, "Why do you help him when

he has so wronged you?" I supposed only too late that I should be wary of her now that I was conscious of Cian's past transgressions against the witch.

The *cailleach* shrugged. "Eternity is a long time. Though I do not trust him, nor do I like him, I cannot deny that having an *Each-Uisce* beholden to me is beneficial, and now a Selkie as well." Eternity was a long while and maintaining enemies for all that time sounded quite exhausting after pondering it a moment. I was rocked by the sudden bolt of realization that I had no desire to spend my existence alone or angry.

The old woman began bustling around the tiny space, gathering things from shelves and cupboards then stuffing them into a woven sack. I drained the contents of the bowl and stood, feeling strong once more.

The witch eyed me with her one bushy eyebrow raised. "See you've got your coat now. It figures the two of you would match. Go on. He stirs." She shooed me through the door without any ceremony. Once I was out in the clearing, she thrust a bundled sack into my arms. "If he grows violent, burn this under his nose. 'Tis a sedative." She took my hand and put a gathering of sticks into my palm before closing my fingers around it. The witch retreated inside, slamming the door behind her. The sound startled Cian, who nearly toppled over in response.

He began to rise, pulling his massive hooves under him so he could stand. Cian's gaze was still alien and distant, I could see in those red eyes with rectangular pupils that he was already assessing ways to get hold of me.

I warily made my way towards him, unsure of myself, and of Cian's strange animal form. I straightened my spine, steeling my resolve. "Cian. I will go with you. I *will* go. But you cannot drag me away like you did before. I will walk with you."

Cian blinked, black lashes fluttering slowly downward before his head bobbed once. I shrugged my coat up around my shoulders, letting the weight of it bring some comfort to me.

"*Bean chéile*. Return with me." His eerie voice still sent shivers dancing across my skin, but at least his vocabulary was increasing. I nodded, reaching my hand out to stroke his snout.

"Yes, you fiend. I will return with you." Cian waited, watching me as I numbly began to make my way back towards the woods. He snorted once before coming up right on my heels. I let the sound of his breath and the beat of my heart drown out all other thought.

"AND OH! THE SONG THE SEA SINGS
IS DARK EVERLASTINGLY.
OUR PAST IS CLEAN FORGOT,
OUR PRESENT IS AND IS NOT,
OUR FUTURE'S A SEAL'D SEEDPLOT,
AND WHAT BETWIXT THEM ARE WE?I
WE WHO SAY AS WE GO,I
"STRANGE TO THINK BY THE WAY,
WHATEVER THERE IS TO KNOW,
THAT SHALL WE KNOW ONE DAY."
— DANTE GABRIEL ROSSETTI

IONA

Cian's obsession with our proximity grew more irritating with each passing minute. Either he was shoving me forward from behind with his gargantuan head, forcing me to trip over the terrain, or he was beside me, his massive body leaning against me with every step, forcing me to walk like a bent over hag.

My frustration boiled to a head, and I hollered at him, "Must you constantly be touching me?" The creature's only reply was a head nod while he stamped at the earth. I longed to hear his voice. *My* Cian's voice. The velvety soft purr of it was only a distant echo in my ear. Would I ever hear it again? I wanted to spar with him, to get his hackles raised as easily as I had done in the past. My heart thumped painfully in my chest as I reached out a hand to run it down Cian's side.

"You are infuriating. Will it satisfy your need if I lay my hand here while we walk? I'm tired of tripping over myself." Cian peered at me sidelong through a fringe of thick black lashes, snuffling in the air. I supposed that was the only response I would receive. I patted his shoulder, heaving a sigh. As long as

I kept some sort of contact with him, he no longer felt the need to herd me down to his river. Thank goodness. I was sure to have bruises from his incessant prodding.

As we walked towards Cian's *abhainn,* the day grew dark and shrouded with heavy clouds. The trees around us were nearly all bare, but some had yellow leaves, shining against the blackening horizon. All the world seemed awash in shades of grey and gold. I pulled my coat tighter around me, my thick hide protecting me from the new chill in the air. Cian huffed and his breath clouded out around us. Then the rain began.

At first it was merely a few drops, the earth releasing a heavenly scent I had never recalled before. Then the pleasant mist became a torrent. The sky opened wide and let a deluge of water pour down over us. It was a small blessing, the storm. I knew well enough that storms like this kept ships safely in the human's harbor, far from my family on the rock. They were safe for a while longer yet.

I quickly became soaked, my hair matted down around my brow and draining into my eyes despite how often I swiped at it, while Cian stayed miraculously dry. The rain on my back wasn't the main problem. It was the path which quickly became slick and treacherous with the barrage of rain assaulting the earth. Tiny rivers cascaded downwards between our feet, washing away the very trail we walked upon.

We slowed our pace to an agonizing crawl, slipping and sliding our way down, then Cian took a misstep and came careening down over me, nearly crushing me beneath him. I let out a frightened yelp before barely escaping his bulk. He faltered and slid down the trail, flailing and snorting in agitation while he tried to right himself.

I skidded down after him. "Cian! Cian, stop."

I caught up enough to place a hand on his back. When his eyes found mine, they were wild with panic. So much of what I saw in him was only animal. It was like staring into the eyes of a seal. There was no—no *Cian* inside those eyes.

"Shh. You're fine. It was just a trip." I patted his sturdy form before pushing him gently off the path. "We'll stop and rest until the rain clears. Come."

There was no shelter for us, no place to hide from the wet while we waited out the storm. Cian stood impatiently, shifting his weight from side to side while I sat on a boulder covered in waterlogged lichen. I fidgeted, uncomfortable with this feeling of solitude.

"Cian, do you know me?" I wasn't sure he heard me over the roar of rain, but he turned and tried to nibble at the ends of my hair, his velvety snout brushing my chin. I swatted him away, pulling the strands from his teeth.

That unnerving low rumble of his once again broke into the air. "My bride."

I was growing tired of the phrase. Cian had many brides. Many loves. I was merely the latest. Or was there more to this? I was a fool. Pure and simple. What other kind of being would dive headfirst into such a situation? A fool in love who would do what it took to bring comfort to her lover. Her very foolish, fiendish lover. I grabbed at his snout, pulling it close to me so that we could peer into each other's eyes. I needed to know it was more than a part of some ancient ritual. It had to be.

He stared at me, and I stared back. "I am Iona. Show me that you know *me*. Please Cian. If you are there at all, please." I searched for any sign that he was still somewhere inside. Cian leaned closer, then blinked in a flutter of lashes. There. A spark of recognition widened his blood red eyes. There was a gleam that reminded me of the first time I'd seen him this way. A creature in disguise. *Each-Uisce.*

"Cian. Why do you not speak? Why are you locked away from me?" Cian snorted, and the intelligence that was just alive in his stare died. I slumped forward, depressed and frustrated. I was so close to once again having that feeling of deep soul connection, but it was just out of reach.

I cursed myself for my stubbornness. So many times, I had wanted to forget my anger and swim up Cian's river to be with him. So many nights spent crying and aching for Cian's touch. I'd convinced myself he had moved on, filled his time with courting beautiful, stupid, human women.

I had been so terribly wrong. We were both fools. Too prideful and self-centered to see past our faults long enough to realize each of us had something the other desperately needed. And what now? What would become of us? Was I to die only to let Cian live on and continue in his dark ways? Would he ever again be the being I knew him to be, or was he lost? There were too many questions in my head, and no one to ask. No way to find the answers.

I pressed my hands to my eyes, pushing against them to stop the burning. Cian nudged my hand, his soft lips feeling for my fingertips. Perhaps he was trying to comfort me. Or perhaps he was trying to latch on so that he could continue dragging me to my potential demise.

I held my hand out, and he leaned into my touch, eyes closing as though my palm was a great comfort to him. I wiggled my fingers, scratching the hollow section of his cheek.

His whiskers twitched at my affection. Once more I found myself the shepherd of another creature in need of my defense. I wished with all my heart that it could be different.

We remained together under the pouring rain for what felt like hours. Cian refused to settle and began to pace in a circle around my boulder. Clearly, he was unhappy with our stopping, but I wasn't about to risk the lumbering creature to fall and injure himself again. There would be no recovering from that, I was sure.

The horse froze, mid stride in his trampled path. Cian's ears pricked up, swiveling this way and that. His intense alertness set my senses on fire. He heard something—or someone.

I stood, reaching for the dagger that hung around my neck as I searched our surroundings. The rain impeded my vision, but there—much too close for my comfort, were three silhouettes growing ever closer to us.

Men.

My knuckles grew white as I gripped the hilt of my knife in anticipation. It had been a while since I'd felt the rush of killing. I hadn't anticipated doing so now, but nonetheless I welcomed the opportunity—the distraction.

There was nowhere for us to hide, and I had little fear. Let them come. I was ready. Cian tried to herd me so that I stood behind him, but I would not allow it. His refusal to leave me alone led to an awkward dance in which I tried to escape his shelter and he stubbornly refused to let me out of his proximity. Exasperated, I stood on top of the boulder, so that he could not hide me away. He snorted and tried to bite at my coat to pull me down, but I dodged his snapping jaw.

"Enough, Cian!" I swatted at his snout, utterly distracted.

"Odd garment choice, is it not, Henry?" The voice was nasally, with an irritating grate. It made me instantly angry. I raised an eyebrow and turned to face the one who had spoken.

"Lass's wearing a sealskin. 'Tis plenty strange. Perhaps she's that faerie Crazy Luella says murdered her man. She's come to curse us."

My head quirked to the side, momentarily confused at his strange babbling before I refocused on the second man who was rotund like a barrel. His breaths came out in heaves that dissipated around him. He would be the easiest to take down. I rolled my shoulders as the killing calm settled over me like a mantle.

"Perhaps we should see what's beneath that lovely coat. Perhaps take that stallion off her hands. She's all alone after all." The third man was a touch more unsettling than his companions. There was a grisly scar running from his brow down to his chin, one eye closed halfway from the old injury. His gaze held darkness and destruction.

He was reaching for something in his coat. Clearly, his decision was made. Cian moved before I had a chance to think. He reared up on his hind legs as he kicked out with his front, sending the fat one down on his backside after shoving a giant hoof into his chest. The man let out a stunted "oomph" before lying flat in the mud.

The commotion distracted both of his companions enough

for me to lunge from my position onto the scarred man's back. I screamed out in a fury as I brought my blade down at the base of his spine. I leapt from him as he fell, blood bubbling up through the gash as his face slammed hard into the muddy ground.

Cian bellowed and began racing after the third man who had run back the way he came. The man turned his head to see the black horse charging and screamed in panic. Cian ran him down, trampling him flat as though he were nothing more than a sapling tree, easily crushed.

I knelt to grab a clod of moss. I wiped my dagger with it, cleaning the blood away. Cian circled back, snorting and frothing with unabated rage. We made a good pair, he and I.

I held my arms out to him after slinging my knife around my neck. He walked into my embrace, resting his head against my shoulder. I could feel his pulse thrumming through his body.

"It's alright Cian. We are safe now. We are safe." We stood like that—in silence— while the rain continued to fall.

"HERE FROM HER SHORE ACROSS HER SUNNIEST
SEA
MY SOUL MAKES QUESTION OF THE SUN FOR
THEE,
AND WAVES AND BEAMS MAKE ANSWER. WHEN
THY FEET
MADE HER WAYS FLOWERIER AND THEIR FLOWERS
MORE SWEET
WITH CHILDLIKE PASSAGE OF A GOD TO BE,
LIKE SPRAY THESE WAVES CAST OFF HER
FOEMEN'S FLEET."
——ALGERNON CHARLES SWINBURNE

Chapter Twenty-Three

CIAN

She with the coal black hair and midnight eyes—my bride—walked by my side. Her strong hands grazed against me, but I could hold her no longer, could not utter a thought aloud that would comfort her. I feared that any moment she would cease to exist, and that I would fall back into darkness. *Bean chéile. Anamchara. Mo mhuirnín.* When she stared into my eyes, I could feel the being I had been once so long ago fighting to break the surface, but it was impossible.

There was only the need to have my bride with me for eternity; all else mattered little. She peered into me, the hope there shining like a bright star, and the aching, oh the aching, how it was mirrored in my own soul.

I longed to touch and kiss her, to feel my arms around her frame. It was maddening. My desperation was only mildly abated by her nearness. It was not enough. It would never be enough.

Her shoulders were tense, pulled up high around her ears, and her brow furrowed low over her eyes as she looked me over. What was in that head of hers? What worries and fears held so much sway over her? I pushed my body against her, wishing to do so much more, unable to give my bride comfort in any real way.

She pushed back against me, as I forgot myself. Forgot my strength and power in this body. So easily capable of doing damage to my bride. I didn't want that. I loathed myself as I remembered with brilliant clarity how I had wronged her. Time did nothing to dull my shame, nor the wanting of her. She wound a finger in my mane absently as we walked together in the darkening woods. The shadows grew long around us, casting her in silver like a cresting wave. A creature of the evening, strange and lovely.

"Cian, can you speak at all? Say something, please. I need to know you are in there somewhere. Please." Her voice, rich and lilting and so bitterly sad, rang out inside me. Rattled around deep down into my core. Her plea lit me on fire from the inside. A rumbling echoed up from my chest, unfurling what had been lost to me for so long.

"Iona." It was all I could muster. It had to be enough.

"THE GREY SEA AND THE LONG BLACK LAND;
AND THE YELLOW HALF—MOON LARGE AND LOW;
AND THE STARTLED LITTLE WAVES THAT LEAP
IN FIERY RINGLETS FROM THEIR SLEEP,
AS I GAIN THE COVE WITH PUSHING PROW,
AND QUENCH ITS SPEED I' THE SLUSHY SAND.

II

THEN A MILE OF WARM SEA—SCENTED BEACH;
THREE FIELDS TO CROSS TILL A FARM APPEARS;
A TAP AT THE PANE, THE QUICK SHARP SCRATCH
AND BLUE SPURT OF A LIGHTED MATCH,
AND A VOICE LESS LOUD, THRO' ITS JOYS AND
FEARS,
THAN THE TWO HEARTS BEATING EACH TO EACH!"
—— ROBERT BROWNING

Chapter Twenty-Four

IONA

"Iona."

My heart soared like a gull in spring. *My* Cian's voice sang out into the night air in a single solitary note. He remembered. My chest heaved and tears sprang from my eyes.

"Cian? Please come back to me. I don't want to be alone anymore." My voice trembled, weary and heartsick with foolish hope. My fingers curled around a lock of his mane in anticipation. I froze and held my breath. All the forest stalled in its machinations while I waited.

And waited.

Cian stamped his hooved feet, sending the deadfall skittering around them. His nostrils flared with effort. *Please. Return to me.*

I watched his eyes stare into nothingness for what felt like ages. Was it truly such a task to speak? He was so far from me and yet so close.

Cian bowed his head. *"Bean chéile."* He was locked away

within himself. But his utterance gave me hope. He could be set free.

"Don't fret, soon you will be yourself again. I won't rest until you are. I swear it." The horse mouthed at my shoulder, and I could almost imagine Cian's fingers lacing between mine. The memories that were faded and forgotten continued to unfurl behind my eyes.

Cian was the only other creature on earth who I'd allowed to *know* me. To see me as anything other than a being of protection and vengeance. As much as I'd loathed it at the time, he had shown me there could be more to life, and what had been missing from mine while living in solitude out at sea. Yes, there was duty and honor in keeping to my calling, but there was *more* that made my existence richer.

Soon our surroundings were blanketed in darkness, and there was nothing for it but to make camp for the evening. Cian stamped around in a large circle, clearing a miniature glen for us. I began scrounging around for any twigs and sticks that had not been saturated, willing myself not to think about how I would be starting this fire without Cian's magic rocks.

I stumbled in the darkness, wishing I had my seal's vision to see through the murk of nighttime. Several times I fell and scraped my bare legs, and I was glad Cian's voice was not working so that he could not laugh at my clumsiness. Instead, he followed me, my private sentinel, watching my every move, searching the trees for threats. I sighed as I tried and failed to snap a too soggy branch over my knee. It was covered in water that flew from the twig and into my face. A hissing rasp escaped from Cian's mouth. It figured the beast would be able to laugh before he could talk.

"Oh hush, you. I don't need a horse laughing at me right now." I shrugged past him, darkly satisfied he couldn't respond. Cian nipped at my elbow, his only available option for a retort it seemed. "If I wasn't so worried about your current state, I *might* find this all much more amusing. Alas."

When we made it back to the clearing, I tossed the kindling aside before I slid down to my hands and knees. My fingers probed the ground for anything with sharp edges. I vaguely remembered the stones Cian using being very angled, black looking things. My hands grew thick with mud as I turned over rotten logs and dug my fingers through the earth looking for two such rocks. "Aha! Got you." I held the two stones over my head as though they were beautiful mackerel I'd captured for a feast.

My fingers were covered in a drying layer of clay, too mucked up to be dexterous. I set the stones aside and moved towards my dark companion. I acted as though I were simply scratching Cian's side, but in reality, I was leaving a trail of muddy fingerprints and smudges all along his torso while I used his hide like a rag to clean my hands and the two stones.

My mouth curved upward in pleasure as I imagined what Cian might do if he wasn't trapped as a horse. As if he sensed my deception, Cian swung his neck back so that he could glare at me, eyes narrowed with intelligent skepticism. He whinnied and shook his entire body, sending the flecks of crust at me.

I scrunched up my nose before wiping at my now dirtied face. "Och! You curr. How dare you. I'm trying to light us a fire! This is how you repay me?"

I shoved my hands on my hips indignantly, waiting, praying for any sort of familiar response. A sign that Cian was merely below the surface. The horse nuzzled my neck with his soft snout. My heart ached. It was purely animal behavior, wasn't it?

Painful disappointment wouldn't keep me from attempting a fire. I knew Cian wasn't going to respond but I continued anyway. "Is that all you have to say for yourself? Just as well." I pushed him to the side and squatted down near the neat little pile of twigs I had created. I exhaled before taking the two rocks in hand and bringing them down hard over the other.

Over and over again I slammed them together, waiting for those strange, beautiful flashes of flame to ignite my pathetic fire. It took so long that Cian circled me several times before obviously succumbing to boredom and lay down across from me. His chin rested at length on the ground opposite the fire. Between impacts I spied his eyelids drifting lower and lower.

Finally, I found the right angle. Sparks erupted from my fists, and I cried out in surprised delight. They showered in spurts over my kindling while I blew gently on the wood, hoping it would catch. Smoke curled up into my face as I continued to fan the minuscule fire into life. Soon tiny orange and gold flames were flaring up into the air.

The snaps and crackles from the fire captured my focus. It used to frighten me. Its heat, its intensity, was unpredictable and dangerous. I was wary of the world, and so broken and angry. I thought about how Cian stayed awake, playing his flute so that I might find rest.

I could almost see his full lips curving into that impish smile while he teased me. I lay a hand over my breast, as if I could press hard enough to put the pieces of my heart back together.

I wanted so much to be the rescuer in this tale. I feared fate would betray me again.

When I had my *own* grand designs, it seemed they existed solely to be ripped away from my grasp. Why would this be any different? Why should I be offered anything aside from my immortal duty? I clenched my jaw, angry at being plagued by the innumerable questions rattling around in my skull.

The fire was damp and choked the sky with black smoke that stunk of rot and mildew. But it was hot, and that was all that mattered. When I was certain it would not be snuffed out, I slowly made my way around the fire to sit nearer to Cian. He was sleeping, still as a mountainside. I didn't want to wake him, fearing he would spring to his feet and immediately demand we continue with his stamping hooves and snorts. I was not about to be dragged to our doom without a wink of sleep.

I pulled the wrapped sack the witch had given me from my back and pulled the fabric away from its trappings. Inside were the dried plants I'd stashed to soothe Cian if needed, and a cut of dried meat. I sniffed at the stiff portion before I ripped a chunk of it off in my mouth. I hadn't thought about what Cian might need to eat, but I supposed he must not have been hungry since he was soundly unconscious beside me. I struggled to chew through the substance. It was tough and salty, nothing like the soft clams and mussels I was accustomed to eating. But it was *something* and I found myself devouring almost all of it before I thought better of myself and wrapped the rest up to save for later.

The night grew colder, so I nestled against Cian, using his body as padding. I pulled my coat around me, hiding my human skin from the chilly air. I leaned back into Cian, resting my head on his stomach. Soon our breathing was in tandem, and my chest rose and fell along with his. The peaceful rhythm was not unlike the lapping waves on the sea as they gently greeted my rock, and soon I was deeply asleep.

The stars numbered in the thousands above us as we watched the tide roll in along the shore. As the waves met the sand, brilliant glittering blue lights flickered upon impact, mirroring the swirling galaxy above. I went to the water, letting it lick at my calves. I wriggled my toes in the sand, sending more flurries of blue shimmers billowing out around me. I turned around to peer at Cian.

I held out my hand as I asked him, "Be with me?"

Cian stood a few feet away, his white tunic untucked and drifting in the midnight breeze. He pushed a slender hand through his blonde hair, though it looked more of a faded periwinkle in the dark. His smile made my stomach twist into knots, and when he reached out to take my hand in his, a surge of heat rushed through my limbs. Our fingers intertwined as he walked into the surf by my side. I leaned down and slapped the sea water up into Cian's face. It gleamed like starlight as it made contact with his skin. Cian laughed and I could have died from the beauty in the sound.

"What is this? Why does the water glow, Iona?" The sound of my name on his lips was divine. I returned his beautiful smile with one of my own. Finally, he asked a question I might be able to answer. Now he was in my domain.

"Perhaps they are the lights of spirits long passed, come

back to play in the waves once more. It does not always occur. Only during the warmer seasons. It is like swimming among the stars themselves, is it not?" I waded further in, the glowing waters lapping at my hips while streams of twinkling particles trailed behind me. Cian held tight to my hand as he followed.

Cian's free hand caressed the surface of the waves, creating eddies that gleamed beneath his touch. I longed to be that water, to feel his hands on me. "'Tis beautiful. Like a dream." He tugged me backwards against him before he wrapped his arms around my waist. Cian's lips brushed against my earlobe, and my body came alive with desire. "Like you. Iona. *Anamchara*. How I've missed you." His lips trailed down my neck, each kiss was a promise of more to come. I leaned backward against him, needing to be closer. Cian's hands roved over my body, remembering, savoring every inch. His touch was tender and heady, and I knew that he meant it when he said he missed me.

Cian gently pushed my coat from my shoulder before bestowing my bare skin with more kisses. He drew my hair out of the way before his lips caressed the nape of my neck, sending me agonizingly closer to bliss. I twisted in his arms, needing to feel his mouth against my own. I slid my hands up his torso to rest on either side of his face. I stared into his crimson eyes, savoring the heat I saw within them as he stared right back.

"I've missed you, too." My words were no more than a whisper before I claimed his lips with my own. The kiss unleashed all that had been locked away within me. All that I had refused to feel for so long—now set free. Cian's arms wrapped tightly around me, bringing our bodies flush with one another. I felt his need for me against my hip as we fought to be ever closer. Cian's mouth parted and my tongue slid inside it, begging for more, more—but he broke away from me.

His eyes burned so bright, cheeks flushed with heat and yearning. He reached up and laid his fingers along my lower lip as he rested his forehead against mine. "Do not leave me. Swear it?"

I panted, passion still coursing like a raging flood through me. "I swear. I swear." Cian's gaze changed. His eyes bloomed with fire, and smoke began pouring from his mouth and nostrils.

"I don't believe you. You will leave. Let me take you. Let me keep you safe. Forever." His arms were locking around my body as he started dragging me deeper into the surf.

I struggled against his hold, beating my fists on his arms. "I promise, Cian! I won't leave, don't do this, don't take me—"

Cian squeezed tighter, crushing the air from my lungs as he rushed the waves. Salt water filled my mouth when I tried to scream out, to reason with him.

Starlight exploded around us as he pulled me down. Into the deep. A black horse awaited me beneath the water. Red eyes glowing in contrast with the silver flecks of heaven drifting around our bodies. I watched my coat drift away from me, suddenly naked and starved for oxygen and so utterly heartbroken.

And then I woke up.

"From the strong will, and the endeavor
That forever
Wrestle with the tides of Fate;
From the wreck of hopes far—scattered,
Tempest—shattered,
Floating waste and desolate; —

Ever drifting, drifting, drifting
On the shifting
Currents of the restless heart;
Till at length in books recorded,
They, like hoarded
Household words, no more depart."
—Henry Wadsworth Longfellow

Chapter Twenty-Five

IONA

Cian woke me with his snout, snuffling away at my ear and neck. I couldn't help but laugh at the tickling sensation. The action was reminiscent of the playful nature of the seals. I missed them always, but at the moment I had another charge. If Cian had taught me anything, it was that all we had was the power of our words and actions. I would not go against my oath to him now.

The morning was coated in a thick frost. Even the ends of Cian's eyelashes were crusted with ice crystals. The sunlight danced across the forest floor, casting rainbows shining this way and that. The fire had died out entirely and was now nothing more than a charred lump next to us. I stood up, dusting off my coat before pulling it tightly around my body. My black sealskin kept the chilly air away from me, just as it protected me from the frigid seawater in winter. Cian's coat was dark like mine, and the light seemed to be swallowed up by it. Two creatures of the Unseen world, forever shrouded in midnight, even as the morning sun shone down upon us.

My dream floundered around in my head. If I died when

Cian took me to the river, would it hurt? Would he remain too heartbroken to fulfill the river's wishes? Or would he continue on just as before, leaving the memory of me to be washed away with the current? Off to find another bride with no regard for my existence, my sacrifice. The ocean had created me to protect the seals, would it do so again if I was no longer alive to fulfill my duty?

My stomach twisted, and a dull ringing sounded between my ears. I hated the unknown, and I was feeling more isolated, fear growing inside me with every minute. My rage and conviction had always kept my bravery aflame, but now all I had to cling to was hope, the traitorous thing.

Cian stretched and rose on his spindly legs. It perplexed me how such reedy limbs were able to keep a massive creature like him upright. They seemed sturdy enough, but I suspected they might be more fragile than they appeared. Cian nudged my elbow with his head, and I wasn't sure whether it was a plea for attention or a call to get moving. I supposed I could do both. I laid my hand between his eyes, gently scratching the soft, short fur there.

Every moment brought us closer to the looming conclusion of this adventure. It made me dizzy when I realized how soon we would be near his cottage. I felt my pulse thrumming in my ears. My body was trying to brace itself for whatever pain it was to endure.

"Shall we?" His long ears swiveled around, and he snorted, but it wasn't friendly. There was a question in his eyes. I cocked my head as I observed his strange behavior. He turned around once before securing a space so near to me that his side was grazing mine. I was about to open my mouth to rebuke his possessive stance when I caught sight of motion through the trees. I froze in my tracks, holding my breath as I waited to get a better visual of who, or what was moving towards us. Then I heard *her*.

Through the veil of frosted yellows and greys was a being shrouded in white. A train of ivory fabric flowed out behind a body that was tall and slender. A woman? She had golden hair that curled down to her waist. A sad, keening wail floated towards us through the air. The sound of it sent a feeling of death down into the pit of my stomach.

She was no human. I swallowed down my fear, reminded myself that she was just another sort of creature making her way in the world. Like I was.

She seemed to sense us. The weeping woman paused a moment before turning her ghostly figure towards the place Cian and I had become rooted. Her skin was as pale as the cloth that billowed around her, but there were crimson tracks racing down her cheeks from her dark eyes, sliding down her neck to mar the perfection of the white fabric on the front of her dress. Her tears were those of blood.

I slowly raised a hand to brace myself against Cian, prepared for whatever was to happen next. The horse stood tall, stoic and foreboding in his own right. At that moment I wished I was able to look as fearsome as they appeared. I was a force to be reckoned with just as they were, though my visage was slightly less intimidating to behold.

The most sorrowful voice filled our ears. "You... have lost much." The creature reached out a bone thin arm, slender finger pointing towards us through the trees. My eyes grew wide. How could she know such things? A sharp cry of agony peeled out from her mouth, silencing all my thoughts.

"Not *you.*" Instantly she was right before us, her finger an inch from my nose in dire accusation. Her teeth clicked as though she were shivering, "Though you have deep heartache in you." Her bloody eyes rolled in their sockets as she turned her gaze upon Cian.

"*This* one. This one carries the deaths of *so many* loved ones. Like a yoke around his neck." Scarlet tears continued pouring from her eyes and she moaned deeply, her spindly fingers splayed wide just above Cian's snout. He stared silently back at her, a knowing look shared between the two. I glanced back and forth, stymied at the familiarity before me.

"What sort of being are you? How can you know so much?" My voice squeaked out of me, sending a rush of burning embarrassment up into my cheeks. We were equals, she and I. There was no reason to be afraid, was there? I had merely been caught off guard by her presence.

The maiden's hand moved to caress Cian's snout. He closed his eyes as if in pain, though he leaned into her touch. If Cian did not fear her, nor would I. Her sobs echoed out into the woods. To a common passerby they might sound like merely a strong wind gusting through the treetops. She was an other-worldly thing. A being worthy of the title, *Unseen.* For I was certain she was a singular thing. A sight rarer than rare.

She turned her stare back towards me, angling her chin away as she considered my question. "*Bean Sighe.* Harbinger of death." She closed her blood-stained eyes and let out a shuddering breath. "Soon now, so very soon." Her chest spasmed as sobs shook her body.

Harbinger of death?

Anxiety bloomed inside me. I prayed she didn't notice. *Soon?* Was she here to warn me of my fate? My gut tumbled inside of me. I didn't want to know the answer.

I thought perhaps clarity would help me steel my resolve, prepare me for what was to come, and yet... desire welled up inside me. The desire to live. It was new and powerful and so immense I felt it would burst from me if I dwelled on it any longer.

The *Bean Sighe* let out a quiet wail and then turned away from us, continuing her strange saunter back through the forest. Cian nudged my hand, his lips trying to take my fingers into his mouth. The odd affection pulled me from my dark thoughts.

I recalled the argument we had after we escaped the mob at the tavern. I'd accused Cian of tricking the women into believing he loved them, when that hadn't been the case at all. The *cailleach* said as much while explaining his history. Tears stung my eyes. I licked my lips, priming them for the long overdue apology.

"If I'd known... I didn't understand what you had to do for all those years. I didn't know that you loved all those women. How can you stand it? The heartache?" I knew he couldn't answer me. I wasn't even sure he could comprehend the words coming out of me, but I needed to try. We continued walking down the hill in silence, my hand against Cian's side. I ached for his response.

"When I left you...it was the worst pain I'd ever known. I became nothing. I was an empty vessel. It was all the more terrible because I then knew I could be more. I could *have* more." I ran a hand along the sleeve of my coat, feeling self-conscious about my next words. "How can you do it so many times over again? To let yourself love *again and again* only to know that inevitably it will end in such a final, excruciating way?" Tears slid down my cheeks. The frigid air around us nipped my skin with the added moisture. When I'd called him out for his actions, he'd become infuriated, and now I knew why. It had nothing to do with his pride, and all to do with his heart.

"I'm so sorry."

Cian snuffled at my cheek, mouthing my skin delicately. We stopped moving and I wrapped my arms around his neck, burying my face in his mane. He smelled of the river.

"There is nothing to cry over, *Anamchara*. It is the way of things." Sultry and dark. Magnificence in every syllable. My heart stopped. I lurched backwards, hooking Cian's giant face by the jaw so that I could look into his eyes.

"You spoke. You, Cian—you spoke?" My eyes searched his, hoping for more. Pleading with every inch of my being.

"Iona. I can speak."

I clenched my jaw, unsure of what to do with my racing pulse. My Cian. He was there. Inside.

"Say something, please. Cian. Speak to me again." I felt a renewed surge of emotion. At first, I'd tried to wall all feelings off, keep them at bay so that I could focus on my task of saving Cian. Later I could worry about the state of my heartstrings. But now—now, with Cian at least somewhat returned to me, the wall was beginning to crumble.

"You look entirely the same, as though we'd only parted yesterday." Of all the things to say, he chose to comment on my appearance? I wanted to weep, while throttling him simultaneously. I nodded my head as the tears continued rolling.

"That's all you have to say? After everything we've—" My voice shook, tremulous with need, with unspent frustration.

Cian interrupted what was sure to be a sound lashing from me. "I love you. I have loved you. And I will continue to love you." My face crumpled as I sobbed, once again hiding my face against his body. "It's not the easiest feat to speak, but for you, I will try." Confusion rippled through me.

"I don't understand, why? Why is this happening to you?" My voice was muffled, but it was clear enough.

"It is a puzzle, but I think you are the key." *Of course.* He'd been fine while we journeyed to and fro across this land the first time. When he'd sworn himself to my cause then lied about helping me find my coat. If my mere presence was enough to awaken his gifts, perhaps it was all he needed. Maybe I would not need to die after all. Relief danced across my mind, but only briefly.

It was never as simple as that. Nothing ever was.

"And you love me too?" Cian's words caught me off guard. I wanted to laugh. What an absurd question.

I swatted his cheek, but my face became a flame all the same. It was not in my nature to be sweet with my words, but I relented. "You fool. Why else would I be here?" Cian stepped away from me and eyed me. Waiting.

I sighed, allowing the words to travel from my heart to his ears. "Yes, I love you. Too much for my own good." I ached to feel his arms around me. To embrace the being I'd mourned for so long. This was not the reunion I'd envisioned so many times. But it was something. The void inside me felt lessened as I held out a hand to him. Cian leaned against it as we continued toward his *abhainn,* toward the ending I was beginning to dread.

Cian's river was black as it coursed down the hill towards the sea, frothing angrily against its shores. The landscape was growing barren in the autumn. The ground was dewy with melted frost and droplets of water glistened in the pale light.

The human village remained largely the same. People traveled between the houses and other structures. I contemplated how many of them had been born and died since I'd last walked the path through their world. How many were now aged and wrinkled, or merely a set of decaying bones to be forgotten to time. While Cian and I remained unchanged, the earth continued.

Time didn't move the same way for Cian and me as it did the mortals below. It didn't suck from us our life forces, nor did it wreak havoc on any other part of our being.

It was an endless march with endless possibilities.

"GLIMMERING AND VAST, OUT IN THE TRANQUIL
BAY....
AH, LOVE, LET US BE TRUE
TO ONE ANOTHER! FOR THE WORLD, WHICH SEEMS
TO LIE BEFORE US LIKE A LAND OF DREAMS,
SO VARIOUS, SO BEAUTIFUL, SO NEW,
HATH REALLY NEITHER JOY, NOR LOVE, NOR LIGHT,
NOR CERTITUDE, NOR PEACE, NOR HELP FOR PAIN;
AND WE ARE HERE AS ON A DARKLING PLAIN
SWEPT WITH CONFUSED ALARMS OF STRUGGLE AND
FLIGHT,
WHERE IGNORANT ARMIES CLASH BY NIGHT."
— MATHEW ARNOLD

Chapter Twenty-Six

IONA

A wave of exhilaration crested over the both of us when we grew near enough to the river that we could hear the water rushing against its shores. We traversed the steep ravine in a series of clumsy leaps and bounds. Manic laughter erupted from my lungs, wild and unhinged.

I never let go of Cian's mane, not for a second. Until I tripped. My toe caught between two rocks, ripping my momentum from me. Cian continued flying ahead down the slope, while I slammed into the frozen earth, all air bursting from my lungs in a painful *whoosh*.

I heard a sickening crunch as my arm made contact with the ground. After flopping painfully into the gully, I tried to free my foot from its trap. When I reached for the rock with my right arm, it crunched again, and I screamed out in shock. There was an unnatural protrusion on the stretch of my arm between my wrist and elbow.

Bone.

I coughed out a strangled whine while struggling to free my

damned foot when Cian finally realized I was missing from his side.

He galloped towards me, eyes wide and burning with panic. I held up my arm to him while pointing at my foot with the other. "I'm pinned and I'm hurt."

Cian danced on his hooves in agitation and worry. He did not speak, instead he grabbed onto my coat with his teeth and began to yank at me, tugging backward.

I yelped when his pulling caused a surge of pain to skitter up my arm and he froze. The look of fear on his face seemed overly dramatic, until I saw three figures rushing toward us from a small house I'd not noticed before. Then I began clawing at my foot, not caring about the pain anymore. Terror at being so vulnerable near humans urged me on to dig myself out. The three humans came into earshot first and I heard a tangle of worried voices chattering—

"Did you see that terrible fall?"

"Absolutely—a runaway horse?"

"We are coming to help! Stop struggling!"

Their words only sent me further into duress as I wriggled like a fish caught in the jaws of a shark. They grew closer, and I realized they were women folk. Two looked to be well into their years, while the third was younger, though I had little to go on.

Women? I'd never encountered human women. Would they be as terrible as men? My mind raced with a thousand choices, but not a one of them stuck. I was trapped, without a properly working limb to do any slashing or stabbing. They grew closer, huddling around me. I braced myself for the attack.

My jaw hung open in silence while the three of them worked together to wiggle the rocks away, shushing and patting me when I seethed with the pain of having the stone grate against my foot. After several tugs and all three women heaving the strangely long stone away from the top of my foot, I was freed. I tried to scramble up and away—anything to put distance between myself and them. And then they noticed I was naked except for my coat.

The younger woman looked about as confused as I felt, while her head turned this way and that so that she could take me in, then Cian. Her mouth opened and closed, wordless, like a carp. The old woman with dark hair and eyes dusted off her clothing and hands, paying me no mind at all. The second blushed profusely and looked away into the woods. She was the first to speak.

"My heavens, youngin' what has happened to you? Come ladies, let's get this girlie and her runaway horse into shelter. Are you not frozen to the bone?" She pulled her shawl off her shoulders and tossed it over top of me as if I was a bit of ground to be covered up. Then she held out a hand. This woman was offering me help?

I looked sidelong to Cian, hoping he had some wisdom he could silently send to me. *He* wasn't even looking at me, the fool. He was busy being nuzzled by the dark-haired lady. It was up to me, then. I almost gave her my broken arm, but remembered, holding it out before me. They each hissed and grimaced as they took in my disjointed limb.

One of them grasped my good hand and clicked her tongue against her teeth before she wrapped a bracing arm around me. Shock at the contact rendered me mute. I remembered how I had chastised Cian for walking straight into an environment crawling with humans, and now I was no better than he was.

Allowing myself to be in the company of human women, no matter how trapped I felt. How amused he must be.

Cian shifted away from the group, head twisting this way and that. One of the women grumbled, "You'll have to get hold of that frightening beast somehow. Where is his bit and saddle? You don't ride bareback, do you? Most unladylike." The younger woman fanned herself as though the idea of my riding style was some kind of sin. I wanted to laugh. What about my existence would not be deemed evil in this person's eyes?

I looked backward to see Cian's nostrils flare wide in irritation. I raised an eyebrow at him before looking back to where they were corralling me. It was a small stone cottage, very reminiscent of Cian's—only the stones were a simple grey and there weren't any living towers of seaweed floating around it.

"Where I go, he goes." I feared to say anything more than that.

The elder one spoke, "Come now darling, we'll get that arm of yours set in a blink, never you mind. And we'll find you some proper clothing to boot." All three women blushed furiously at the mere mention of my lack of dress.

My amusement faded when I noticed Cian's growing agitation. He began stamping back and forth, holding his feet up as though he might rear back. I twisted out of the woman's hold and held my hand up to calm him. When he put his front hooves to the earth all intelligence had fled from his eyes. He was afraid I would no longer return; the beast was taking over him once more. I reached up and hooked a finger into his nostril, yanking his face so that I could look directly into his eyes.

"Shhhh now. I'll be back to you sooner than you know. I

need to fix this bend before we can be together. It wouldn't do to have a broken bride, now would it?" I held out my damaged appendage so he could freely see its wrongness. His teeth clamped down on nothing, begrudgingly accepting my declaration as truth.

"Good. Now, go find a place to rest. We'll be together soon. I'll be right inside." I turned back and saw that only the dark-haired matron remained. She'd witnessed my entire conversation. I bit my lip, waiting for her to call me *monster* and banish us from her home. She eyed my person up and down, a black look flashing across her features before walking through the doorway. Cian nudged my back, urging me in. The sooner I was looked after, the sooner we could leave. And so, I willingly walked into the den of my enemies.

The women led me to a room in the back of the cottage that was bare save for a bed on a metal frame and a massive piece of driftwood hanging above the small hearth. Upon my entry, I was immediately overwhelmed with gentle hands and cooing voices as they coaxed me out of my coat. I utterly refused to let it out of my grasp—I slid awkwardly into a lavender dyed shift, holding my sealskin for dear life in my good hand while I shoved the other arm painfully through the sleeve.

The younger woman, who I learned was Beatrice, seemed dreamy if not absent-minded. Perhaps my presence had shocked her into the strange stupor. The woman with dark eyes who'd witnessed my conversation with Cian said her name was Helen. She was the only one who truly put me on edge. There was a rigidness to her that churned in my mind. An aura of danger surrounded her. The woman who was fair and quite beautiful in her old age was Roisin. She seemed to run the house, and everyone in it. Both the other women deferred to her in all things, or simply stayed out of her way as she rushed about gathering herbs and cloths and such.

I tentatively followed all orders, afraid that the smallest thing might give my identity away. I needed to escape as soon as possible. It wouldn't do to reveal my true nature to those so close to both mine and Cian's homes. It could spell disaster for us if humans learned we could be captured. They planted me on the bed, propping my feet up and covering me in a festoon of blankets. Beatrice put an exceedingly warm cloth over my brow.

She asked, "Where are you from? We've not seen visitors from the south in ages." I swallowed, trying not to make eye contact with her. I'd never liked peering into human eyes. Their stare was so different from those of the seals and other sea creatures I spent my days around. But Beatrice did not look cruel or stupid.

"Emm. Not far from here actually. The other side of the river." Not a lie, technically. Beatrice nodded, patting my shoulder. The gesture sent pain ricocheting up and down my arm, the ache reverberated out of my broken skin. She winced in realization of the pain she'd caused me.

"Oh! I'm so sorry, what a silly goose. I'll let Roisin do the tending, I'm awful at this." Her face turned scarlet as she hurried away from the bed. Roisin was at my side in an instant, her sudden appearance jarring. Her eyes were so pale in the darkness they seemed to glow. They were piercing in a way that unsettled me.

"Hold out your arm now. This will hurt, but only for a moment. I have to reposition the bone back to where it belongs. You don't want it sticking out like that, otherwise the arm will be lost entirely." My eyes widened, terrified at the loss of my appendage. Swimming with one less limb would be quite a feat. Maybe impossible.

"Do not fret—shh, it will be fine. We have all the tools here to ensure your proper recovery. Are ye ready lass?" I nodded and gritted my teeth. Roisin took my wrist and bicep in her hands. I watched her take a deep inhale, then in a terrible rush, she wrenched my arm. The bones crunched and I wanted to vomit when the broken ends ground together as they made their way back to their natural position. I shuddered, willing the bile in my throat to subside.

"There now. Helen, fetch us some tea while I wrap her arm up. That's a good lass." She cooed and clucked while she twisted a cloth tightly around my arm. She finished my binding with a sling, trapping my injured arm against my chest. "You'll not want to move that for at least a month. Or you'll risk re-injury."

A month? Surely not. I was immortal. Bullet wounds had healed sooner than that. A broken arm should be no problem for me.

The dark-haired woman—Helen—returned soon enough with a cup of steaming liquid. She was careful to avoid my touch though she stared deeply into my face. A raw hatred poured through her gaze. I refused to look away from her, instead silently challenging her to provoke me. My glare was enough to send her out of the room without comment. There was a nagging feeling in the back of my skull, beckoning me to pay attention, but to what I couldn't say. What harm could a mortal woman do to me?

I set my cup aside then tugged my coat up around myself like a blanket, letting the silky skin caress the bottom of my chin and jaw. I felt like a fish corralled by a pair of hungry seals. The two remaining women were peering down at me, each with her own scrutinizing expression. I shifted further beneath my coat, wishing to be far away from them now that I had been tended to. I needed to make an escape, and soon. Cian would not be patient for long and I was in no hurry to spend more time with humans than was necessary.

Roisin seemed to understand my unspoken thoughts, or at least some of them. She pushed my cup back into my hand. "Drink that dear, it's got willow bark in it—for the pain. We'll get back to preparing for supper, won't we?" She glanced at Beatrice then hustled her out of the small room.

"Twilight and evening bell,
And after that the dark!
And may there be no sadness of farewell,
When I embark;
For though from out our bourne of Time
and Place
The flood may bear me far,
I hope to see my Pilot face to face
When I have crossed the bar."
— Alfred, Lord Tennyson

Chapter Twenty-Seven

IONA

I sniffed at the tea, wary of anything given freely by humans. It was pungent yet botanical. I decided my pain was not great enough to warrant a tincture. Pulses of bright agony surged through me when I tweaked my posture the wrong way, but I had survived much worse.

I thought momentarily about the gunshot wounds that had torn through my body. My side and shoulder had been permanently marred with the scars, but the aches were gone. A broken limb was not enough to hinder me on my quest to fix other, more important things that had been broken. Pain was part of healing—the suffering, the discomfort. And I would take it gladly.

Murmured gossip bled through the walls as the three women continued to no doubt discuss my odd intrusion into their lives. I mentally promised not to invade their lives any longer. It was time to leave.

I briefly considered sneaking out, then scoffed at the absurdity of the idea. I was not some prisoner to be held captive. There was nothing that would stop me from leaving. I stood then draped my hide around my shoulders. The heavy skin of my coat settled against my frame as though it were embracing me.

My feet carried me swiftly to the threshold of the cottage. The women paused in their conversation, clearly becoming aware of my nearness. I merely turned my head, nodded once, and whispered, 'Thank you. I'm going now." Not a single one rose or tried to stop me. A parting just as strange as my arrival.

Outside, the air was damp. My breath clouded out from my nose in a sigh, relieved to be away from humans and their suffocating dwelling. I surveyed the fields, searching for Cian's silhouette.

"It's time to go now, Cian. Where've you gone off to?" My voice was carried aloft in the early evening air. It wasn't long until a great horse came sidling around the back of the cottage. When his gaze landed upon me, he picked up his pace until Cian was by my side. "There you are."

I ran my hand down the length of his snout. I waited for him to respond, but his eyes were back to that strange animal blankness. Whatever magic he'd gained had been leached away in the short time we'd been apart.

My heart sank into my stomach. We were so close to ending this. I feared there would be no true relief for either of us, but I once again grasped for that feeling of hope, that feeling inside my gut that longed for a happy destiny, no matter how futile.

I coiled my fingers gingerly in his mane as we turned from the cottage and headed towards the distant roaring I knew was his *abhainn*. I tried to imagine Cian's face, with his angular features and smiling eyes; his singular dimple and his golden curls. I wanted nothing more than to run my hand along the length of his jaw, to press my lips against his. I had to believe I would see him again, touch him again, soon.

"I know what you are! *Maighdean-mhara*. She Who Murders Our Men." The words rang in the air like a gunshot, fired directly into my skull. I whipped around towards the harsh voice that barreled out at us from the cottage. It was Helen, standing at the door. Her face was crimson with rage as her hand thrust accusingly out in front of her, pointing angrily at me. "You've taken our men for too long. Mark my words. Your days of killing are numbered."

My blood ran cold, the ancient killing calm rising up inside of me like a rogue wave.

"How dare you threaten me, *human*." I spit the words at her, as if they were acid on my tongue. "*Your men* befoul my sea, destroy all they touch, and take whatever they choose, damning all consequences. They deserve their fate."

Helen stepped towards me, hands dropping to her sides where they curled into tight fists. "No—no, you do not get to tell me what *my* son deserved. He deserved better than a slit throat not a mile from his home on shore. He deserved a full life with his family. His children. His wife. *You* are the destroyer. A she-devil who destroys lives without pity or remorse."

I reached up to finger my blade where it hung beneath the layers of fabric, ready for blood. I bared my teeth in warning, but her words rang true in my ears. I hated her all the more for it.

Before I could unleash my fury upon her, Cian barreled towards the woman, crimson eyes nearly on fire in his skull. Helen stumbled back, catching herself on the doorframe. He stood between her and I, forming a perfect living barricade.

There was something so frantic in his eyes that he pulled all my thoughts away from the confrontation and back to my quest. There were more important things than putting human women in their places. Cian needed me. He began nudging me with his great neck in an effort to get me to climb atop his back. I did as he bade, and in an instant, I was clinging to him as he galloped out of the pasture and nearer to the river.

He could not outrun Helen's last cries. "Soon, Selkie! You'll find yourself back in hell soon enough. Count on it."

Cian did not slow until the cottage was far behind us. I supposed he must still be able to comprehend language, for I doubt he would have reacted in such a furious manner otherwise. I peered over my shoulder every few minutes to be sure we were not being followed. There were no others sharing this stretch of open space with us. That foolish woman was merely angry and had no real means of seeking revenge, that I was sure of.

Though she would be right to claim her vengeance. Just as I was right to claim mine. There was no other way to make amends. I pressed my cheek against Cian's neck, sighing as I admitted to myself that was not entirely true. There would always be exceptions. His warmth flowed into my skin. I could feel his pulse, fast and powerful, surging through him just beneath the surface, much like the river he was tied to.

Wild and ancient.

Beautiful and deadly.

I wondered if Cian understood the precipice we stood before. I almost asked aloud but thought better of it. I did not know if he could respond to me, or worse yet—if I could bear the weight of his words. I would go to the river with him because I loved him. There was nothing for it. Whatever that meant for me... it did not matter. There was an empty space inside me, echoing and pained, that would never be filled unless I was with Cian. If that meant there would be an end to this existence of mine, then so be it. He would not deter me. No one would.

Despite my resignation to my fate, my heart began thundering inside my chest when we grew near enough to the river that we could smell its banks and feel its sway on the air temperature. My fist tangled viciously in Cian's mane when we caught the first sight of the frothing current, white and violent.

The rain had filled the river to the brim, and it raged like an endless riptide. Once again, I was stricken with the sensation that this river, much like the sea, was an entity all its own. And it was *angry*.

Cian's body grew more rigid as we continued to near it. I tried to dismount from his back, but he reared upwards, screaming out in warning. I froze in my seat, unsure of what was required of me, afraid to be parted from Cian, and so I remained.

We edged along the boulder speckled shoreline, the smell of cold freshwater and mud already filling my nose. Cian danced atop the rocky ground, his hooves finding the invisible path he must have walked for hundreds of years. I tried to swallow down the growing lump in my throat, tried to find my voice to ask questions, but I was mute—choking on the unknown.

Cian turned his head back to look at me out of the corner of his scarlet eyes only once. I nodded silently, knowing only that he needed my permission. Something in his look flickered, a spark of recognition. It was gone in a moment before he bowed his face low and waded into the roaring *abhainn*.

This was it. This was the end.

I forced myself to breathe, forced myself to hold fast to Cian.

The water bit at my toes, hungry for more of me. It swelled up around us. It lapped against Cian, ready to embrace him like a mother cradles her child. Cian's pace slowed to a ceremonial march, and little by little, he brought me further into his domain. I remained still, terrified but unwilling to depart from this path I had chosen.

The river pulled and pushed, as if a thousand hands were trying to force me away from Cian. To rescue or to drown, I knew not. I wrapped my good arm around Cian's neck while I held the other crushed close to my chest. The pain from the break was a burning flame compared with the coolness of the water. The contrast made me breathless and dizzy. I tried to take even breaths, tried to stay staunchly adamant in my decision. I was a fearless Selkie. Death was merely another moment awaiting me. It would only be a moment. I would return to the sea, on the currents of the river, then I could rest in the endless nothingness of darkness. It would be alright. If there was to be anything more, anything greater than this, I'd welcome it.

When the water came up to my shoulders, pulsing and impatient, Cian's body was entirely submerged. For a moment I was alone. I felt a bolt of panic surge up from my core. I was about to die.

And Cian would be the one to kill me.

Would I even allow myself to drown? Such a foolish act when I was, at my essence, a creature of the deep just as Cian. Love was foolish, and I was the queen of all fools. What was I doing here? The river swelled and a foamy wave crested over top of my head before I had a chance to gulp down any air.

The world grew garbled and muted. Water rushed numbly all around me as Cian dragged me down to the murky bottom of the river. I opened my eyes to see where fate was leading me, but the water was dark and churning. Cian was hardly visible in all the black, but I felt him, strong and warm and alive.

Let this be enough.

He'd brought me to the river, given me over. I fought the urge to let go, to untangle myself from this insanity and swim away from my death. But then I imagined the curve of Cian's lips, his smoldering stare as he burned through every last one of my defenses and gripped tighter to his mane. That woman was right. I had only ever taken life. Never had I truly saved one.

What little air I had left in my lungs would have to be enough. Enough to bring together the fractured pieces of our lives. Enough to heal and restore what had been taken from us. What we had taken from each other. My chest grew tighter, heaving with the desire to expel my last breath, but I held on. Just a little longer now.

The night is dark, the waters deep,
Yet soft the billows roll;
Alas! at every breeze I weep —
The storm is in my soul."
— Helen Maria Williams

Chapter Twenty-Eight

CIAN

The river welcomed us home with lapping water that tenderly embraced me. Kissed my skin with icy lips while cradling us both. Gently at first, but then it grew frenzied— excited that finally, *finally* my *bean chéile* had been restored to us. For so long the *abhainn* had gone hungry. Starved from ancient promises made and not kept. Too many nights spent on the wrong brides, the wrong women entered the river, tasting of false love and fleeting desire but now—now we were complete and so close to being fulfilled and redeemed and satiated.

I could feel my bride's strong arms holding tight to me as I brought us down deep into the murky depths of my *abhainn*. She held fast to me as I swam further away from the sun, and closer to my home. The blackness swallowed us whole in a delicious descent away from the world above.

And then something changed. A memory, hazy and forbidden, danced behind my eyes. A name, and a song, sorrowful and enchanting. Agitation over the flickering image forced me to slow my descent. Something in me cried out. I *needed* to remember but couldn't. My mind swam and spun, *searching, searching, searching,* for who I so desperately sought but could not name.

Then I saw her.

My body went rigid in the water, stalled completely with remembering. Imprinted on my eyelids was the image of a bonny lass. Though strange to behold, nonetheless captivating. She wore a crown of bleached coral and *creathnach* atop her inky hair. Pale skin dotted with endless freckles. Eyes black as obsidian, curious and ancient.

Iona. *My* blessing. *Anamchara.*

The sudden realization of what I was doing stole the air from my lungs and ripped me from my thoughts. *No.* Not like this. I could feel her, still astride my back as she began to lose her grip. Water no doubt filled her lungs to the brim. The wedding of my bride to the river, almost complete. The ancient ritual of deep sacrifice so ingrained in me that it was all I was. Another death to grant me the same empty life, so that I might continue to tear my heart to pieces, and tear someone's life from them. But this—this I could not—would *not* bear. She was like no other being on this earth and deserved so much more than this wretched end. Nor did I want to exist in a world where she was not.

Iona. Iona. Iona.

In a flash of surging bubbles, I reversed course. We had been under for so long, Iona had only barely made it to my cottage before, with the help of my powerful body to pull her swiftly under. My instincts to take her life had been so sure. Repulsion for my deep-rooted longing to give her over to the river set my insides afire. This was all wrong. I needed Iona. Alive.

Save her. Save her.

The thought was as strong and singular as my rushing pulse. I blindly searched the river, probing the space around me for the woman I dragged into the water. The woman I so loved and craved and needed. My snout found a silken coat first, and then a slender shoulder, curved and cold against my skin. I opened my eyes to see straight into the glassy black gaze of the immortal I'd pined after every day since she'd left me. Those eyes now stared ahead, unseeing, like so many before her.

No.

It would not be this way. The river could not have her. She was *mine* and mine alone.

I tugged Iona's body near with my teeth and began to kick furiously up towards the surface. Damn the river, damn my life. Without this infuriating creature in it, there was no point anyway. How dare she think to leave me like this now? Iona the eternal protector, thinking to sacrifice herself for the likes of me. I cursed my nature and the warring desires I'd fought so long against. So long I'd stayed away from her, pleading with my very nature to forget her, forget the ache inside me that would only be assuaged by her—her death, her life.

And now she'd drowned. No—I, the beast and coward that I was, I had drowned her. Snuffed out her life. For my own.

No.

I would not accept this fate. Not anymore.

I feared the way Iona's hair flared out around us every time I paused to thrash my legs and propel us onward would haunt me forever. How her head lolled lifelessly atop her shoulders, so wrong and devoid of her vitality it made me want to retch. I pushed my body to its furthest capacity—every single muscle burned beneath my skin as I forced my limbs to move faster than they ever had. Each kick and stroke felt maddeningly slow, no matter how I tried. I refused to let myself believe what I felt in my bones. *It's too late.*

When I broke the surface in a sloppy splash of panic and sheer will, I'd lost all sense of reason. I tumbled clumsily over stones and rocks, slipping while I dragged Iona's limp body out of the river by her arms as fast as I could. Her hair was slick over her face, eyes closed, and mouth open as if she were merely sleeping. A horse could do little for her now. I'd not the strength before to make the change, but now, necessity and instinct forced me to become human. How it ached to shift from the horse and back into that of a man after so long being trapped in the body of my animal self. Limbs twisted and shrank and rearranged themselves, bones melding into another form, a form that could employ arms and hands for saving. The shift was quick, but every second felt like eons. My instincts took over entirely, and soon I was slamming my fists down upon her chest in a frenzy. I pressed my lips to hers, forcing great gulps of air into her lungs. If I were able to somehow push my very life into her, I would have.

"No, Iona. You don't get to leave me again. *Breathe.*" Her body trembled with each thrust of my hands, but her chest did not rise. Again and again, I would not stop. My face grew wet as tears began tracking down my face.

Agony. It was agony. It was my nature to forever grieve my loves, to find them and wed them and then let them die and rot away. Now I was here, leaning over a creature of salt and sorrow, fierce as the edge of a blade, rejecting the very essence of my purpose. I wanted it no longer. I wanted only Iona. And she was dead.

I could not subdue the heaving sob that wracked through me down to my guts. Exhaustion seeped into my bones paired with the sharpest ache in my heart. I went to lay my head down on Iona's still bosom when my eyes caught the ends of her coat sleeve. It had fallen low enough to cover most of her hand. Her fingertips were just as I remembered them. Pale and strong, scarred yet beautiful.

Iona could have easily just pulled her sealskin up over herself and swam away, free of me and of death. But the fool chose me. She chose my fate while sealing her own.

My hand brushed against hers and I grimaced as I tugged her coat up around her body. It was a piteous attempt at putting her to rights the best way I could. I gently laid her coat over her torso so that it closed over her breast, concealing her body up to her clavicle. I wrapped my hands around hers, placing them, one over the other, at her stomach.

My beautiful *bean chéile.* Iona.

I couldn't help but to run my fingertips along the length of her sealskin. I wanted to remember the feel of her coat so fine and lovely. As my hand caressed her shoulder, I balked. The sealskin began to *close* up around her prone form. I lifted my hand then held it just above her, afraid that any movement may break whatever spell was being worked.

As Iona's coat hid her human form away and transformed her body, the river began to eddy and swell behind me. Tiny tributaries raced through the gaps between stones. At first it was merely a trickle, but in moments water was pooling around us. My head jerked from side to side, trying to make sense of what was happening. It was as though a great rain had fallen and flooded the river to heights of which I had never seen. It seemed the very river had reversed in its course. The sea had forced itself upriver to witness Iona's death.

When I looked back down, Iona was no longer a woman at all, but a black seal, perfectly sleek and frozen in death. The river had nearly overcome her, rising past her flippers and over her head. I reached out to cradle it from the oncoming flood, but I was held fast by some unseen force. I fought with strength I no longer had, furious to be held prisoner by anything whatsoever in such a moment of desperation.

The swollen mixture of sea and river surged over us both. It completely obscured Iona from my sight as it lapped at my neck. Panic sent my blood boiling, fearful that the river had come to claim its prize—my Iona. But then, it receded frighteningly fast. As if something had sucked it out to sea. In all my existence, I'd known within my soul the river was a living, breathing, demanding thing, but never had it acted in such a bold manner. I was dumbfounded. The world held so many secrets, so many wonderful, terrible things, and though I did not understand what was happening, deep within myself I knew it for what it was. *Magic.* An ancient and mighty magic the likes of which few had ever seen.

The air became charged. Strange voices speaking ancient words in reverent whispers swirled in the wind and through the trees on either side of the river's shores. The sky grew dark, and clouds tumbled overhead in a writhing mass of violets and blacks. The temperature plummeted instantly, forcing the air out of my chest in a panicked rush.

A deep roar filled my ears. I twisted back to see what was

causing it and was met with a churning wall of emerald water that towered above us, high as the moon herself. There was no time to brace for impact, not that I was actually able to move. Instead of immense force and pain, all went dark. All went silent.

A voice spoke into the void. A voice I'd always known, yet never heard. *"Dorcha agus éadrom, grá agus gráin, síocháin agus foréigean. Is éard atá san iarmhéid ná éagothroime. Is é an bás an saol. Is é an saol bás."* The words repeated in an endless echo, drowning out all thought, devouring my attention entirely.

Dark and light, love and hate, peace and violence. Balance is imbalance. Death is life. Life is death. A pearl of gray light appeared before me and I knew, I knew with every inch of me it was Iona. *Mo mhuirnín.* The pearl grew into an orb, and then a rolling riotous ball of light. It burned my eyes to look upon it and yet I found that I could not look away. A bright burning sun hung before me. Its brilliance was astounding. I reached a tentative hand out, hoping very much to feel Iona's presence within the light. There was no fear, only hope, treacherous and seductive in every way. A blinding strobe of illumination turned the abysmal world white.

I was wrapped in a blanket of warmth, as though the sun was shining on a summer's day. I was forced to shut my eyes tight, no longer able to look out at my white-washed surroundings. The world seemed to sigh, and the whispers, the song, the light winked out like the stars do when the sun creeps up over the hills. My body was nearly drained of every drop of energy, and yet there was a raw power thrumming within me. A pulsing drive to simply *know* for certain that which my heart was crying out for confirmation.

I was left on my hands and knees, slick stones digging into my palms. The river was once again behind me, the sea retreated to where it came. I could hear it coursing down the hill once more in its natural rhythms.

I realized I had been soaked to the bone for the first time in my living memory. It was as if I had been washed clean. When I looked out ahead, searching for the seal woman whom I loved, her body was no longer prone before me. Instead, I was confronted by a pair of lean freckled legs. Then a gentle, yet strong hand pressed down upon my shoulder.

"But how—?"

Iona knelt before me, entirely naked and utterly glorious. Her eyes had a gleam in them that stole the breath from me. Slender fingers curled up under my chin, as she brought her face nearer to mine.

"Magic." I felt her breath whisper across my lips before she placed hers against mine. There were so many things I had wanted to say to her, so many regrets and apologies and professions of love and adoration. Iona's kiss held every response and every emotion I'd yearned to experience. I wrapped my arms around her, caring for nothing else in the world save for this moment. This feeling of earth-shattering completeness.

Iona cried out, and I pulled away, frightened that I had caused her pain.

"It's just this arm—I broke it, remember?"

Confusion rippled inside me. Still broken after that ancient magic? A sour smile marred her loveliness, if only for a moment. So much had transpired in such a short while after eons of nothingness. Would life always be so tumultuous?

I searched her expression for any greater hint of suffering

before laying a smattering of gentle kisses up her wrist to her shoulder, then at her neck, before finding my way back to Iona's delicious, beautiful mouth. Her good hand found its way into my hair, fingers tangling in my curls with a slow deliberateness that sent shivers up and down my spine. I let my hands wander over the subtle curves of Iona's body, savoring the touch and feel of each and every inch of her.

Our kisses grew more feverish as the moments went on, and the time spent apart weighed heavy upon us. The many nights I'd spent searching for her in the faces of different women, pining for what I knew I would never find in any other. Years of pent-up desire begged to be unleashed. Iona leaned into me, pushing me back down against the rocky shore.

Our lips parted momentarily enough for her to gulp in air and stare down at me. Her black eyes were brooding as she peered into my face. "I didn't think I would ever get to look at you this way. I thought it was the end of me."

I swallowed down the raw emotions that threatened to overtake me.

She reached up to trace the line of my lower lip. I held deathly still, wanting so much to take her fingers in my mouth, to nip playfully at her and to forget all the aches within my heart, all of the black emotions that had eaten me alive while we were separated, but this was a reckoning—though one I wanted to avoid. I braced myself for the lashing I deserved, but it did not come. Instead, Iona's hand slid down to my chest where she laid her palm flat over my beating heart.

She stared into my soul, those black eyes deep wells of emotion. "I wanted you to come for me. To go against my threats and find me. I wanted so much to be with you. I still do." I pulled her back into my arms.

Before I brought my lips to hers once more, I whispered in holy reverence, "*A chuid,* I would never go against your wishes." A single tear raced down her cheek, wiped away easily enough by my thumb. Her mouth twisted into a smile before her eyes wandered back down to my own. Our bodies melded together as she kissed me.

An eternity could have passed us by and neither one of us would have minded, until Iona froze unnaturally on top of me. Her head jerked up and I saw panic in her eyes. Confusion rippled through me; the heat of our passion quickly disintegrated when I realized why she behaved so. A man held a musket at her back. There was a mob of humans swiftly descending upon us in a frightening number.

A woman's voice echoed across the river stones, raw with hate. "I told you your days were numbered, Selkie. Your wretched life is at an end." The dark-haired woman rushed forward, nearly falling over herself in an attempt to get close enough to Iona. Her face was wild with anger, twisted. There was no time to react as the woman from the cottage spit into her face. Then, we were overtaken.

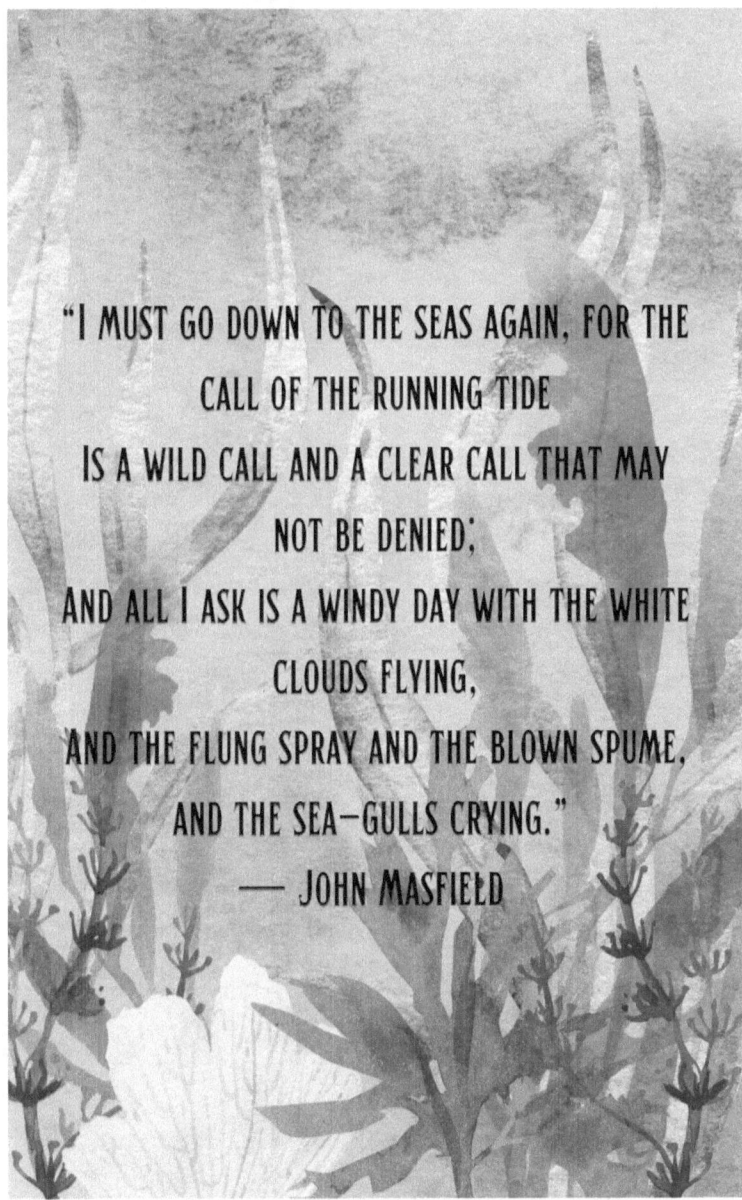

"I MUST GO DOWN TO THE SEAS AGAIN, FOR THE
CALL OF THE RUNNING TIDE
IS A WILD CALL AND A CLEAR CALL THAT MAY
NOT BE DENIED;
AND ALL I ASK IS A WINDY DAY WITH THE WHITE
CLOUDS FLYING,
AND THE FLUNG SPRAY AND THE BLOWN SPUME,
AND THE SEA—GULLS CRYING."
— JOHN MASFIELD

Chapter Twenty-Nine

CIAN

Too many things happened in a brief span of time. I thought my soul fled my body. Incomprehension and fear turned my limbs to stone. I did nothing but watch as Iona's hands flailed, fingers spread wide in a frantic attempt to grab hold of me while another man surged from the crowd, wrapping a scabbed hand roughly around her bicep. He forced her backwards, closer to the chaos. My mouth hung open, gaping in horror while I scrambled to gain my footing and reach for her.

The man dragged Iona into the writhing mob of angry mouths and arms all reaching, searching to get a piece of my Iona with their claws and fangs. It was at that moment I saw humans the way Iona might. *They* were monsters.

"Caught her in the act!" A woman, pale haired and sour faced, came rushing from the mob with a flaming torch in her hand. She waved it wildly about before me, the heat from the flame biting at my skin. She shouted to the others, "We saved this poor sod from the succubus of the sea!" A roaring chorus of cheers sent my head spinning as Iona wrestled like an eel caught between two rocks. She snarled and spit, snapping her jaws—savage thing she was—while more grubby hands snatched at her still naked body. Like she was a prize to be portioned out among them. The feeling of dumb confusion wore away and seething revulsion took its place. Wrath curled its icy fingers around my heart, sealing all its tenderness away.

"No—unhand her! Let her go, *damnit*!" I bellowed as loudly as I could, pushing the magic of my Glamour into every syllable but my words were lost in the din. They fell flat to the earth, trampled in an instant. There was blood in the water, and the humans smelled it. Nothing I could say or do would stop what was already in motion. The sea of hate and rage was deep. Iona had seen to that with the trail of dead sailors and hunters she'd left in her wake.

It did not matter how my body ached, the deep exhaustion clawing at every inch of me. I would get to her. I would save her. I'd allowed myself once to believe she'd left me, but never again. I would not stand idly by while the most singular creature I'd ever known was picked apart by a mindless hoard of humans.

My lips curled back in a furious snarl that tore out of me when I grew close enough to Iona that I could reach out and wrench her free of all those who held her, but before I could, Iona's black eyes flashed as she craned her neck to make eye contact with me through the crush of bodies. They were round with terror, her mouth open as she gulped in air. Her agony sliced me to bits. There were no words that could be uttered. Her expression stalled me in my tracks.

I began again to surge for her, damning all other consequences, only wanting her in my arms once more. Again, she glared at me. Plain on her face, clear as crystal, I knew she wanted me to wait. I bit the inside of my cheek, tasting blood as I raged at her silent insistence. Above every powerful instinct and ancient need, Iona was a protector.

Damn her for all her bravery and stoicism. The crowd undulated and Iona was swallowed whole before I could get to her. I did not have the luxury of time to speculate the humans' planned course of action, nor could I spare a moment to contemplate anything beyond the relentless urge to get my Iona back. I started to follow the herd of humans. I stalled in an abrupt realization that Iona's precious coat lay behind me, still rumpled on the river stones from her resurrection.

I stumbled back, and without thinking, pulled her coat over my own shoulders. It smelled of the sea and of Iona. The coat seemed to sense that I was not its intended. It felt strange against my body, cold and alien. Soon she would wear it again, and all would be right in the world.

Something small and gleaming between the rocks caught my eye and I snatched it up. Iona's blade. She would be wanting that before long.

Thankfully, night slammed down against the earth, shrouding the landscape in unassailable darkness. Its sudden arrival forced the mob to slow in their death march towards the village. It also made blending in among them a tad easier, though I would take no chances. I sent a silent plea into the air, hoping to have a sliver of my gifts returned to me, afraid that my ability to use Glamour had been diminished forever.

I flexed my fingers before I slid my hands through my hair, then down my body. To my relief, I could feel the slight charge of magic as I dusted a fine coat of Glamour everywhere my hands touched. Soon I was dry, ruddy faced and ginger headed, clothed in the simple, efficient garb of a farmer. When I was certain I had my disguise secured, I bounded ahead to the nearest spectator. There were so many angry humans around us, the hatred was palpable. Whatever they had planned, it was to end in terrible bloodshed unless I intervened.

I cleared my throat, preparing to sound the part as well as look it. "What's all this about? I heard the hollerin' from my door." The man I asked was elderly, his face puckered up with indignation and too much drink. He made no sign that he'd heard me at all. A streak of silver flashed across my vision. He was holding a knife, *quite* sloppily in his left hand. His arm swung to and fro with every step he took. I had to lean out of his reach to avoid being slashed with his blade. He was so far gone, I doubted he could comprehend speech. He would soon be in too much of a stupor to do anything useful with that blade, and if he wasn't—I doubted his aim would be true enough to land even a scratch on the Selkie.

I jogged around the side of the mob, looking for a more coherent human to interrogate. I must have gotten close to where Iona was, for I could hear intermittent howling quickly paired with cruel jeers. *Oh, they would indeed regret this.* I allowed myself a moment to fantasize darkly about the terrible retribution that Iona would unleash upon these fools once I'd rescued her. I pushed those thoughts aside when I saw two gangly girls who tottered beside one another, arms interlocked. Clearly, they were bosom friends, in attendance for the sheer entertainment of witnessing someone's torture and demise. I swallowed my disgust before I once again attempted to glean whatever information I could.

"Hey girlies, what's the meaning of this? Can't be a parade

I've missed, eh?" The girls barely tore their eyes away from the mob ahead of them long enough to register my existence. The one closer to me glanced at her friend, then responded.

"They've caught a Selkie. She's the one who's been destroying the boats and killin' the men. It was the three widows up the glen who found her out."

Ah. Damn. I cursed myself for trusting them, for putting Iona into such danger. "Well then, what's to be done about it?" I had to shout for them to hear over the roaring throng.

Her reply filled me with renewed terror. She seemed horrifyingly giddy as she said, "When the sun comes up, we're going to throw her into the sea." They didn't mean they were going to just return Iona to her home.

I stalled, feet rooted to the earth. They were going to *push* her from the towering cliff at the end of the village. A fall from such heights spelled death for any creature. I knew the humans would make certain of it. I gritted my teeth as the unbidden image of Iona's shattered body beneath the abusive surf flooded my mind.

Damn caution. Damn any kind of plan. I would lay waste to this entire town if it came down to it. I needed to get to Iona, *now*. I barreled between the girls, forcing their arms to untwine. I pushed and shoved my way between the crush of bodies. Despite the night's cold air, the proximity to all these humans paired with Iona's coat had me sweating and panting. Elbows dug into my back while people threw curses at me for stomping on their boots. I made my way for the center of the crowd, judging my proximity to Iona by the growing intensity of her growls.

When I found her, my stomach constricted. Four men held

her by her shoulders and her thighs. Iona writhed slowly now. She must have been exhausted. Still fighting against them with all she had. I knew she would until her final breath left her lungs and *that* would not be happening again anytime soon. Iona's speckled skin was bruised, violet and indigo bloomed in ugly blotches across her body in the shapes of her aggressor's hands. Her broken arm was tucked into her side like a chicken wing, but at an odd and painful looking angle. It had probably been further broken.

Iona thrashed her head left and right, teeth bared in glorious defiance. Her eyes found my Glamoured visage in the sea of faces and held. *Och, mo mhuirnín.* Even hidden beneath my layers of magic, she saw me. Her brows knitted high upon her forehead, and I realized tears streamed from her eyes, their tracks stained brown on her cheeks from the dust kicked into the air.

She sobbed, a fitful wrenching sound that tore my heart from my chest. I nodded in silent understanding, sending her a false yet unrelenting smile. She nodded her head in response, sending a strangled laugh out into the night. *Soon.*

We entered the village center. Terrible, churning hoard of angry, foul-smelling humans, ready to kill a creature so fine and singular it was surely a sin. The fools. The absolute fools. To destroy one blessed by the sea itself, surely was a giant step towards ruination. I tried my best to remain close to Iona, but the crush of the crowd made it all but impossible.

A haggard old thing screeched over the cacophony of voices, "Lock her away! At first light we'll have our justice!" Whoever the old woman was, she held enough sway with the villagers to elicit an ear-splitting cry of macabre joy. The crowd parted around the four who held Iona fettered between them, allowing them to walk to a dingy building tucked off the main path.

One of the men holding Iona's leg dropped her abruptly, summoning hisses of anger from the three others as she was suddenly flailing with one less guard to keep her from escaping. She didn't have much time, for the first man flung open the building's door, and the other humans followed him. I heard Iona howling. I could see her pale limbs slip into the darkness beyond the threshold, and then, the door slammed shut.

I refused to believe that she was in danger within those walls. It was the men who ought to be afraid.

I knew that firsthand.

"NOR SOLE THE GULLS IN CLOUD THAT WHEELED
CIRCLING ONE SNOW–FLANKED PEAK AFAR,
BUT NEARER FOWL THE FLOES THAT SKIMMED
AND CRYSTAL BEACHES, FELT NO JAR.
NO THRILL TRANSMITTED STIRRED THE LOCK
OF JACK–STRAW NEEDLE–ICE AT BASE;
TOWERS UNDERMINED BY WAVES—THE BLOCK
ATILT IMPENDING—KEPT THEIR PLACE.
SEALS, DOZING SLEEK ON SLIDDERY LEDGES
SLIPT NEVER, WHEN BY LOFTIER EDGES
THROUGH VERY INERTIA OVERTHROWN,
THE IMPETUOUS SHIP IN BAFFLEMENT WENT
DOWN."
—HERMAN MELVILLE

Chapter Thirty

CIAN

I melded into the unruly crowd while my mind raced through every possibility, every opportunity, and every risk involved in the task that lay ahead. I tried to focus, to think but the air was so filled with vitriol and disdain for Iona, my thoughts scattered about, too abstracted by my simmering ire.

Though the night had already descended upon us, in my rage I conjured a heavy velvet curtain of tangible dread to ensconce the mob, draping everything and everyone in a horrid void-like darkness. If any held out a hand hoping to catch a glimpse of their fingers, well, they'd be greatly disappointed. Let them see what eternal darkness awaited them. Let them taste my wrath.

The humans fell into a stunned silence. The acrid scent of terror tinged the air and coiled in my nostrils. Delectable malice coated my tongue. It had been so long since I'd had such a unique opportunity. Iona was always bringing me novel experiences, whether intentionally or not.

I cleared my throat as I summoned a voice as beastly as I

could imagine and then thundered, "ALL WHO STAND HERE SHALL BE JUDGED BY THE SEA HERSELF FOR THE MOLESTATION AND CAPTURE OF ONE OF HER BELOVED CHILDREN." My voice sounded more like thunder clapping, or a cliff face peeling from the bedrock and cascading in a violent rush into the sea than it did an actual voice. I nearly surprised myself with my own ferocity. I held my breath, waiting for the humans' reactions.

A symphony of screams peeled out, confusion rippling through the abyss. I felt my Glamour growing thin. It was the most I could muster after having gone so long with an empty well to glean magic from. Power-spent and fatigued, I was forced to rein in the darkness. When the sky lightened to its natural hue, the old woman yelled again, destroying my efforts to foment hesitation among them.

"Must be the Selkie's devilry! She's trying to trick us into sparing her." she shouted, and a glob of spittle clung to her chin. "Do not be fooled by her Satanic games. She's not to be trusted, that one." I nearly ground my teeth to a pulp listening to her drivel. Her words had all but unraveled the terror brought on by my magic.

The crowd of angry dullards subsided. They began heading home to their warm beds where they could dream up all the terrible things they wished upon my Iona. As they meandered away, I swept into the shadows between buildings, waiting.

Not long after the town center was cleared of any remaining humans and there was hardly a living soul awake, I crept out from my hiding place. Around the corner was the squat little building where Iona had been thrown. At its door, a man slumped on his side, an empty bottle limp in his hand. A laughable watchman. Curious, it seemed there should be at least two men guarding such a formidable, evil creature. They were clearly suffering from illusions of grandeur. It would take far more than a few drunken buffoons to hold Iona for long. It was a truth I'd learned for myself after much difficulty.

The man was so far gone there was little need for me to do anything more than step over him as I made my way to the door. My fingers wrapped around the steel handle, their true appearance jarring me at first. I must have removed my Glamour when I'd pulled my magic back.

I intended to reveal myself to Iona once inside the building, so it was only a small matter. I supposed magic wielding was like using a muscle. After so long without any control of it, my ability must be somewhat atrophic. I was only momentarily troubled by my awkward shift in ability, for the darkness of the building set all my other instincts on edge.

The interior was intentionally oppressive. The masonry itself gave off a feeling of supreme cruelty. It was all bars and stone walls, with no windows to let in fresh air or natural light. The atmosphere was damp and chilled, ripe with human stench. I gagged at the idea of spending any more than a few moments in this dank prison. Surely it was better to die outright than to live any number of days in such hell.

I didn't make it any further when I sensed what must be the other watchman. He was standing inside the cell, the barred door flung open behind him. He flipped a silver key between his fingers while leering at a pale figure standing defiantly in the corner of her small prison.

I felt for Iona's blade. The string that had hung from Iona's neck was twisted several times around my wrist. When I palmed the hilt, every thought in my head vanished. I stalked towards the man who was reaching a pathetic hand toward Iona as though he might be able to claim her, to control her for even an instant.

His voice snaked out of him, and the very sound of it made me all the more wrathful. "I hear if you lay with a man, he gets to keep you forever. 'Sat true, Selkie?"

I didn't feel an ounce of guilt over the possessive fury that turned my sight red. I was going to rip him limb from limb. Iona glared at her captor as she stepped nearer to his embrace. I moved into a killing position, holding my hand up, up, positioned just behind his neck, ready to pierce his vertebrae. I clenched the dagger in my fist, steeling my resolve.

Iona purred, and it was veiled with death. "Would you like to see?"

Her hand snaked around the man's neck and after one brutally violent tug, he fell at my feet. I gasped in shock at her swift movement. Equal parts impressed and unnerved, I peered down at the dead man for only a moment. When I looked up again, Iona's beautiful black gaze met mine, brimming with tears.

I held her knife up for her, feeling relieved and sheepish all at once. "I brought you your knife, *Anamchara*." Her eyes flitted away from my face to take in her dagger. She reached for it, securing it around her neck while her face crumpled. "Ah, hush now *A Mhuirnín*. You're safe —well *almost* safe. We've got to get you out of here." She leaned against me, pressing her face against her coat. I ran my hands down her arms as gently as I could. I held my desire in check, for I wanted so badly to give her comfort. But the worry of causing further pain if I were to touch her many bruises and that treacherously broken arm stopped me from the onslaught of passion that welled inside of me.

Her words were low and muffled against my chest, but I understood them all the same. "You came for me."

"I merely followed my heart." I smirked, trying to bring any sort of light I could into the blackness of the cell.

Iona snorted. "You are a *fiend*. Now give me my coat." She tapped my arm impatiently, ready to be whole again. The fur was sinfully soft beneath my fingers while I pulled it over Iona's frame. It was like a glove, made to fit Iona and only her, sliding over her skin, the finest seal coat ever to be worn. She shuddered audibly as she ran her hand over her other sleeve, trying to tuck it under the crooked elbow of her broken arm.

When she was satisfied that her coat would not fall loose from her damaged limb, she looked back up at me, an eyebrow raised. "It smells like shit and death in here." There was a tiredness in her eyes, deep and terribly pained but she too was making an effort to bring us both comfort in whatever way she could. She cocked her head to the side, and I knew a question was sure to follow.

"What's next?"

For a moment I hesitated to share all her options, before reminding myself to avoid acts of stupid heroism. Iona would lead, as she was destined to.

"What's next is, well"—I wrapped an arm around her waist, guiding her out of the cell and around the limp corpse beneath our feet—"up to you, of course, Miss Selkie. They've wronged you greatly. Vengeance would not be an unreasonable course of action." I cleared my throat, anxious to say the rest. "And I'd be there, beside you." Her head whipped upwards, and she eyed me, considering my words.

It was a long while before she spoke. "What would make this ache within my breast disappear?" She held her hand up to her chest, pressing it flat over her coat. It was a solemn question, one I knew she'd never asked before. I began to shake my head, wanting her to say more, but she cut me off. "Were I to make a wound deeper than the one they've already inflicted upon me, what peace would I gain?"

Her voice shook as she continued, "They deserve their revenge. I've done violence to them, and now, by all rights, they have every cause to slit my throat." She dropped her hand and wrapped it around mine. Her fingers were cold against my skin. "I have existed in an endless cycle of death, killing, revenge. This was all I knew. It was all I thought I was capable of." I patted her hand reassuringly, wanting, needing her to say more. Iona sighed and said, "I won't forfeit my life, but I cannot go on as I have. I will not lash out simply because *my* life amounts to a penance in need of payment." Iona shrugged her shoulders, tugging her coat up around her ears before she stepped towards the door.

I pulled back against her waist, hoping to slow her pace. "While it is a relief to know I won't be needing to take part in the culling of an entire human village, I want to caution you."

Iona's black eyes rolled around in her head, no doubt frustrated at all she had endured and all that was to come before the next setting of the sun.

I bobbed my head in understanding before continuing. "If we do nothing, they will *always* seek you out. We could stop it. We could make it so that we never have to fear this village." Iona didn't look back at me this time, but I knew she was listening. "And we won't need to kill them all, either."

"Cian—you've got an idea, don't you?"

I leaned in close to her, my lips grazing her ear. "Can selkies read minds?" She leaned into my caress, heating my blood. I didn't need to see her face to know she was smiling. "There's a man, unconscious outside the door. Let's leave him there to find his friend. We need to find a place to wait out the dawn. Timing is of the essence and there is much to discuss."

"AS I WEND TO THE SHORES I KNOW NOT,
AS I LIST TO THE DIRGE, THE VOICES OF MEN AND
WOMEN WRECK'D,
AS I INHALE THE IMPALPABLE BREEZES THAT SET
IN UPON ME,
AS THE OCEAN SO MYSTERIOUS ROLLS TOWARD
ME CLOSER AND CLOSER,
I TOO BUT SIGNIFY AT THE UTMOST A LITTLE
WASH'D—UP DRIFT,
A FEW SANDS AND DEAD LEAVES TO GATHER,
GATHER, AND MERGE MYSELF AS PART OF THE
SANDS AND DRIFT.

O BAFFLED, BALK'D, BENT TO THE VERY EARTH,
OPPRESS'D WITH MYSELF THAT I HAVE DARED TO
OPEN MY MOUTH,
AWARE NOW THAT AMID ALL THAT BLAB WHOSE
ECHOES RECOIL UPON ME I HAVE NOT ONCE HAD
THE LEAST IDEA WHO OR WHAT I AM..."
—WALT WHITMAN

Chapter Thirty-One

IONA

With Cian's arm firmly wrapped about my waist, I stepped out of the fetid darkness and into the sea swept night. The scent of low tide hung heavy in the air. The brine called to me and eased my frayed senses into a strange state of calm. I stepped lightly over the man who lay snoring on his side just in front of us. His breathing stalled once, twice, but his drunken wheezes resumed after Cian and I cleared him.

The weight of my coat was of great comfort, but even beneath its fine heft, I still felt as if my bones might shake apart from the chill in the air. Or maybe it was in me—the deep cold of terror that had filled me the moment those hands, those terrible hands pulled me into hell. It wasn't likely to leave my mind anytime soon, no matter how much I'd like to forget.

I moved a little closer to Cian, hoping to absorb some of his body heat. He was so warm, and so wonderfully alive against me. The nightmare of the last several hours had all but eclipsed the euphoria of finding each other again, of surviving. Now that we were once more side by side, I felt a flame building inside me, slowly but surely it would burn away the horrors I'd experienced.

The tender sensation of his palm pressed firmly against my side fueled my every step, though exhaustion threatened to pull me under. How I wanted to bring myself ever closer to Cian, to reclaim him as my own, and simply leave this place behind us but I knew Cian was right. With such long lives as ours, it would be impractical to leave things as they were.

I whispered, "So... what exactly are you thinking?" Before I could utter another sound, Cian stuck his pointer finger before his lips, commanding me to silence my chatter. For a moment, I wished he was still trapped as a horse without such an attitude, but I relented. I'd be a liar if I said I didn't enjoy it.

He ushered us down several side streets until we arrived at the base of a hill shrouded in trees far away from the center of the town. There was a crumbling stone wall lining this copse of forest, and the ground was littered with slabs of rock, thrust into the earth with foreign etchings carved into their surfaces. Cian's hand remained steadfast about my waist while he surveyed the surrounding area. His head swiveled this way and that, searching for any sign we'd been followed. Then we waited.

I held my nose to the air. With my coat on I maintained a seal's sense of smell. There was no hint of any nearby humans in the wind, but there was a strange malodor seeping up from the earth. Death. My instincts sparked to life as I reached out for Cian. "I don't like this place."

Cian's lips flattened out as he nodded in agreement.

He kept his voice low as he spoke, "'Tis a cemetery, *A*

Chuid. Humans collect their dead and bury them in the ground."

I frowned at the idea of someone collecting my body and then stuffing it below the earth. Doomed to be kept prisoner, never to see my beloved ocean again.

I wrinkled my nose. "*Why?*" The utterance was thick with disgust. Cian smirked, an amused light shining in his crimson eyes.

"They like to come back and visit."

Strange. The sentimentality was completely unsettling until I thought about the pathetically short lifespans of humans. How easily they died, and how frequently. I could not say that I wouldn't like the chance to visit my beloved dead, to speak to them once more, even when they could no longer hear me. Peculiar, nevertheless.

Cian wandered ahead. Clearly, he'd been here before. He knew the layout well enough to find a portion of the cemetery that was obviously far older than the rest. Here the earth smelled ancient, moldering and forgotten. A tree with long slender branches that kissed the ground stood among a disintegrating collection of slabs that I assumed marked the places where bodies had been buried.

Cian put out a hand to pull the tree's limbs aside so I could walk beneath them into the secret alcove created by its sweeping growth. Cian followed me, letting the curtain of leaves fall, hiding us from the world of the living entirely. He turned around, smiling like the predator he was as he ran a hand through the length of his hair.

"Here's the plan. We need a...a... hmm, now—what would I be calling what we need?" He tapped his chin, pondering what I did not know. "A diversion? A decoy? Yes! Yes, a decoy. The humans will not be satisfied if they do not feel they have avenged all those men you've skillfully dispatched. We need them to believe they've done away with ye." I sighed, unsure of what he was suggesting, though I feared I might know.

Cian arched a pale brow, gauging my level of awareness. The look on my face must have been one of incredulity for he continued to elaborate, "We snatch one of the many terrible humans from the village, and I Glamour them to look like you. We shove them back in the cell, and escape before anyone is the wiser. There. We shall be free, and no one will ever search for ye again." Cian waited expectantly, holding both hands up as if he were offering the idea in his palms.

I rubbed at my eye with my one good hand, dissatisfied with his explanation. "So... you're suggesting we kidnap someone so they can be killed in my stead?"

Cian licked his lips, sensing my souring mood. "Yes. One of the *terrible* humans who was going to kill *you*, if you'll recall." Now his hands were planted against his hips, preparing to spar with me.

"And where are we going to find this human? Shall we knock on doors and ask if anyone inside attended the mob earlier? Or are we to assume guilt of all who dwell here?"

Cian shook his head, then pinched the bridge of his nose with his thumb and forefinger.

"I don't know Iona, but we've got to hurry. The sun will rise, and that cell will remain empty unless we do this. Now."

I growled in frustration, hating with every ounce of my being that I was obligated to make this choice. Killing had always been an instinctive act, a necessary step to defending the lives of my kin. I'd never planned someone's death in such a cold manner. The calculation of it made me nauseous.

This was Cian's realm of existence, not mine. As if he could read my mind, he yielded, taking my hand in his. "I know it's dreadful, but it's the only option. Come." Cian pulled me out from our hiding place, unwilling to allow me to protest, and charged ahead until he stopped so abruptly, I slammed into him.

I cried out in pain when my broken arm crunched audibly against his back. I could hear Cian sucking in air, wincing because he knew full well what that sound was, yet he did not turn. Instead, he reached a hand backward, as if he intended to keep me shielded behind him.

"It's no use trying to keep her hidden! I heard everything, you *monsters*. Killers, the both of you." I recognized her voice immediately. *Helen*. The unforgivable wench who'd sold me out to the hoard of blood thirsty heathens.

She waved her torch in the air as she yelled, "But you'll not be doing any of those things you've got planned. I'll be sure of that. You're both going to burn. I'll be sure to tell them all how you are more than creatures of death. You're Satan's spawn. Demons straight from Hell!"

Helen turned, opening her mouth as if to call out for aid, and terror mingled with rage as I ripped my dagger from my neck. Hundreds of years of blind fury roared through my body while I sprinted around Cian, lunging for the woman with my knife angled ready to pierce her wretched heart, to stop her from taking what had only been so fleetingly mine.

But I was brought down hard. My chin hit the ground before the rest of my body. Cian had used his long legs to sweep mine out from under me. My lungs were flattened, forcing all the air within them to leave at once. As I struggled to inhale, I looked up to see him holding the woman in a crush of his biceps. Her neck was positioned in the crook of Cian's elbow. She wheezed, slapping her hands lamely against his arm a few moments before going completely limp.

I jumped to my feet, still short for air and instantly angry at his usurpation. "How dare you—"

Cian's mouth twitched again, threatening a smile as he said, "How dare I see an opportunity and rise to meet it *instead* of slashing it to death with my knife?" My mouth dropped open. *Heaven and earth and all the hells below.* I silently cursed myself. He was right. Cian smiled, realizing he had bested me.

"Miss Selkie, I believe we've found the perfect candidate to secure our plan's success."

I studied the unconscious woman's slack countenance. Of all the humans to visit this place, to attempt to destroy us, the one woman who'd wronged me, found her way to us. The serendipity was not lost on me, nor was the guilt of cold calculating murder. The witch had been right. With an immortal lifespan, one must do what it takes to go on.

My chest now ached right along with every other inch of my body. Let this encounter be the last to bring me any more physical misery. Cian smiled broadly, his sharp teeth gleaming in the dark. "Now you've seen reason. I shall remember the expression upon your face for as long as I shall live. It will linger in the halls of my memory titled as: *The Moment I Was Right.*

I smirked, having actually missed his arrogance. "And that will be the only way to ever see it again, I'm sure."

Cian snorted as he dropped the human unceremoniously

on the ground. I felt a slight shift in the air as Cian began to create a Glamour. He swiftly ran his hands along her form, transforming the belligerent cow into a perfectly identical version of me, down to the very last speckle.

It was a strange sensation, peering down upon myself. "Is that truly what I look like?"

Cian stood upright, dusting his hands on his pants. "Well, she's got all your coloring and freckles and such, but there's no magic on Earth that could replicate such a fine creature as you, no matter how talented the wielder." I felt my cheeks burning as I reveled in the feeling of being adored. I swore I saw a hint of crimson wash across Cian's face before he turned away, hauling the woman up over his shoulders.

I followed him, zigzagging around the monuments of death that littered our path back towards the village. Soon, soon it would all be done with.

"FAR, FAR OUT LIE THE WHITE SAILS ALL AT REST;
LIKE SPECTRAL ARMS THEY SEEM TO TOUCH AND CLING
UNTO THE WIDE HORIZON. NOT A WING
OF TRUANT BIRD GLIDES DOWN THE PURPLING WEST;
NO BREEZE DARES TO INTRUDE, E'EN ON A QUEST
TO FAN A LOVER'S BROW; THE WAVES TO SING
HAVE QUITE FORGOTTEN TILL THE DEEP SHALL FLING
A BOW ACROSS ITS VIBRANT CHORDS. THEN, LEST
ONE MOMENT OF THE SEA'S REPOSE WE LOSE,
NOR FURNISH FANCY WITH A THOUSAND THEMES
OF UNIMAGINED SWEETNESS, LET US GAZE
ON THIS SERENITY, FOR AS WE MUSE,
LO! ALL IS RESTLESS MOTION: LIFE'S BEST DREAMS
GIVE CHANGING MOODS TO EVEN HALCYON DAYS."
— HENRIETTA CORDELIA RAY

Chapter Thirty-Two

IONA

The sky was a threatening periwinkle by the time we made it back to my former prison. The man who had been posted outside still lay there completely unbothered by the stirrings of predawn, not to mention Cian's labored breathing after having carried our *decoy* as he referred to her, all the way there.

I hid in the shadows behind a cart while Cian went into that terrible oubliette to deposit her into the cell. On our journey to the village, I thought perhaps Cian had actually killed the woman, but he assured me that he had only rendered her unconscious. It would not be long now until she met her fate.

While I waited, I searched within myself for any ounce of regret or shame for choosing to sacrifice this human, and I found none. There was a pinch of discomfort, at having my hand forced one way or another. There was a version of history where none of this would have been necessary, but then no one can travel back in time. Cian was right that it was unpleasant to know her death would arrive soon, but she would already have bled to death in the cemetery if Cian hadn't stopped me from taking action.

I nearly jumped out of my coat when Cian's voice sounded directly behind me. "It's done. Won't be long now until the village rises, ready to throw you off the cliff. I think it's best we leave before they arrive. Don't want anyone catching a glimpse of you now."

I worried my teeth against my bottom lip, anxiety gurgling in my guts.

"What if they realize they've been tricked? Could your Glamour come away without you knowing?"

Cian kissed the top of my head before smoothing my hair down with his hand.

"The people want death. They will believe our ruse, because they *want* to believe it. Humans do not seek truth as they like to claim. Mostly they seek self-gratification. I s'pose we could find ourselves a hiding place far from here to observe..." My heart thudded against my ribcage, and I realized it was fear that had my pulse racing. Never again did I want to see such rage or feel swept away as I had by their malicious claws and sharp words. I had no desire to witness a mob of people overtake any soul, wretched or otherwise.

"Cian... I can't—I can't stay, but we need to be sure. *I* need to be sure." I looked up into his eyes, silently pleading for him to understand. To know what it was in my heart that I was too proud to speak aloud.

He nodded grimly, looking out around us at the growing dawn. "Go back to the cemetery. I'll meet you beneath the willow tree. Go quick now and stay hidden. Wait. First, come here *Anamchara*." He pulled me into his arms and wrapped me in a fierce embrace that made me ache in every way.

He pressed his lips against mine, a kiss that stole the breath from my lungs. My toes curled as we kissed, the heat between us growing with every second. His hands gently cradled my head as he swept his tongue into my mouth. When Cian pulled away, the air became charged as he hastily draped a Glamour about my body. He breathed heavily as he worked. "You'll blend right in, should anyone see you."

I held up a hand, which was no longer freckled at all, and ran my disguised fingers along his jaw, savoring the touch and feel of him.

I hated to be parted from him for any length of time but agreed. "I'll be waiting." Cian nipped at my nose, conjuring a smile to bloom across my lips.

"I won't delay this time." He wrapped his hand around my wrist then turned my hand upward, planting a tender kiss in my palm before letting me go.

I could feel Cian's eyes following me even after I turned down an alleyway. The sun crept up steadily over houses and buildings, creating trails of steam that curled into the sky like fingers attempting to touch the heavens. I pulled my coat ever tighter around me. Cian had Glamoured it to look like a simple fur coat, shabby and worn, a far cry from my elegant sealskin. I knew it for what it was despite its altered appearance. It was my shield and armor, even as far as I was from the sea.

At first, I scuttled along, crouched low to avoid detection, but as the streets began to fill with people all heading to the village square, I realized my behavior was more likely to call attention to myself than anything. I stood upright, dusted

myself off, threw my shoulders back, and gave my best imper-
sonation of Cian's saunter. Someone so confident in their
demeanor could not be under any speculation.

Several men looked my way, but when they caught a
glimpse of my face, they abruptly shifted their glances to their
feet or in another direction. One young man even grimaced
when he made eye contact with me. It was only after falling
victim to several more frightened expressions that I decided to
find something with which to catch a glimpse of my reflection.
After peering into a dirty puddle, I realized Cian had taken
great liberties with his Glamour.

The bastard had made me hideous. I recalled his earlier
teachings on the dangers of being a single female in the presence
of humans, and his desire to keep me safe by pretending to be
my husband. I huffed with dismay as I realized this ugly disguise
was the way Cian thought he could shelter me. To all who
looked upon me, I was a one-eyed hag with a terrible scar
peeling down across my face.

I'd never considered myself vain until that very moment. I
wanted to bury my face in my hood and crawl away in shame.
Cian must have felt so pleased with himself. He would regret
this. Whatever bravado I had mustered fled from me as I
continued to shuffle down the lane and out of the village in a
rush of embarrassment. *That fiend.*

People flooded past me in the other direction. They were
heading towards my execution as I escaped it. Their giddy
chatter set my teeth on edge. It was one thing to take life, but to
revel in it as though it were entertaining? My stomach tumbled
inside me. The sooner we could leave this place behind, the
better.

The developed, human touched world gave way little by little to verdant nature, tendrils of muted green and gold coaxed me to safety. Golden rays of purest sunlight stretched across the horizon, barely kissing my skin, reminding me of the gift I'd been given. The magic that it was to be still breathing, still living. A breeze blew in from the north, bringing with it the heady aroma of the sea. As I walked towards the wild each step felt lighter and lighter.

The cemetery was different in the light of day. There was an aura of peace within the decaying walls. Birds flitted to and fro from their gnarled little nests wedged between the crumbling stones. The bare branches of the willow tree swayed on the wind. I walked towards it, weary and ready to rest hidden beneath its bows. A flicker of movement caught the corner of my eye. A solitary band of fog hung low, writhing and alive. A train of white gossamer slithered behind someone as she floated over the grass. *Bean Sighe*. My skin pebbled from her sheer presence.

The specter must have sensed me, for she turned towards me, extending her milky white fingers in my direction. "You were meant to be dead," she moaned, a mournful sound that nearly broke my heart. "I saw it. You drowned so terribly, so tragic. So lovely." Tears of thick blood snaked down her face.

I swallowed my fear, and replied, "Yes. I did." *Bean Sighe* angled her head, visibly bewildered.

She appeared to look past me, or through me. I wasn't sure which, when she asked, "Are you a spirit? Or have the ancient ones resurrected you?" Her words sparked new curiosity in me. My brows knitted over my face while I pondered her question. The ancient ones. The sea? The river? Perhaps.

"I think it was the...ancient ones, as you said. Magic. Though I don't understand why."

She let out an ear-splitting cry, the deepest sound of despair. It echoed against the stones around us. My body went stiff as a board in response to the sound, instantly sending sparks of pain through my already aching muscles.

"Best not to try... too many wonders to conceive of." The ghostly creature turned away from me, continuing her way through the sloppy arrays of stones scattered on the ground. Her mournful cries continued to sound long after I'd lost sight of her. I hadn't realized I was holding my breath until I'd released it, my chest stinging with relief. *Too many wonders to conceive of*, to be sure. I leaned my body against the wide trunk of the willow tree, savoring the sensation of rest. The morning stretched on before me, and I began to grow anxious in waiting for Cian's return.

He'd said to wait here, that he wouldn't keep me. Surely there would be no trouble. Cian had assured me our plan was fool proof. Still. My nerves jumped and skittered under my skin, and I grew more desperate for his appearance with every minute. My eyes scanned the horizon, constantly searching for movement. Had he been caught up in some terrible mix up? Or had the idiot found his way into one of those awful taverns again? Frustration and worry warred inside my mind, wearying me even further.

I'd resigned myself to return to the village to seek him out and drag him away by the ear if needed. I rose up from the ground and stood on trembling knees. I tried to harness the skeptical anger that was brewing under my skin, let it fuel my weary body as I searched for Cian. I walked beyond the stone threshold and immediately began laughing.

Cian was meandering up the hill with a rather bulbous basket in the crook of his arm. When he looked up at me he startled, nearly dropping the whole thing as he clutched his chest in surprise. "Heavens! I'd forgotten how, erm... Glamoured you were."

My nostrils flared in renewed irritation. "You mean how *ugly* I am? Yes, I'm aware." A flood of giddy relief crashed into me as I rushed to him. He held out an arm and pulled me in tight before he peppered my forehead and cheeks with kisses.

"You could be the ugliest thing in all of existence and I would still want you."

"Liar."

He chuckled as he ran his free hand down my cheek and over my shoulders.

"Perhaps. There. My bonny *bean chéile,* restored to me at last." He kissed me again, his lips whispered against mine, reverent and lovely in every way. "I've brought wrappings and such for your arm... and lunch."

He continued walking up the hill, past the cemetery, towards his *abhainn.* I scoffed, suddenly impatient and terribly curious about what sorts of things he might have stolen that would constitute a meal for us. "Are we to walk all the way to your river before we see to our needs?"

Cian whipped around, face scarlet and eyes twinkling in a wicked way that sent my blood boiling. "If you'd prefer, we can meet our needs here in this very field, if you don't mind an audience?" He gestured to the several animals grazing in the distance.

My voice squeaked in a very unappealing way. "I meant my arm. And our bellies. When was the last time you ate?"

Cian's blush remained but he smacked his lips and ran his tongue over his teeth.

"I think perhaps the last thing I ate might have been a mouthful of hay. You're right. Picnic it is." I raised an eyebrow in puzzlement. *Picnic?*

Cian plopped down on the ground, crossing his legs before he began disassembling the bundle of things in his basket. He laid out a swath of fabric and several jars, then began removing what smelled like salted meat and an assortment of other items that smelled wonderfully delicious. I found my mouth watering quite profusely. Our journey had not been one of comfort and leisure, and my stomach was emptier than it had ever been.

Cian motioned for me to sit, before speaking. "First your arm. We'll need to set it again *Anamchara*. It will hurt. Drink this first." Cian pried open a bottle, took a swig from it, then handed it to me. "It will numb you a bit, take the edge off anyway. And make you more amenable to my charms."

The devil smiled at me, and my heart began to beat harder in my chest. From nerves, fear, or lust, I couldn't quite tell. I took the bottle from him and drank deeply. It was spiced and bitter, coating my mouth instantly. It burned as it went down my throat. I coughed and sputtered, hating the smug look on Cian's face, and loving him all the more for it.

"I'm ready. Just do it." I took another deep pull from the bottle, savoring the heat now, hoping to let it distract me long enough for Cian to readjust my bones. His touch was firm yet gentle. He tugged once, brutally, and my twisted wrist felt at least somewhat right. He tugged again, and I felt a snap as the sinew in my forearm realigned. It was agonizing, but then there was a tinge of relief. Cian wrapped my arm in layer upon layer of fabric, ensuring it would not move accidentally, all the while I continued to drink the mysterious contents in the bottle, growing more relaxed with every sip. When I finally handed Cian back the bottle, his eyebrows shot up in surprise at the lack of golden liquid within.

"Ah, *mo mhuirnín*, 'tis pure whiskey you're drinking, anymore and you may pass out."

"It tastes terrible. I like it." My words were soft, and my head felt hazy. Cian's smile was calm and beautiful across his perfect face as he began to rummage through the food. He handed me something soft and fluffy with a cut of dried meat hanging across the top of it.

"Have a bite, Iona. It's beef on bread. You'll like it, I promise." He was right. It was rich and salty and delicious, though a tad tough to chew. I had bite after bite in silence while Cian did the same. We were both famished.

When my belly felt full and my mind was calm, I leaned against Cian who sat beside me, idly sipping from the bottle we were sharing. "What is a picnic?"

"This is a picnic."

"What? Setting bones and eating on the ground?"

Cian sputtered, laughter caught in his mouthful of whiskey. "Eating outside on the ground is a picnic. The bone setting was a rare treat."

"Ah. I see. Cian?" He looked down at me, waiting for my question. I had to know, had to be sure it was done. "Was it— did it happen just how you planned?"

He grimaced slightly and said, "Yes. Just as planned. It is

done. We are free." I nodded in silence, feeling a deep peace roll up and down my body, releasing the mounting tension that had been threatening to take me over.

Free.

My blood thrummed through my veins like a song, my very being feeling lighter with immense relief. "What do we do now?" I looked into his eyes, adoring how the sunlight glittered in his beautiful blue irises.

Cian pulled me close, sheltering me beneath his arm. He pressed his mouth to the top of my head, and answered, "We live."

"Though I am old with wandering
Through hollow lands and hilly lands,
I will find out where she has gone,
And kiss her lips and take her hands;
And walk among long dappled grass,
And pluck till time and times are done,
The silver apples of the moon,
The golden apples of the sun."
— William Butler Yeats

Epilogue

IONA

Time passes strangely. Sometimes in spurts. Some days can be cataloged by the unique traits ingrained in them, but more often than not, it moves on in a blur of similarities. Sunrises, sunsets, the phases of the moon. The tides, the seasons in their cyclical rhythms taking us on a journey we often and so easily forget once it passes us by. In my life there is the time before Cian, and the time with Cian. That is what matters.

On a brilliant summer day sometime later, I found myself gliding through the sea, my coat secured around me as I swam with my kin, bobbing in and out of the surf as they played and searched for food beneath the waves. I followed them, always finding joy in the sheer movement of my musculature as I navigated the current.

Cian joined me, making a grand splashing entrance from the rock above. His mighty black frame sent fish scurrying away into the depths, searching for shelter. He took no pleasure in hunting; I knew he merely wanted to be by my side. I pivoted so as to swim alongside him. To any human wandering the seaside our appearance would be unsettling, but that world mattered little to us.

Cian's snout nudged playfully at my own, as I sent bubbles trailing out from my nose. I raced as fast as I could to the sandy shore ahead, and Cian followed, trying his best to outpace me. He was no match for my speed. The water sparkled behind me in a glistening wake. Cian wasn't as graceful, but his power made up for it. The water churned around him, formidable and treacherous. It did not matter how fierce he was. He lost our race.

I let my coat slide from my shoulders, allowing my human legs to carry me up onto the shore. The sun had warmed the sand and it felt heavenly under my feet. I set my coat down and stretched out on the beach, savoring the sun's rays against every inch of my skin. It wasn't long until Cian emerged for the waves. Not an ounce of water to be found on his person.

"There's so very little in this world that has captured my attention in such a way, and you, *bean chéile,* are the most enticing creature I've ever beheld."

I smiled, a shark ready to snatch up her next meal. "Then by all means, come, let me satiate you." Cian's smile was fiendish and wonderful as he laid next to me, sparing no time before he ran a hand down my naked body possessively. I pulled him to me, claiming his mouth with my own.

He pulled away long enough to reply, for he was always to have the last word. "It would be my utmost pleasure."

The End

Acknowledgments

To you, the reader— Thank you for choosing to spend your time with this book. It is the most wonderful feeling in the world to know there are other readers out there who enjoy stories like mine.

The very first person to look at every page I've ever written deserves my deepest gratitude, and all my love. Mel, thank you for being my number one fan at every step of the way. I am so grateful you're my sister (And that you have excellent taste). I would have never considered myself worthy of publication without your constant support and encouragement. You will never know the true depth of my appreciation. Cian and Iona would have never made it through without your endless stream of excitement and your ability to tell me exactly what I needed to hear when I needed it most.

Thank you to my AWG girls; Amélie, Andrea, Carrie, Dareth, Laura, Nicole, and Sophie— you are always the best supporters! I am eternally thankful for your inspiration and your friendship. It has been such a joy to share every part of this journey with you all. I will always be grateful for the time spent together as we hone our craft and celebrate writing. Monday nights are my favorite part of the week, thanks to you all.

This novel is out loose in the world thanks to my phenomenal publishing company, Lake Country Press, and the unstoppable Britt Weisrock. Your passion for my work gives me life. I am a fantasy author because you believed in me, and my story. You've made my wildest dreams come true, and I will never ever forget that. Thank you also to my LCP siblings—You are all amazing in every way. I am endlessly grateful for your camaraderie!

To my lovely friends and beta readers who agreed to slog through earlier drafts of this work and give me the best feedback ever; Genalea, Carrie, Beka, Hannah, Gabrielle, and Dareth. This novel is what it is because of your willingness to help me make it shine.

My editor, Tara Sexton, who expertly combed through my work, ensuring it was the best it could be— thank you for polishing this book into the sparkly thing it is today.

To all the incredible people I've met from the online writing community, You made this experience so much less lonely. I will always remember the support you showed me.

Not every romance writer is keen to have their family read their work, but I got lucky, My family eats it up! I am so glad to be surrounded by such open minded people who can't get enough of love, or revenge, for that matter. I love you all dearly. Your unending excitement for me as I embarked on my publishing journey has been much needed fuel for my creative fire. I hope to keep making you all proud. All my love.

When she's not writing or reading, Kait is studying for her PhD at the University of Arizona, where she's focused on exploring Youth Literature through an educational lens. In her free time she likes exploring the desert or cuddling up on the couch with her writing assistant, Germain the tabby cat.

http://www.kaitwaterhousewrites.com/

instagram.com/kwaterhouseauthor
tiktok.com/@authorkaitwaterhouse